GW00871570

THE DRUM HOUSE MYSTERY

By

Tom Askey

ShieldCrest

ISBN 978-1-913839-50-5

MMXXI

A CIP catalogue record for this book
is available from the British Library.

Printed and bound in the UK

Published by
ShieldCrest Publishing
Boston, Lincolnshire,
PE20 3BT, England
www.shieldcrest.co.uk
+44 (0) 333 8000 890

Contents

Chapter One

Murder in the Surrey Hills

"You're going the wrong way, mate." The inspector handed the ticket back to the solitary passenger sitting awkwardly on the edge of his seat. "They shouldn't have put you on this train." Colley bristled. He glanced at his reflection in the window and saw that his face still looked haggard.

"Tell you what," continued the inspector, "I haven't seen you, right? You get out next stop and go back to the junction. Then ask somebody to put you on the express." He reeled off times from a grimy pocketbook and went away.

Silly mistake that, confusing the platforms at Victoria. Better get out now. No sense in wandering farther away, even though Colley had allowed two days to reach the coast. He was still uncertain of the new artificial leg, despite what the doctors said about trying a journey further afield from London. Switzerland ought to be far enough to stop their nagging. And he couldn't even board the right train at the beginning of his journey. Just as well he had not booked overnight at Dover, if he was to waste time wandering around the Surrey hills.

The two-coach electric pulled through the chalk cutting into the station. Colley alighted, not without difficulty. The two or three other travellers had already rushed away before he managed to cross the footbridge and find the exit barrier. The only official in sight was arranging parcels on the other platform. On an impulse, perhaps an echo of old training, Colley withheld his ticket from the pile left by trusting midday passengers. Wondering quite why, he sensed that it would be needed. Later.

He shivered in a sudden breeze. Strange how cold the wind blew on this secret downland, barely twenty miles from London. He had forgotten. Some memory in his good leg took him across the grass to the road fork. He had meant to wait patiently for the next train back to the junction, but habit led him up a quiet lane, deep in the chalk. This was plain foolishness, but the feeling of adventure beckoned him on. He found a good hiding place for his travelling bag under a box tree at the very edge of the down. House names at driveway ends, thinly scattered, recalled those long ago days when he had passed them every working day.

Then he was back at the Drum House. No officious board now marked the entrance, lying about its true purpose in bland government lettering. Instead a brass plate glinted, discreetly among the fir trees and barberry, announcing the Cammering Foundation. Never heard of it, but it was worth a look around for old times' sake. The main house was much as he remembered it, an eighteenth century folly, utterly impractical for living in without the later additions, but still remarkably handsome. The Victorian additions, being inconspicuous, hardly spoiled its line. But the old huts that he knew, across the sloping lawns, had been replaced by two post-war brick blocks. Decent and undistinguished, but probably far more convenient.

The receptionist fluttered. He had no appointment and knew nobody to ask for. His business was vague, but he looked too presentable to be sent away lightly. And of course, this wasn't her job, she shouldn't really be here, but someone had to be. It was too bad that they could never find good juniors in this area. All the brightest girls commuted into town, to much better paid work. The Foundation should not have to see visitors like this -. A buzzer interrupted her.

"Mrs Kingston? Have someone bring the folders to the conference room, as soon as possible."

"Sorry, Sonia is still out at lunch." What did he think he was playing at? There was no hurry. The meeting wasn't until four o'clock. She wished she had stayed in her room. Or gone home for lunch. "Oh, I see, I'll bring them myself." She faced the unwelcome visitor. "One moment, Mr - er - Dale." She waved at a chair and disappeared through a rear doorway.

Colley had recognised Irene Kingston at once. Twenty five years had greyed her hair, but she still had that cherubic face at odds with her superior manner. The former copy typist had stayed on, it seemed, when this Foundation thing had bought the property. She probably ran the place now. Usually very well, he was sure, but at the moment there was some kind of upset. She had shown no sign of recognising him. He had lost a deal of weight and his accident had left him looking prematurely aged. There was of course also the tin leg. That was probably more noticeable from the way he walked than he liked to think. Odd though that she had not known his voice. Oh well, put all that back into the past, he thought.

Nothing stirred in the entrance hall. Ten minutes passed. Fifteen. Colley had now missed his intended train. Nearly an hour till the next. Time for a quick look around the old haunts. Once through the inner door, all was new. A white corridor clinically divided the rooms into little desk-filled cubicles. One at the end of the row was quite grand, larger than the rest, and carpeted wall to wall. This was probably the den of the chief clerk or administrator, whatever he might be called. All the cubicles were quiet. He could see they were empty, their doors being left ajar. Lunchtime was obviously leisurely. How different from the old days! They would have been court marshalled for not locking their doors even to go to the lavatory. Colley returned to the entrance hall, pausing at the main door. Were the turret stairs still there, he wondered? A door panel, hidden behind a coat rack and an elaborate display of dried flowers, opened at the first push. Stairs led up into the gloom, dusty as ever. The clinical atmosphere did not extend here, and everything was now familiar. Yes, he remembered the narrowing climb past the first floor doorway, but the steps were steeper than he recalled. Not that he was having any real difficulty with them, he told himself, though he was quietly panting for breath as he opened the top door and stepped on to the gallery.

A familiar roof stretched above. Fifty feet below lay the drum-shaped hall, no longer a grand saloon but divided by screens into a central area with anterooms on each side. The distinguished furniture, quite valuable as Colley recalled though they had not treated it respectfully, had been rearranged as a boardroom table and surrounding chairs. Mrs Kingston bobbed about, setting papers on the table. One side room was empty. A heavily built man emerged from the other.

"Good afternoon, Sir Matthew," came her voice, clearly audible up among these rafters. The acoustics of the building were excellent.

The other gave no response and walked out behind her towards the entrance hall. Mrs Kingston had not looked up from her task, but followed him out after spending a few minutes longer in arranging the table for the coming meeting. It was not until afterwards, long afterwards, that Colley realised what was odd about the little episode unfolded below him. The stand-in receptionist was strangely familiar in her tone with the obviously important Sir Matthew, whoever he was. Far more than one would have imagined, even from such a superior secretary. Their footsteps echoed briefly around the high ceiling. Then a distant door closed, and all was silent.

The afternoon light was fading, but a wayward beam of sunshine shot like a searchlight from a high window into the space below. The anteroom furthest from the entrance door was suddenly lit up. Colley was just turning away, thinking to explore the outside rampart, when the pencil of light beneath him caught on a peculiar patch on the carpet. Then he saw clearly what it was. Fifty feet below him, under the empty Drum, lay a body, spread out and lying face down.

All that Colley heard was his heart pounding in his chest. At first he thought someone had fallen, but after a time there was still no movement. Then sudden voices echoed. He sprang up, as quickly and silently as he could manage. But now he was a tired man, exhausted by the walk and then the climb. He should not have come here. Colley staggered up the short wooden staircase to the outside gallery and gently prised the door panel open. From this vantage point he surveyed the surroundings in the failing light. The Drum House, as he remembered so well, stood isolated among several acres of lawns. No-one was in sight. He rested behind the stone parapet.

Colley began to realise that he was in a peculiar position. Voices came from the two figures he had last seen below him. They emerged, talking excitedly on their way to the car park. The man she had called Sir Matthew was giving Irene Kingston a lift. He would not however ponder that puzzle now. He had to make his way out, and back to the station. The man on the carpet had not moved. Colley thought that he ought to go down to see if there was anything that he could do for him. At least he ought to raise the alarm. Despite awkward questions, and the unlikely answers he would have to give, that would be the right course.

Slowly, his body aching and sore, Colley descended the spiral stair. As he reached the turning just above the first floor landing, a white-coated figure appeared from the doorway and rushed downwards. Colley shrank back. He was close enough to read the name "Dr Sedgfield" on the coat label, but the man did not glance upwards. Colley felt sure he had not been spotted in the dim light. Scuffling sounded somewhere near the bottom door, which had been flung open. Colley withdrew quietly back up to the inner gallery door and sat down. He could not get out safely till the man had gone. He leaned against the inside of the door and waited, eyes closed.

Suddenly a loud noise downstairs roused him. He crept out from his hiding place and listened. The staircase was now in complete darkness. He could not see his wrist watch, but guessed he must have dozed off. Cautiously he descended. His leg was stiff but less painful. He should be able to make good progress once he had found his way out of the building. No further sound came from below. Down he went, step by step. Soon he passed the first floor doorway. There was no proper door there now, just a curtain partly screening the entrance. Slowly he examined it, feeling his way around in the blackness. There was nobody there. The space beyond the curtain was as dark as the staircase, and as empty. No light entered it from the Drum on the farther side. It seemed to be some kind of storeroom. He went out

5

again and continued his cautious descent of the staircase, step by step, holding on to a guide rope fixed to the outer wall. Counting the steps, he calculated that he must be nearly at the bottom. Suddenly he stumbled and clutched at the rope. Recovering his balance he prodded gingerly with his good leg at the obstacle. It was soft and yielding. Since he had entered, some kind of cloth bag, quite large and heavy, had been placed on the bottom few steps.

Colley paused to consider this setback. If he could squeeze himself past, he should be able to open the bottom door and get out safely into the entrance hall. He tried, but in the total darkness that proved difficult. He failed completely to pass on the outer side. The object had become entangled with the guide rope, and he dared not shift it in case it became dislodged and fell noisily down the remaining stairs. He remembered that the bottom door opened inwards. Slowly he moved himself to the other side of the obstacle. Here the wedge-shaped steps narrowed, providing little foothold. He just found room to pass but had to cling to the object to steady his descent. His palms pressed into the cloth. Inside something yielded to his pressure. He pushed himself backwards down the last few steps and gently opened the door. Light seeped through from the front hall. He looked at the object that he had been pressing down on, and froze! It was not a cloth bag but a body of a man!

With the bottom door open as much as he dared risk, Colley forced himself to examine the corpse. It lay on its side, the face being mostly hidden in the angle of two steps. The right arm was caught in the guide rope. The man could not have been dead for long, and there was no sign of any injury. Dead however he certainly was, and bundled roughly on to the staircase.

Footsteps sounded outside the main entrance. Colley quickly withdrew back into the staircase and closed the door behind him. Someone bustled about noisily in the reception hall. Colley held his breath, dreading that the staircase door might be flung open at any moment to reveal him bending over the corpse. Nothing happened. Colley quickly dragged himself back out of sight upstairs, passing the body easily now he knew where it lay. Still nothing outside. He climbed back up to the inner gallery and peered down. The lights had been switched on. No-one was in the main room below, and the anterooms were both empty too. Colley began back towards the staircase. Then he returned and looked again to make sure. There was no body now lying in the far anteroom.

In the silence, Colley descended the steps again, painfully, pushed once more past the dead man, and opened the bottom door. Quickly he crossed the marble floor. He had just opened the entrance door, when a piercing scream echoed through the building. He had only time to drop behind the coat rack before the inner door flew open. From under the coats, Colley could see a flapping white coat, and heard a shrill voice telephoning from the desk.

"The Drum House, yes. Quickly! There's been a terrible accident, terrible. Hurry, please hurry! My name is Garton, Dr Garton. Yes, certainly. I'll meet you at the gate."

The outer door was flung open, and footsteps died away down the drive. Colley looked out cautiously. There was no-one about in the reception hall. He stepped outside and rounded the curve of the building. A group of people appeared, running across the lawns from the service block, three men and a girl. Another ran up behind them. They paused briefly, and all of them started to run quickly towards the Drum House. Someone must have telephoned them, but who? The white-coated man who raised the alarm had made no other call from the reception desk.

Colley dived into a small shrubbery outside the door. Within a minute, the four runners arrived and rushed into the house. Agitated voices rang round the high roof, and orders were rapped out. Colley waited no longer. Nothing could be usefully done by him. He decided to get out quickly and avoid inquiries that would only complicate, and perhaps delay, the imminent investigation. He ran down the lawn path on the far side of the house, in and out of bushes, and flung himself into a thick belt of woodland. He paused and listened. No-one was following. With luck, he had not been spotted. He peered out from behind the trunk of an old beech tree. The man who had raised the alarm was running back up the drive, following a white van which was flashing a blue light. Then silence again. Birds started singing in the wood. Colley hobbled along an uncertain path, and found himself at last on the road, about a hundred yards from the station.

It was becoming quite dark when he discovered the hollow at the edge of the open down where he had hidden his travelling bag. He knew the place well, there being no other box tree on this part of the common. The broken gate still creaked nearby. The same discarded rubbish still littered the near side of the tree. True, there were more footprints in the mud by the lane than he remembered. He thrust his arm into the dark void under the tree. He groped wildly around. He took out his arm, looked around him, and searched again in the darkness. There was nothing there. His travelling bag was gone!

Colley drew back into the bushes, and shivered. Panic rose inside him. He strove to keep the shaking under control. He had been so sure that nobody had seen him, even the white-coated Dr Sedgfield. What had he been doing snooping up in the Drum? Well, that was a fine question for him to ask. Colley smiled despite himself. Then the smile vanished again. Someone must have seen him and taken his bag. Had he been followed, from the station, or from the house? It seemed highly unlikely. There was no-one about when he arrived, and of course no-one was expecting him. He felt reasonably certain that he had not been spotted running away from the Drum House. There was too much hullaballoo, and no attention would have been paid to him even if he had been seen. Not as yet, at any rate. He shivered again. It was bad luck losing that bag. Surely there was nothing sinister behind it? A tramp or some passing walker must have taken it. Where? To the police? Well, it contained nothing to identify him, no name and address label. There was certainly no sense in hanging around here. He must get away as quickly and quietly as possible.

Brushing himself down, and looking as casual as he could manage, he walked briskly along the chalk pathway to the railway station. A train was just drawing into the platform. Cars lined the roadway outside the railway offices. Children's voices sang through the air, coming towards him. Mothers were meeting school children returning home. No use his going that way if he wanted to stay unnoticed. He turned off towards the main road. The train lights faded into the distance in a hum of grating wheels. Colley paused for breath. He was exhausted, but would somehow have to collect enough strength from somewhere. His leg throbbed, and he began to shake again. The light was failing rapidly now. Lights loomed out of the November mist. He must get on. He walked cautiously at first, but gradually desperation made him bolder. He must get on.

He ran stumbling down a hidden side track that he didn't see until he was upon it. A rough path, full of flinty lumps of chalk. Fresh tyre marks showed in the white mud. Silently he rounded a bend, and saw the railway far beneath him in a cutting well concealed with bushes. Fifty yards down the line a gang of railwaymen hacked at the ballast between the rails. The electric current must have been shut off from the third ground rail. Then a shout rang out. Colley froze, praying that he had not been seen. The workmen were standing back to the side of the railway. The lights of train carriages approached, passing directly beneath where Colley stood. As the train reached the men, it stopped where the section had been disconnected. They started collecting their tools and flags. Work had finished for the day. The train had made an unscheduled halt between stations to pick them up. In a minute the electric power would be re-connected, and they would be gone.

Colley crashed down the steep slope, bringing with him an avalanche of chalk and debris. He had no time to wonder whether he had been heard. He dragged himself along to the train, and staggered blindly to the last coach. It would be just too bad if he were seen now. Perhaps they would take him for another workman. He must have looked thoroughly dirty and tired. He clambered up unobserved. The guard and driver were looking the other way, making sure that that the railway workers were safely aboard. In another moment they would all be gliding away. With immense effort he managed to open a carriage door, and threw himself inside. The compartment was empty. That was a real stroke of luck, he thought as he lay panting on the dirty carpet, among the gum stains and trampled cigarette ends. The train jerked forward. Pain shot through his whole body. After a few minutes resting where he had landed, Colley recovered sufficient strength to place himself shakily on the seat. Nobody came. He was safe!

Thirty minutes later, having tidied himself as best he could, he crossed the platform at Clapham Junction, and boarded a train, some train, any train. Three hours later, complete with new luggage and basic necessities, he boarded the Channel ferry. Three days later he reached his destination, a tiny cottage hidden in a valley, a few kilometres from the shore of Lake Geneva.

Chapter Two

The Meeting in Palmyra Square

"So what makes you believe my story? You don't find it incredible, considering I'm the only person who seems to have ever seen the body? Nearly three weeks ago, and this is the first time you've heard about it." Colley sat calmly in his wheelchair, waiting for my answer.

"I'm not sure," I replied eventually. It was hard to match his description of the weary fugitive on the downs with this groomed and confident gentleman at ease in his cosy study in front of a blazing log fire. I could not be completely frank about what I thought. I had never seen him before today, knew nothing about him, but I could not conclude that he was lying. His story was so bizarre that it had to be true. I decided to switch the subject. "You must have been surprised when I rang your doorbell, and you found me there holding your travelling bag. Yet you never twitched a muscle."

"Surprised you had found me. Pleased to get my bag back safely. Thank you once again, Mr Steward." He was secure on his home ground, in his snug London mews house, not far from Gray's Inn Road in a quiet Georgian backwater. Even so he was remarkably composed. Some unforgotten training lay beneath his steady gazing at me in the firelight.

"You are thinking that you know almost nothing about me, no doubt," I said, more than anything to break the silence. Outside the window, snowflakes drifted through the twilight. "You're wondering what I am - policeman, private detective, blackmailer?"

"I'd say that you are a scientist of some kind. That thoroughgoing curiosity, that persistence, they're quite unmistakable. You're wearing a city suit and carry a furled umbrella. So you are a manager of some kind, an administrator in a scientific organisation. And no, I don't think you're here to threaten me. You came either from a sense of duty or to tidy up loose ends, or both."

I smiled. He was entirely right. "I qualified as a pharmacologist in Glasgow twelve years ago. I missed London however, and took up a position in a teaching hospital. Steeped in tradition but depressing, and I was badly paid. Fortunately I met Professor Garton there. You will have heard of him, I'm sure. He's become rather famous, writing and broadcasting."

"Dr Augustus Garton? I know the name but I've never met him. He was a colleague of yours, you say?"

"Oh no! Not a colleague exactly. He was far more senior even then, although we discovered mutual interests in music and occasionally we went to concerts together. It helped him as he doesn't drive, and found it awkward making cross-country journeys by public transport. He offered to share my driving expenses, but naturally I couldn't accept his kind offer. I enjoyed his company, and learned much from him during our months together at the hospital. I missed him greatly when he left to move on to higher things." I paused. "But I'm sure you know all this already." He made no comment to deny it. "I can't begin to imagine how you found out. You have a brilliant brain."

"Quite easy," he laughed. "I'm no mind-reader, no super sleuth. I worked out in my mind how you came to trace me. It was not because of what I *have* but what I *lack*, namely my right leg! From that it was simple enough to deduce the kind of person you had to be. A few phone calls confirmed it all. Do go on, please. Dr Garton asked you to join him at the Drum House after he transferred to the Cammering Foundation?"

"Yes. It was unexpected but I was delighted. I could not of course have expected to contribute much to the research there. So I was relieved to find that my post was administrative. I moved out to Surrey and took lodgings at the home of a Mr and Mrs Dixon, and I have lived there ever since. I'm not married and have no close family, you see.

They are a nice couple. Mrs Dixon is quite deaf, but a splendid cook. Her husband is rather a bore, but welcomes my company and my conversation. I think they must have rather sunk below their former station in life. Otherwise they would hardly be living in that expensive district yet need to take in lodgers. Mr Dixon is more sociable but he begins to tire easily. I've even noticed stifled yawns during our evening chats. Fortunately my work at the Foundation is demanding, being involved with hospitals and charities all over the world. I'm never at a loss for occupation, and it is surprising how the years have rolled by."

"How did you come across my travelling bag? There must be quite a story about it and how you came to return it to me here."

That puzzled me. I was unsure how much work he really had put into finding out about me. Although confined to a wheelchair at times, it was apparent that his mind was amazingly active. Indeed I subsequently found that being immobile seems to enhance his powers of concentration in working out problems that baffle me. Colley now calls it my "paw work", chasing around after things I don't altogether understand and become muddled about. Like a terrier dog, once I'm started. The metaphor is not one I particularly like, as I understand that terriers are not outstandingly intelligent!

"There's not much to tell you really," I said. "I must have come across the bag soon after you hid it under the box tree, from what you say."

"I don't suppose you remember it clearly, but I would be interested to have any details. Very interested indeed, as a matter of fact."

"Actually I remember it well", I began. "I don't often go to our local railway station. I live in the opposite direction, and if anything needs collecting, staff are available who travel there each day. However, a parcel for Professor Garton happened to reach the station after everybody had arrived at work. Professor Garton was worried, as the parcel contained samples he required urgently. I volunteered to collect it, as nobody else was available. The building was unusually deserted."

"As I noticed," said Colley. "Otherwise I would never have got through the front hall on to those stairs."

"Most of the staff were away on a half-day training session. Mrs Kingston had stayed behind and was rather agitated. Sonia had taken another long lunch break, and had been absent all afternoon without permission. She was visiting her boyfriend again, we thought. Just as I reached the edge of the common, I realised that I had not made certain - h'm - necessary arrangements before setting out. Suffice it to say that I withdrew from the road into the bushes. On my way back I found the travelling bag under a box tree, quite rare now on our part of the North Downs. The bag was pushed low down, well hidden."

"I didn't want some vagabond pinching it," said Colley. "Yet isn't that just what did happen?"

"I considered it better to leave the bag where it was while I went to the station. On my way back, having collected the professor's parcel, I looked under the tree for the bag, but it had vanished. I was certain I had the right spot, but there no sign of it anywhere, just muddy footprints. Mostly mine, I suppose. Naturally I thought that the owner had retrieved it, or that someone had taken it. Either way, there was nothing more that I could do. On reaching the entrance hall at the Foundation, I was astonished to find the travelling bag there, pushed behind the reception desk! Not really hidden, but I would not have noticed it if I had not dropped one of my gloves. I suppose I was intrigued. I had wasted time looking for it - oh, I do beg your pardon, I forgot it was your property - not really *wasted* - and it puzzled me".

"The terrier had his teeth into a bone," Colley smiled, but was not convinced by my explanation. "You could have watched to see who collected it."

"No, there was another reason too." I began to explain, when the telephone rang. Colley wheeled himself over to his desk and picked up the receiver. "You'll have to excuse me in a few minutes," he told me when the caller finished. "Of course you looked into the bag?" "What told you that it bag was mine?" From long habit Colley was sure he had left no identifying tags or documents inside. That had consoled him when thinking about it during his fortnight in Switzerland.

"You embarrass me," I said. "Must you press the point? I knew it was yours - can we leave it at that? No? Well that's reasonable. I suppose I would want to know, if it were mine. I made, er, inquiries."

"Where? What brought you here? Yes, I must press you. It is important that I know." Colley rose to stand. He became emphatic. "It's important that I get a clear picture of you - what sort of person you are. Excuse my saying this, but you are a complete stranger to me, and I must find out what brought you here."

"Please sit down. All right, I'll tell you. It was because of the surgical pads in the bag. I appreciate that they were unmarked, quite anonymous indeed. But I recognised them as being a necessity for, er, someone in your condition. Somebody with an artificial leg, recently fitted. I knew at once where they were made, the exact workshop. Need I say more? We did a lot of work at that hospital a year or two ago, and I still have contacts there. I made a phone call. They gave me the name of Mr Collingwood Dale."

A sudden change came over Colley. He leaned forward, angrily. "You mean you abused their confidence! You used your privileged position to get them to tell you. It's disgraceful. It's -."

"I'm truly sorry, you must believe me. I didn't mean that. Yes, I see now. A matter of trust, yes. I behaved badly. But my inquiry will be kept confidential, and there were certain reasons -."

"What possible reasons could make it right? It's my bag and my problem. Do you think I'm proud of my tin leg, not being able to get around and do what I want to do, what I have to do? Why can't people just stop fussing, trying to help?"

He was making me angry. Perhaps I had misjudged him. Perhaps he was another patient scarred by losing a limb. A strong active man, now reduced to depending on others. But why all this self-pity? Surely there was still a great deal he could do for himself. He did not seem to be short of money, and was clearly intelligent, interested in all kinds of matters. Perhaps I had mistaken him. Indeed he was rather letting himself down, acting in this way, before a total stranger.

Acting! Yes that was it! He was playing a role to test my reactions. I had been taught about this tactic on training courses. Well he would not be disappointed. Two could play that game! He was testing me, for some reason not yet apparent. But I would find out if I kept calm inside.

I continued expressing my regret, but firmly persisted. "I did no wrong in finding out who you were, and in returning your bag. Its contents would have been a loss to anyone, not irreplaceable but expensive to replace. I acted discreetly, even if I was privately curious about the whole incident. And private is how I have kept it. I want no recompense or even thanks. No-one need ever know anything about the bag, nor how you came to lose it. I am naturally curious, but I shall ask no further question. And I shall most certainly make no further inquiry." I hoped that I had not been too much on my dignity, but I was not used to this play-acting.

"It's all very fine to say that!" Colley retorted, "but you will have told all your cronies up at the Foundation." He paused, for breath I thought. "No-one else knows? Are you quite, quite sure? Nobody? Not even your precious professor friend?"

Colley was better at the game, and I had to be careful. "How dare you," I exclaimed. "I now regret ever seeing the wretched bag, and still more that I thought to return it! You do Dr Garton an injustice to insult him in that way! A friend, a real friend, who has been extremely kind, both personally and in my career." I was beginning to warm to my task. "No-one knows," I continued. "I'm telling you for the last time. It is entirely private as far as I am concerned. Do you think I cared what you thought? You did not come into the picture at all. It was a personal inquiry that interested *me!*"

Colley looked up, puzzled. "I didn't come into it? Then whose feelings were your concern? Not mine evidently." He was stalling now, calculating whether to confide in me, whether I was worthy of his confidence. I must confess now that I was fascinated.

"Mine, my own feelings. I had a duty to myself." But I had to tell him, I thought, even if he made no response. There was no other way to discover his purpose. "I was curious about the bag," I added, after a long pause, "and worried, frightened even."

"Frightened?" Colley's play-acting crumbled. Now he was interested. My persistence had worked. "You scared? What had you done? You merely found a travelling bag and left it. Nobody is interested in you – not in the slightest".

"There you are quite wrong," I announced calmly. "Someone is very interested. Someone is trying to kill me."

For a long time Colley stared at me. I was glad then that the telephone had forestalled my telling him earlier. Something of my feeling may have communicated itself to him, for he picked up the phone and dialled. "I can't manage this evening after all. Sorry. Something very urgent - yes, very important. Tomorrow's fine. Same time?" He put down the receiver and offered me a drink. Gladly I accepted. I felt exhilarated, for I had broken his composure, and somehow that gave me great pleasure. I was eager for him to continue, gratified that I had managed to stop his play-acting.

"I owe you an apology, Mr Steward." He paused. "May I call you David?" Colley's voice came gently across the room. "I had to be sure of you, who you are, and what your motives are. I realise now you know that. I had to be able to trust you. I had to be quite sure you could step into a strange and perhaps hazardous situation without flinching. I am not at all surprised that you are in danger. Will you tell me more about the attempts on your life? I need hardly say that everything -." He broke off suddenly. "No, first I'll tell you how I come to be involved in the affairs of the Drum House. You must think me impertinent to be so inquisitive."

"Well, I can't give confidential information about our work at the Foundation - ."

Colley handed over a sealed letter addressed to me personally. Inside were instructions from a senior Foundation director, Sir Carlo Waybridge, to give Mr Collingwood Dale my complete co-operation in anything concerning the Foundation, and to keep the matter totally confidential.

Colley saw my amazement. "Waybridge is known to me personally," he explained. "Several weeks ago he asked me, in strict secrecy, to find out what is happening at the Drum House. He's concerned with recent developments there and how certain people are behaving. I made inquiries, and told him you would be well placed to help, once I had checked you out. He agreed, and prepared that letter for you. I take it that you will comply?" I nodded my head in agreement. He smiled and shook my hand. "Then perhaps I can now destroy the evidence?"

Again I nodded, and handed back the letter. He burned it in the fireplace and broke up the ashes. "I will do everything I can to help." Nothing more was said for several minutes. I turned this strange request over in my mind. Colley fiddled about at his desk, watching my face all the time. Waybridge I knew by name only, as he had not attended board meetings since I joined the staff. Extremely shrewd, he was reputed to have made an immense fortune from speciality pharmaceuticals. His name was influential in international medicine, and more recently in politics. Small wonder that Colley was interested in whatever was bothering the great man. Yet merely known to him, and not perhaps a personal friend."

I was the first to speak. The room had grown cold. Outside, snow flakes collected on the window panes. I should be travelling back home, I thought, yet made no attempt to take my leave. Dazed by what I had been told, there was still much to hold me in that room, sitting in the dying firelight. "You must be wrong about seeing the body from the gallery and on the stairs," I reflected aloud. "The same body? Yes, surely it must have been. One is more than enough. For the Foundation, I mean."

"For anywhere, surely," replied Colley. "It is strange that none of you has seen the corpse. Or, rather that none has reported it. Surely someone found it. I assure you that I did. Saw and felt it. It was no hallucination, I can tell you." Colley lapsed into silent thought. I waited for him to speak. We had only met that afternoon, yet seemed to have been friends for years. He was already treating me as a worthy colleague.

Indeed the meeting proved to be a turning point in my life. Despite several dangerous situations it landed me in, I never regretted returning the travelling bag to its owner.

Chapter Three

Death in the Laboratory

Colley continued to brood in silence. Suddenly he eased himself from his wheelchair, stirred the dying fire and threw on several logs from a pile nearby. Wood crackled and cheerful sparks flew up the chimney. The room brightened and grew warm again. He looked up, questioningly.

"So why bring in the police if there is no body? What made, whoever it was, Dr Garton, do that? I saw their van come up the drive, flashing its blue light."

I smiled, gratified to give Colley information. "That wasn't the police. It was an ambulance. One of the researchers, a chemist, had collapsed. It was a dreadful accident, a terrible way to die. And so, well, undignified."

"A researcher? What was a chemist doing in the Drum House anteroom? Don't all your chemists wear white coats? The man I saw wore an office suit, with a jacket. I should have thought all the research staff worked in the laboratory block?"

"That's where he was," I explained. "He didn't die in the Drum House. He was in his own laboratory. The old man suffered a massive heart attack, apparently. He had been working alone at the bench. When he was taken ill, he pitched backwards, smashing into his apparatus. He was badly cut by the broken glass, very severely in fact, but he was dead before he fell."

"The old man, you say? Let me guess. It was not Dr Kaltz by any chance, was it?"

"It's strange you should say that." My words drained the smile quickly from Colley's face. "At first we all thought it was Kaltz," I continued, "but it turned out to be Paul Mountford. His head and shoulders were a dreadful mess, his face barely recognisable. Poor man, it was so sad."

"Mountford? I don't think I've heard you mention him before."

"No. He was a close colleague of Kaltz. They had worked together for a good many years. His death was a quite a loss to the staff at the Foundation -."

"But not to the scientific world in general, I guess, from your tone of voice?"

"Oh dear," I replied. "Is it so obvious? I'm afraid you're right. He will be missed, undoubtedly, but he was not very well known. He had done some good work of his own, many years ago. He was really just an assistant for Dr Kaltz."

"There was an inquest?"

"No. His doctor said he could have gone at any time. He had a severe and incurable heart condition, and he had overtaxed his strength badly."

"Why did you think it was Dr Kaltz when you found him? Were you expecting it to be him?"

"I didn't discover him myself. I happened to be in the service block at the time, not the laboratories. There were papers to be signed by one of the scientists going abroad. It was the professor who actually found him. Poor old Mountford. Sedgfield had been searching everywhere for him, he said. The alarm had gone off in the laboratory block. Some of the apparatus had caught fire. Dr Garton didn't see him lying on the floor at first. It was the merest chance that he passed the door, he said. There was a terrible mess where Mountford had crashed down off his bench stool. Blood and glass all over the place, and burning chemicals. Sedgfield wanted to get the fire brigade as well as the ambulance, but the professor insisted that our own men were able to tackle the fire, as they indeed were. Later in the day he agreed to have the county fire people in to check, as a matter of form for the insurance cover. There wasn't a lot of damage to the building, as it turned out. It was lucky that Dr Garton was quickly on the scene, and Sedgefield close behind him."

Colley looked solemn. "You say they were close colleagues, Mountford and Kaltz?"

"Yes. I'm sorry to smile, but it was an old joke at the Foundation that they had been together so long that they had grown to look like each other. You know, just as pet dogs begin to resemble their masters in time. They were much of an age, but Mountford was the junior partner, as it were. Very much so."

"Did he resent that?"

"It didn't seem to bother him at all. Mountford must have known that he was less gifted. He had far less insight into the problems of research. He was pretty shrewd, though he was getting a bit decrepit. Yes, he must have realised that. They worked well together as a team, and still published good work, even though it was mostly Kaltz who had the ideas."

"How did Kaltz treat Mountford? Was he bossy?"

"Far from it. No, they seemed to be on the best of terms, good friends. It was one of those partnerships where each of them had long since settled what their individual strengths were, their expertise, and they shared out the work accordingly. Not that they appeared to have any sort of *formal* arrangement as to how they worked, you understand. They just knew each other's thoughts intuitively and never got in each other's way."

"So they kept close together, you mean. Pooling their thoughts, discussing their theories, firing ideas off each other all the time. That sort of thing."

"On the contrary. For most of the time they worked quite separately. In different rooms in the laboratory block."

"Not next door to each other?"

"No, strangely enough their laboratories were at each end of the block. It's a long building, and they could hardly have been much further apart. They did meet quite often, though. Sometimes they even lunched together. When they bothered to eat, that is."

"Did they take their lunch in the staff canteen, with all the others?" asked Colley.

"No, no. That wouldn't suit them at all. They would go off together somewhere in the village. Mountford usually drove, though he wasn't supposed to. Kaltz is an appalling driver. Nobody else would want to go with them."

"They had established a familiar routine then, a well-worn pattern?"

"Yes. I think Mountford would have preferred working more closely. He was rather sociable, you know. He liked to chat. Prattled on a bit sometimes, and talked rather wildly at times. Kaltz worried that he would give too much away. Before they were ready to publish their findings, I mean. None of us took much notice. Yes, I do think Mountford was lonely."

"But Kaltz isn't - either sociable or lonely?"

"He certainly isn't. He simply lives for his work. Always busy, almost frantic most of the time. There are hardly enough hours in the day for him to do everything he wants to do."

"He's in good health, is he? For a man of his age, I mean. Still well and active, with no thoughts of taking life easy?"

"Yes indeed. He seems to be quite fit. He should have retired years ago really, but after Cammering gave up and went to live in France, Kaltz wanted to keep the old traditional partnership alive and active in modern medical circles. The general public, of course, had forgotten them both, long ago." I paused to reflect. "It was a great shame that Mountford died the way he did. It was so undignified. He would have disapproved. Kaltz certainly did."

"Disapproved? That's an odd way of describing it."

"Perhaps so, but Mountford was such a courteous, old-fashioned sort of scientist. Just like Kaltz. Great pride in his work, you know, and in the traditional ways of conducting oneself. He was a law unto himself, of course. You could never get him to obey official procedures. He disregarded all the rules of the Foundation, in the way we had to work. It was such a pity that he was so badly scarred. The fall into his apparatus had smashed up all his apparatus. He was severely lacerated, quite badly cut about. I didn't see him, you understand, but the professor told me. Poor old Paul Mountford! At least he would have wanted to die still working."

"What about Dr Kaltz? He must have been pretty devastated. Tell me about him. Somehow I can't get a clear picture of him into my mind."

I was surprised how Colley had switched his interest so quickly to Kaltz. It was Mountford that we had started discussing. Perhaps he was getting confused. After all, I thought, he didn't know any of the personnel, even by sight. The staffing was rather complicated, in the way it had grown up over the years, mostly through personal contact as in my own case. We never had any formal policy for taking on people. It just depended how hard one argued the case, and what was in the budget. And of course who you knew to be available and, well, suitable. So I made no comment, and went with the drift of Colley's inquiry.

"Old Kaltz was very upset indeed. He had always been rather eccentric, but now sometimes he seemed positively unhinged. Not that we saw much of him. He simply shut himself in his laboratory, literally I mean. He practically lived there. He only emerged late in the evenings to go home, long after we had all gone. But working hard, certainly. Indeed he appeared to be twice as busy."

"You say he was part of a team, Dr Kaltz I mean. I suppose he must have been famous, even outside his own somewhat specialised circles?"

I smiled. "I can see that you are no scientist. Yes, he was famous all right. Cammering and Kaltz. The great team, Nobel prize-winners forty years ago. Their discoveries in immunology saved thousands of lives, tens of thousands."

"Cammering set up the Foundation, I understand," said Colley. He's dead now, I take it. Did he work at the Foundation with Dr Kaltz?"

"No to both questions. Cammering is still very much alive, although I believe quite frail. He lives in the south of France, out in the wilds in a small cottage, all alone except for an aged housekeeper and her husband. He has no family that I know of. His wife died many years ago, and there were no children, or any relatives."

"What will happen to his money when he dies?" Colley wondered.

"Ah, now that I do know," I replied. "It's public knowledge that he has willed it all to the Foundation. There'll be some personal bequests I understand, to long-serving staff and so on. But the Foundation gets the bulk of it, and quite a considerable fortune, they say

Colley pondered for some minutes, without saying anything. Then he suddenly asked, "Why did you say that *no* was the answer to both questions?"

"Did I? Oh yes, I remember. You asked if they worked at the Foundation together. They didn't. Cammering retired when it was set up. He had been busy with all the arrangements, of course, but that was mainly done through his lawyers. I suppose he was feeling old and worn out, and no wonder. It was about then that he bought the cottage and we hardly ever saw him here."

"He didn't come back to England very often?"

"No, not even to London. Nor to any of the international symposia. Kaltz is a complete contrast. He has always been quite indefatigable. Always working. No other life at all. We always said that he worked enough for two men! Still publishing valuable work, beavering away at the Foundation, in the background and out of the public gaze. Never one for the limelight - quite unlike Cammering in that respect! At least, until recent years. Cammering and Kaltz. Now they're largely forgotten even in their own field. So much progress has been made since their heyday. But historic figures, of course. Cammering and Kaltz!"

Colley gave no sign of sharing my enthusiasm, but then he was not a scientist. So I said nothing for several minutes, and nor did Colley, who sat lost in thought.

"How did Cammering take the news about Kaltz?" he suddenly asked. "Badly, I suppose. From what you tell me, it would be the end of a great partnership, even though he must have realised the famous days were over."

"Kaltz? You mean Mountford." I was baffled by Colley's lack of attention to what I had said, and more than slightly nettled. "I've told you already, Kaltz is working away in his laboratory -."

"Sorry. All right, Mountford."

"I don't know. The professor sent a message at once, but I don't recall that we have had anything from Cammering at all. That's odd, now I think of it, I suppose."

"Not necessarily," Colley came back quickly. "He's probably not in good health himself. No-one has been to see him recently from the Foundation, I suppose?" I had to confess that nobody had visited the old man.

Colley wheeled his chair vigorously around the room, squealing and rubbing the fine carpet. It irritated me, but I did not like to interrupt him. I felt pretty foolish now about my outburst, and hoped I hadn't made a fool of myself. I glanced at my watch.

There were still questions that I wanted to ask, and time was passing. Soon I would have to be thinking of leaving the comfort of Colley's study to catch my train home. The wintry weather outside seemed to be getting worse. I decided that I had to take the lead.

"That body you found on the stairs," I ventured. "You're sure that it was the same one as that you saw in the anteroom?"

"Yes, pretty sure. He was wearing the same kind of dark blue suit. I didn't see the face clearly in either place, so I'm unlikely to recognise him from a photograph, if that's what you are thinking. Why do you ask?"

"Well, it seems so unlikely that anyone would take a corpse out of the anteroom and move it to the stairs."

"That's less improbable than there being two similar bodies," Colley began. "Although, I wonder…" He tailed off and lapsed once more into silence.

I tried again. "I mean, if there were two, perhaps - ."

"No," interrupted Colley. "You may be right, of course, as we have so few facts at present, but I think we have to keep down the number of assumptions. Let's stick to the simplest explanation, at least until the evidence proves it wrong. It's more likely that there was the one body, and that it was moved. There was plenty of time for the murderer to shift it. I was up in the gallery for a long while. I may have passed out. No, I don't think there have been two killings. At least…" He paused, and then went on. "At least, not yet."

"So the murderer decided to move the victim out of the anteroom to the staircase for some reason. Why do you think that was?"

"Because there was some disadvantage in leaving it in the anteroom. Probably it was more likely to be discovered there."

"Yes, but it would have been found on the staircase, sooner or later. I mean, I know it's not used as often, but eventually the body would have been discovered, even here."

"That's an interesting point, or rather what follows from it is. Because the body was shifted to the stairs and then moved again somewhere. That tells us something important." Colley stopped pushing his wheelchair around the room and faced me. "You do see what that is, don't you?"

"I must admit I don't. Neither spot is really a good hiding place. The staircase is marginally better because it's less often used. That's all."

"Exactly!" shouted Colley. "And the villain knew that just as well as you do! The murderer is someone who knows the layout of the building very well, someone who knows very well how the building is used. In other words, someone on the staff of the Foundation!"

"Not necessarily," I said. "It may have been a lucky chance. After all, the staircase is dusty and looks unused, whereas the anteroom is kept clean and polished for constant use. An outsider could have spotted that."

"An outsider, though, would have left the body, if not in the anteroom, then on the stairs, and made good his escape as quickly as possible. It would hardly have mattered where he left it, so why waste valuable time in moving it? There might not have been much time to get away. An outsider would be uncertain of the layout of the place and of who was likely to appear and when. It could have been, what would you say, half an hour at least before it was spotted in the anteroom - ?"

"Yes, if, as you say, the body was lying on the floor. It would be partly hidden by the table in that room, and the windows are rather high in the wall."

"...And possibly several hours before it was found on the staircase? An outsider would want to get off the premises as rapidly as possible."

"Yes," I admitted. The timings seemed about right. I didn't like to think about it much, but Colley seemed to be correct. The murderer *must* be someone inside the Foundation, a member of staff we all knew, a person we had all trusted. The very idea repelled me, and I shuddered.

"There's something else, you know," Colley continued. "If it was an outsider, then the body would have been found on the stairs long ago. After all it's over three months since I discovered it, and the body has *not* been found, neither in the anteroom nor on the staircase, nowhere! After I left the building, some unknown person fetched the body from the stairs and disposed of it in an unknown place. Now just remember the scene. The whole place was buzzing with activity following the discovery of Mountford lying dead in his laboratory. Any stranger around the Drum House would have been noticed by half a dozen people at least. Yet no-one has reported anything unusual. No, my friend, I'm sorry to say that this is the work of an insider, someone who knows the building and the movements of the staff extremely well."

I shivered again. Colley noticed my distress, and wheeled himself away to stare out of a window.

"This is a bad business, David. There's some terrible undercurrent moving at the Foundation, some secret pressure building up over months, perhaps over years. I know that it's your world, your life. But some dreadful conflict has been going on there, right in front of you."

"And I have seen nothing! It's been happening under my very nose, and I've been too stupid to notice." I felt utterly cold and miserable.

"Not at all. You must not take that attitude. It's very important that you do not - to the Foundation, to yourself, even to me." Colley stopped for a few moments and I savoured his reassuring tone. "You have not been stupid at all. I would say that you have been very observant indeed, perhaps too much so for somebody's plan. All you have to do is to remember what you saw. Somewhere along the line you hold the solution. I don't doubt that you are a valuable witness. You will have to watch carefully now, without seeming to act differently from usual. Don't arouse any suspicions. Be very careful, my friend. You *can* do it! And when you do remember anything you think important, or find anything strange happening, please, please let me know at once!"

"Do you really think I can be useful, important even, in this terrible business? I feel so, well, so incapable of dealing with the situation. So isolated."

"You can rest easy about that straight away. You won't be alone at the Foundation for much longer, and already it's not just a matter of you and me working on the case. I won't say more now, but you will soon see that I'm right. And do remember to take care, observe, and don't do anything at all out of character. No matter what happens."

"You don't think we should inform the police, do you?" Although much reassured, and quite excited, I was still uncertain as to the correct course of action to take.

"Leave that entirely to me," said Colley, "and to my associates. As yet we have no firm evidence. It's only my word for what I saw - one witness, uncorroborated. And things that you believe happened to you. That I believe did happen to you. But you could be mistaken. There may be some other explanation. Now is not the time to act."

I began to feel better. It gave me a warm feeling to realise that I had a vital role to play, even if I couldn't yet fathom out what was going on. I was not alone. Colley *had* to be trusted, and I did trust him.

After a lengthy silence, I stood up and we shook hands. "I really must be on my way now," I said. "I have a train to catch. The weather is getting worse." Colley seemed indifferent, still lost in his own thoughts. I began to wonder if he had forgotten that I was there. The fire had died down and the room was quite dark, and growing cold. I stood up , ready to go. Colley came to with a start. "Yes, of course. Sorry." He moved to a window. "We shall have a white Christmas at this rate. Good of you to come. Thanks once again. Sorry I can't drive you home."

I waved my dismissal of his suggestion. He seemed to be saying the words almost mechanically. He had all but forgotten that I was there. His mind was still on something else. It was something to do with me and the Foundation. And something I had said. I felt uneasy.

"Yes," he said at length. "It's very good of you. There's usually a taxi at the end of the square, or you'll find one in Holborn." I said my goodbyes, and promised to keep in touch with him.

I didn't bother with a taxi. The snow had stopped falling and the slush was already melting in the gutters. I could easily catch the bus in Holborn that would take me to Victoria station. I hurried towards Staple Inn. The street lights glowed and the cold air was exhilarating.

I had gone at least a hundred yards down Gray's Inn Road before I remembered. I had told Colley nothing at all about my own adventures!

Chapter Four

An Unexpected Visitor

"Go back to bed, Mr Steward, and I'll bring you up a hot drink and some paracetamol. You really shouldn't be up and about with a chill like that."

Mrs Dixon wanted me out of her kitchen, where I lingered over an aimless breakfast. No doubt she was concerned about my unusual lethargy, but I knew that I was disrupting her tight schedule. Mrs Scutter was due to arrive at any minute to do the cleaning, and she liked to be out of the house when that happened. Otherwise much tea would be drunk but little actual work done. On Fridays, Mrs Dixon took herself off up to the village shops, and stayed there until the three hours contract expired.

"I'm off now, Mr Steward. I've left a note for Mrs Scutter to say she's not to disturb you. Shall I ring them at the Foundation and say that you won't be in today?"

"No, that's all right. Thank you, Mrs Dixon. I'll ring when I have finished my breakfast. Then I think I will go back to bed, as you say." I did feel rather unwell.

John Merryman answered the phone. I had forgotten that Mrs Kingston was away. Sonia had failed to appear yet again. She had been absent from work now for three days, with no message or explanation. Arnold Springer had still not returned. A feeling of desolation swept over me. One by one my team, that I had carefully built up over the years, was crumbling away. Indeed the whole Foundation seemed to be dissolving rapidly.

"I should be all right for Monday, John," I explained. "In fact I feel better already just for talking to you." Perhaps my illness was as much in my mind as anything. Certainly there had been a lot of stress recently. By mid-January we were, as usual, catching up on the backlog from the Christmas shutdown. Yet the feverishness was real enough, and I did not want to miss a single day at the Drum House. Events might begin to unfold swiftly, and I wanted to miss nothing, not only for myself but also on behalf of Colley. I gave Merryman a few instructions, and asked him to leave everything else for my return. If something important happened, he was to phone me at once. I felt that something was about to happen, and that Colley might be in touch again shortly.

I sank back into my pillows and dozed. I was aroused by a loud ringing and hammering at the front door. At first I ignored it, but then realised that there was probably no-one else in the house but myself to answer. By now Mrs Dixon would be enjoying herself making her round of the village, and catching up with the latest gossip. Mr Dixon was away for a few days at his brother's. The noise persisted. I glanced at the clock. Quarter to ten. Feeling refreshed by my sleep, I got up, pulled on my dressing gown and went on to the landing. I was just about to go downstairs, when the kitchen door opened, and Mrs Scutter appeared. I did not want to be drawn into conversation with her, so I withdrew to my room.

"It's all right, Mr Steward," came a yell from below. "I'm going to see who it is, making all that noise." The door opened and there came the sound of agitated conversation from the front hall. I could not hear what was said, however. Nor was I particularly interested. If it was important, I would be told all about it in due course, as I would even if it wasn't.

Feeling much better, I sat up reading my newspaper for some time, possibly an hour. Then I decided to wash and dress, and went downstairs to the sitting room. The kitchen door opened again, and I called out, in as loud a voice as I could manage, to tell Mrs Dixon that I was there.

"It's me, Mr Steward," shouted Mrs Scutter. "Mrs Dixon's not back yet from the village. Can I get you anything, like a cup of tea?"

"No, thank you, Mrs Scutter," I replied quickly, remembering that what she made was nothing like a cup of tea. "Did you answer the front door bell a little time ago?"

For a moment there was no response. Then Mrs Scutter herself appeared in the sitting room, tying the strings of her apron behind her back. She was red in the face and aggrieved. "Most certainly I did," she exclaimed. "I never heard such a carry on in all my life. No respect for people's front doors, some folk. What Mr Dixon would have said I do not care to think, really I don't."

"Who was it? Was there any message for Mrs Dixon?" I was becoming quite interested, especially as the caller seemed to fluster Mrs Scutter more than might have been expected, even though she did have a notorious short fuse. I thought I ought to get the message relayed correctly, just in case it was something important to the Dixons.

"Wasn't for Mrs Dixon," retorted Mrs Scutter. "It was a person for you. Very hot and bothered as well, but I said you were poorly in bed and on no account to be disturbed. Mrs Dixon left me clear orders on that subject. I wasn't having any nonsense. You should be in bed, Mr Steward, anyway. Not lolloping about in here."

Thinking it might be Merryman, or someone else from the Foundation, I waited for the fuss to subside and then returned to the subject that interested me. I asked her who it was who had called.

"Person by the name of Mountford", she announced. "No message. Just the name. Mountford. Said you would know. Something to do with the Foundation."

Mountford! I shot up in my armchair. It couldn't be, surely. Was it a joke?

Mrs Scutter looked perfectly serious and anxious to return to the kitchen, ...her tea was getting cold. In any case, she never joked, and seemed to have no sense of humour, even a malicious one. "Are you sure, Mrs Scutter?", I gasped. "Are you quite, quite positive that was the name?"

"Sure? 'Course I'm sure! Should know, me that's worked for the Mountfords up at that great big place of theirs these past seven years!"

I just could not take it in. There must be some mistake. I had seen Paul Mountford dead in his laboratory, horribly dead. I had attended his funeral. We all had. What could this mean? And what was so urgent, and why did he want to see me, of all people? A cold sweat came over me. I was scared by a sudden new thought. I went into the kitchen to question Mrs Scutter again.

"This visitor, did they - did they - well, leave any message at all? No? No message?" I was utterly relieved to see Mrs Scutter shake her head. But my heart started pounding away again as she continued.

"No, there was nothing. Except to say they'd be coming back. Calling again, later today. I hope it's not this morning. I've still lots of work to do, holding a body up like that. Mrs Dixon will be back before I can turn round."

I shuddered again at the mention of a body, and hoped Mrs Dixon would come back quickly. I did not want to be alone in the house when my strange visitor returned. I tried to read, but it was no use. I could not concentrate. I turned on the radio and tried to relax. The music was not to my taste, and I was restless. Eventually I returned to my reading, and must have dozed off again, for it was twenty minutes to eleven when Mrs Scutter re-entered the sitting room and roused me.

"Someone to see you," she told me. I thought for the moment that I would faint or at least pass back into some semi-conscious state. Perhaps I was only dreaming anyway. Perhaps -

"You look ghastly!" said a loud cheerful voice. "Time you got yourself sorted out!" Colley threw himself down on the sofa. I felt the blood gradually returning to my cheeks. "What's wrong with you? They told me it was influenza, but you look as though you've seen a ghost. It must be your guilty conscience. Maybe you are the villain behind all these goings-on at the Drum House."

"Don't talk like that, even as a joke," I said. "It's not funny!" Colley looked puzzled. "Sorry, I'm not feeling very well, and I have had a bit of a shock. I'm very glad to see you, though. Very glad indeed."

"I'm sorry myself for giving you such a fright. What's happened to make you so jumpy? That's not the 'flu. Don't tell me - ". He lowered his voice to a whisper. "Don't tell me that there's been another attempt on your life! No? Well that's something to be thankful for, at any rate."

"Did you think there might have been?" I asked. I wanted to know what was in Colley's mind. "I thought you had come for some important reason." He tried to look hurt. "I see no comforting grapes in your hand for a poor invalid," I added.

"You'll soon be all right and back at the Foundation, sleuthing away," he laughed. "Anyway, terriers don't eat grapes, even when they're off colour! No, I really wanted to hear about what happened. You said someone tried to kill you? You dashed off so quickly from Palmyra Square that you forgot to tell me." He stopped smiling and stared anxiously at me. "It's important. Very much so."

"It's certainly important to me. But I got the impression at the time that you weren't particularly interested. In fact, I wondered if you thought I had imagined it or if I were concocting some yarn to compete with your own adventure."

"It crossed my mind, but not for long. You're not that sort of person. Anyway, there's a good reason why someone close to you at work might want you out of the way."

"Now I'm really worried," I told him. "Come on, you've got to tell me what's going on, or at any rate what you think is happening. You must have worked it out by now."

"Not entirely," Colley said, thoughtfully, "but it's only fair to tell you what I have discovered. First, however, I want to hear your story." He settled down comfortably. There was no sign of trouble with his leg, and he had obviously walked up the hill to see me without difficulty.

He sat back and waited patiently for me to begin. I postponed telling him about the impending visit of Mountford's ghost.

"The first occasion was at the end of October. I remember it well because it was Halloween. We were having a party at the Foundation to celebrate - you know all the usual things, masks, pumpkin faces and so on."

"A little undignified for such an august institution, surely? I should never have thought eminent scientists got up to such things. Do you often have parties there?"

"No, we certainly don't. It was organised at the last minute by some of the laboratory staff. They have children at the village primary school, and they had organised it with the teachers. They are not allowed to use the school itself, for insurance reasons I think. I don't really know, and haven't usually taken any interest. The normal venue is the village hall, but that was closed for urgent repairs. The professor said they could use the grounds at the Drum House - he's an honorary governor or something like that. He thought it would be good public relations."

"And was it a great success? I should have thought the parents would have been overawed by the grandeur of the surroundings."

"Oh, they didn't use the main buildings. In fact they shouldn't have gone inside at all. The idea was that they used the lawns around the Drum House. But it poured with rain. The whole thing was a disaster. The children went home early, but some of the parents stayed behind to help tidy up and dry out. We went into one of the laboratories for a drink - just a cup of coffee, you know, nothing alcoholic. We just sat by the benches talking. It was all unofficial, and not really allowed, but somehow we just drifted in and stayed a while chatting and waiting for the rain to stop."

"So you had got involved, although you say you didn't normally?"

"That's right. I can't remember who invited me. I'd been working in my room on some ideas I had for a publicity booklet. Yes, that's it.

I was parking my car, which I'd taken because it was so wet. One of the scientists was parking next to me, and he asked me if I'd like to come along later. I suppose they were trying to regularise the situation, though I could not have given them permission. However, I saw no harm in it, as Dr Garton had authorised the party in the first place. It was a bit pompous of me, looking back, but I thought it would be as well if I were there, to keep an eye on things."

"Can you remember which scientist invited you?"

"Yes, it was Harry Staniforth, but they were all keen for me to join them when I got there. It was quite late, about eight-thirty. I'd been anxious to finish a report that was overdue and I wanted to clear it up that weekend."

"So what happened? You had a convivial evening, no doubt, drinking cocoa and munching sausage rolls."

"It was rather like that," I laughed. The chemists were reminiscing about college days. Some of them had been students together. The time passed pleasantly enough. Someone suggested a last drink of coffee before we plunged out into the night. It was still pouring with rain. All the cups had been washed and packed up, ready for taking back to the village hall, so we used glass lab beakers. They were all quite new. Palmer and Fletcher-Smith got them out of store and washed them. I went out to the lavatory, and they had already made the coffee when I returned. Some of the staff had gone home, and the others were in a private huddle discussing their research, so I picked up a beaker that had been left for me and took it into the next bay. I'm not so used as I was to drinking hot liquids from glass beakers. Your fingertips gradually become normal again when you've been out of a laboratory for a few years. You lose the hard skin pads you acquire from handling hot apparatus, you know. Anyway, the fact is that I spilt my coffee. It went on to the floor, but fortunately nobody noticed. There was still some liquid left in the bottom of the beaker. I wiped up the mess without attracting attention and re-joined the others. When I finally left, I remembered the beaker I had left in the next bay, but the others were setting out for home, having washed up. So I took the beaker back with me. As it dried, white crystals formed in the bottom, that were rather peculiar. Certainly not sugar crystals, and anyway dried sugar isn't like that. I kept the beaker and had the crystals analysed. It turned out to be lead acetate. The so-called *sugar of lead* because it's supposed to be sweet. But I've never tried. It's highly poisonous!"

"You think somebody - one of the staff there in the laboratory - deliberately tried to poison you?"

"Well, what else could it be? The stuff was close at hand, as it's used in some of the inorganic analysis they do. None of the other beakers could have been poisoned, or we would soon have known about it. There could not have been any confusion with the real sugar. They used cubes from a box."

"How very odd! It certainly looks serious for you. No wonder you're jumpy. But who did the analysis for you? I take it you did not tell any of the men in the lab what had happened?"

"No, I wanted to make some discreet inquiries. I told the professor of course, in strict confidence, and he analysed the crystals himself. He has the apparatus in his room, and I could not have done it so inconspicuously."

"H'm. What about the other attempt on your life? Did that happen soon afterwards?"

"Yes, about ten days later. I was again working late in my room. Very late indeed, on that occasion. It was past eleven o'clock, perhaps just before midnight. I don't often stay so late, but I was still busy with a report - the same report as a matter of fact that I was doing at Halloween. It was naturally very quiet. Suddenly I became aware that someone was moving about in the board room, at least that was my first impression. I went quietly along the passage and into the room, you know under the great Drum."

"Yes, I know it very well, and those stairs!"

There was nobody in the conference room or either of the side rooms, but as I was going out again I heard a sound in the far anteroom, quite loud, like something falling over. I rushed back in but there was nothing there, nor anything that I could see out of place."

"How did you manage to see? Presumably you hadn't switched the lights on."

No. There was a full moon or nearly. Bright moonlight shone down from those windows high up in the Drum. It was as clear as day. While I was bending down peering at some curious fragments on the carpet, I heard another strange noise. An object flew past me, just grazing my left shoulder. I picked it up, and to my surprise found I was holding a heavy piece of wood. I recognised it immediately. I dashed back into the corridor and stood under the entrance arch."

"You recognised it, you say? What was it? Something had fallen from high up in the Drum, I guess."

"That's right. I happened to have been looking at the old drawings of the Drum House a day or two previously, doing an inventory for the insurance company. It's a job I only have to do every few years. I recognised the object at once. It was a piece of wooden handrail from the inner gallery. It's carved in an unusual way, to allow for all the curves and shapes in it. The whole railing is made up of short sections, separately carved and then fastened together. Originally it must have been glued into a single piece, but many years ago it was screwed together for added strength. And safety of course."

"Not so safe, though, if pieces descend on you. The piece that fell was presumably large enough to do considerable damage."

"It would have killed me had I been a few inches further over. I think I had just moved slightly. I recall wobbling on the carpet. The floor is rather uneven."

"Don't you think it was purely accidental? What convinced you that someone was up there trying to finish you off"

"Because of what happened afterwards. I picked the piece up and put it on a table in the anteroom. A screw must have been sticking out of it, probably dislodged as it fell. Anyway, its pointed end was still sharp and caught in my jacket sleeve. I took it out carefully so as not to tear the cloth and, for some reason slipped in into my pocket. I still have it locked up in my desk. I didn't stay to investigate further. The whole incident had unnerved me, and I began to feel vulnerable standing there alone in the moonlight. I went back to my room, gathered up my things and left rapidly for home. The next morning, I went up to the gallery as soon as I arrived. There was no-one else in the building, as I had deliberately come in very early. The handrail was intact! Someone had retrieved the fallen piece and replaced it. However, they missed the screw that I had kept, and there was a brand new screw in its place. From that day to this, I have never spoken about the incident, and nothing has ever been said to me."

"Can I just go back to something you said a little while ago, please? You say you noticed some fragments on the carpet before the rail fell. What did you make of them?"

"They were like long splinters, about six inches in length. Roughly removed from some old wood. Yes, heavy splinters, that's the best description I can give. Quite sharp at the ends. Not that I tried them, but some were sticking deep into the carpet."

"What happened to them? Do you have any?"

"No. I never saw them again. They had gone next morning".

Colley stayed silent for a while. I wondered if he really believed my story. Then he said something that made it clear that he did. "You will have to be very careful. Make no mistake about it. Someone is determined to do a serious mischief. Be very watchful, but act as you always do. On no account give anybody the idea - ."

A door slammed upstairs. Mrs Scutter had finished in the bedrooms and was coming down to attend to the sitting room. Our confidential chat was over. Colley quickly said his goodbyes, rather more loudly than strictly necessary, and departed. I went back up to my bedroom and lay down. It was only then that I remembered that I had forgotten to tell him about my other visitor. He was due to return at any moment, and I heartily wished that Colley had stayed!

There was a noise again in the entrance hall and a low buzz of voices. I heard heavy footsteps dragging upstairs to my room. Mrs Scutter was on her way to announce another arrival.

"There's that person here to see you again," she announced without preamble or apology for disturbing me. She did not seem bothered or scared, just disgruntled because I was still there, getting in her way. I was a confounded nuisance to her. She worked better alone, rushing round doing the necessary minimum, but welcoming any interruption as long as it was feminine chat. That was why Mrs Dixon went shopping on Friday mornings. Both ladies would be perfect in their timing. Mrs Scutter would just happen to have her coat and hat on ready to go, but waiting discreetly to be paid, when Mrs Dixon opened the front door.

"Oh, tell him I can't see him now, Mrs Scutter," I called. "Unless it's Mr Merryman or someone else from the Foundation." She stood her ground. I felt the fever returning. My head swam, and I tried desperately to think of some reason for not letting the visitor enter. I hoped Mrs Dixon would return soon. It was all to no avail. I gave in.

"All right. I'll come down. Ask him to wait outside while I go into the sitting room. I'll see him there." Mrs Scutter left, shaking her head, as though I had finally taken leave of my senses. I went downstairs and entered the sitting room. Soon I heard her re-crossing the hall. Footsteps followed, coming towards the sitting room. I took a deep breath. She came in, quite nonchalantly except for her assumed air of servility that was entirely bogus and put on to try to impress the mysterious visitor.

"Mrs Mountford to see you, sir." She paused. Silence hung in the air. Then she turned to my visitor and sniffed loudly, with obvious disapproval. "Hope you've had the 'flu already." She withdrew to the kitchen, nodding knowingly at me and deferentially closing the door behind her, smiling.

"Please sit down, Mrs Mountford," I managed at length when my power of speech returned. "I don't think we have met before, have we, in all these years? Oh yes, of course I saw you at the funeral. We were all so very sorry."

"I'll come straight to the point, Mr Steward, if you don't mind. I'm Eleanor Mountford. Paul Mountford is, er *was* I should say, my husband. I can't get used to realising I'm a widow now, with nobody at all." Her eyes filled with tears.

"Please tell me if I can help," I responded softly. "Is there anything that I can do? Would you like some coffee? I dare say Mrs Scutter could make some for us."

"No thank you, although it's kind of you to offer. I just wanted to talk to you. You see I have nobody now, nobody else to tell. I don't like to impose, but there's nobody."

The widow sank back into a chair opposite me. Her manner was odd, rather subservient, deferential even. Quite unlike old Dr Mountford. There had never been anything humble about him. She was also younger, much younger surely, and then something more. She was frightened.

"I've just got to tell somebody, and there's really nobody else. Paul always thought highly of you. Said you had a sensible head on your shoulders. Knew how to keep your thoughts to yourself. Not like some I could name - that Arnold Springer - and that sly old bird Garton - not to mention stuck-up Mrs Kingston, as she calls herself. No, Paul thought you were a good sort, a bit cautious perhaps, but a real gentleman."

Not wanting to become involved in gossip about my colleagues, I swallowed hard, cleared my throat, and said with as much sympathy as I could muster, "I'll do what I can to help you of course. What is it that's worrying you? Is it a financial problem, money? I need hardly assure you that what you say will be kept totally confidential."

Would it though, I thought. Supposing I ought not to keep it to myself, whatever it was. Mountford had been close to Kaltz, and he might have to be told if it concerned him or the Foundation. Sir Matthew too might need to be informed. And there was Colley to consider. I began to feel wretched about the whole interview and wished she had not chosen me to confide in.

"No, thank you. It's not money. That's no problem at all." She smiled fleetingly. I noticed then that, despite her humble manner, she was wearing good quality clothes, expensive though serviceable shoes and coat, and had with her a smart new handbag. This widow was rather an interesting paradox.

"I just wanted to come down to the Foundation, one day to suit of course. I want to collect my husband's things, please."

"His things!" I spluttered. "Surely you already have all Dr Mountford's personal belongings. I made particularly sure that you would." I had certainly asked someone to do it. Springer, Merryman, Mrs Kingston - I couldn't immediately recall which of them had been given the task.

She had received nothing. That was very strange, I told her. Mrs Mountford stood dejectedly in the middle of the sitting room. I felt tremendously sorry for her. For all the material comforts she had, she was utterly alone. Mountford had always kept her in the background. Perhaps he felt slightly embarrassed, having, in a way, married beneath him. People at least might think that, old-fashioned though the idea might be. Perhaps he wanted to keep work and home firmly separate. Yes, that would be it, and very sensible too. I thought that was just what I would do myself. Mountford always did have a lot of common sense. That way he could cope daily with Kaltz and Cammering. A man of sound judgement, and clearly of some small mystery, for he must have had some private income above his salary. I felt uneasy, and wanted more time to think. I wished that I had bothered to have got to know Mountford better when I had the chance.

I told Mrs Mountford that I would certainly look into the matter, and assured her that she would have Dr Mountford's effects as soon as she wished. I hoped privately that there would be no wrangling over what had been his own property and what belonged to the Foundation. Kaltz could be awkward if he thought Mrs Mountford wanted laboratory notes or equipment. Still, that was for the future.

We arranged that she should come to my office on the following Wednesday. By then I should have recovered fully, and would have had the chance to deal with the backlog on my desk. I said my goodbyes and returned to my bedroom, still feeling uneasy. What was it?

I rang Merryman. After a few minutes on other matters I asked him what had been done about Dr Mountford's personal effects. Merryman went quiet for a moment, and then seemed flustered. "Mountford? Oh, that! Arnold Springer said he would attend to it. Very keen he was to sort it out. I was glad to let him. I bet he had a high old time arguing with Kaltz. Not to mention the merry widow."

Chapter Five

The Man in the Gallery

"**Y**ou're jumping to conclusions, you know, without first checking the facts. I've spoken to you both about this before, and I do hope that I shan't have to mention it again."

Dr Sedgfield was winding up his tirade in the laboratory of his two senior assistants. I had not intended eavesdropping on the three of them, but I was trapped as I reached the door of the building. If I went on into the laboratory it would be obvious that I had overhead at least something of what was said, while if I stayed until they had finished I might hear something I should not. It would be very embarrassing if someone else came up while I hovered about.

It was an unusually mild morning for the middle of January, quite sunny but with threatening clouds. A local thunderstorm had evidently been brewing for some time in Sedgfield's laboratories, and had now burst. I decided to take the chance and wait outside the open window, patiently waiting for a better time for me to go inside.

Staniforth had already been taken to task, and now it was the turn of Horning to receive the outspoken criticism of Sedgfield. Something unusual must have upset him to become so outspoken. Sedgfield was normally so easy-going and mild-mannered. Probably some internal politics with Kaltz or the professor, I thought. I heartily hoped I would not get involved if it was.

"It's not enough to reach the right conclusion, Horning. As I've already explained to Staniforth, even if that is correct, it's no good basing it on faulty readings. It's only by chance that you've confirmed the answers you were after. You might just as well have guessed the figures."

46

There followed a burst of speech from the other end of the laboratory that I could not hear properly. Indeed I should not have been hearing any of this conversation, I told myself. Still, I was stuck there until it finished. I could not interrupt nor tiptoe away. There was no cover to retreat across the lawns should any of them look out of the window.

I heard Sedgfield continue. "I'm not saying that at all, Horning. No-one is accusing you or Staniforth of concocting the readings, but you know perfectly well that you can't just pick and choose. If what you find goes on to confirm your theory - which incidentally I think is right, a nice piece of work, in fact - you can't simply select the observations that fit in and reject those that don't. There was another pause and more half-heard comments. "No, of course you can't take on trust what somebody else has said. They may be wrong, whoever they are. You've got to have the evidence yourself. At least half your readings were not reproducible. That should have told you that they might be false. Yes, I know it's embarrassing to have them picked up and checked by Dr Kaltz and found to be wrong. But if he can get the correct readings, so can you."

Horning was obviously very upset at the suggestion that either he was not taking enough care or that he had actually cooked the figures. Staniforth added that it was humiliating to have brought in Dr Kaltz at all, without at least referring to them first.

"Dr Kaltz is entirely within his rights to come in and verify anything that we do in this Foundation. You know very well what the procedures and rules are." Sedgfield was trying to calm the situation down, having made his point. It was interesting that he sided now with his assistants. No doubt he too suffered from Kaltz's interventions.

More expostulations followed, and I just caught the mention of Kaltz's name again from one of the younger men, when the figure of the great man himself appeared in the doorway. I rather think that Kaltz saw me waiting outside. At any rate, he turned back towards his own room. The conversation inside had died away.

"I don't mean to be hard on you men, you know," Sedgfield concluded, "but don't ever take anything on trust. Always check what someone has told you."

Horning was still mumbling discontent to Staniforth as they went down the corridor to their own rooms. "That nosy old man, he's nothing but a busybody, poking and prying into other people's work. You'd think he could find something better to do with his time."

"Now you really can't say that about Kaltz, whatever else," commented Staniforth. "It's a wonder to me that he can find time to look at your work. He's always at it, nineteen to the dozen! Never goes home at all, so Sonia says."

"Well she would know, wouldn't she! Of course he goes home." Horning lowered his voice. "As a matter of fact, I've seen him slinking off quietly, locking up and looking all around the place before disappearing up through the woods to his place."

"You must have been working very late yourself then! What were you up to, might I ask? Currying favour with Sedgy by working overtime? He wouldn't even notice. Or were you trying to impress Kaltz? Either way, you're doing yourself no favours."

"Don't be so daft! I'd forgotten my squash racket. I brought it into the lab first thing and shoved it in my locker with my sports gear. It must have fallen behind the stuff in there. I didn't take it with the other things when I left at night. I usually go straight on to the club after work."

"I'm not a bit surprised. The rubbish you keep in your locker. Kaltz will have a fit if he checks up on that!"

Sedgfield did not at first hear me come into his room, although I had knocked on the door and waited briefly. He paid little attention to the details I had to discuss with him, so I cut the meeting short, thinking to postpone it till he was in a receptive frame of mind. He was clearly more upset by Kaltz's intervention in his assistants' work than he had disclosed to them. His was an awkward job, I reflected, now that Mountford was dead. He had to do that old boy's work as well as his own. Nobody wanted to have to co-operate that closely with the human dynamo if he could avoid it. I felt sorry for Sedgfield. Things couldn't go on like this.

A shower had dampened the ground while I was inside the laboratory block. Now that I came out again, the sun shone brightly as I crossed the lawns back to the Drum House. I had forgotten whatever I had discussed with him, but I could not get Sedgfield out of my mind, nor his remarks to the assistants. They were wise words, and the young men would do well to take notice of them. They should be careful to check and re-check. Then neither Sedgfield nor Kaltz could catch them out and their conclusions would be sound and useful to society. I hoped I would always verify observations in my own work. I knew that the professor did. He took great care, pride even, in doing so. Experience was a great teacher, I reflected, and so was the professor. So was Colley. They were alike in that.

The thought must have stayed in my subconscious long after my thoughts turned to other matters concerning the Drum House. That body, for instance, the one that Colley had seen from the gallery and found on the stairs. Who was it, and why had it never been seen again? Where was it now? Why had nobody been reported as missing? It was very baffling. I ought perhaps to inquire more closely. After all I was the administrator and had special responsibility for the Drum House and what happened within it. Should I not call in the police? There was little evidence that anything untoward had ever happened. No dead body anywhere. Mountford's death was not exactly unexpected, tragic though the circumstances were. I would have to consult Colley and get his views. We could so easily make fools of ourselves and of the Foundation, if we acted hastily. Colley would know what was best.

I hurried on across the lawns. My feet beat out a regular tread, pounding into my brain. "See what Colley thinks. See what Colley thinks." I quickened my pace. "See what Colley thinks." It was going to rain again. I'd better hurry. "See what Colley thinks. Think what Colley sees."

What? Another thought came to be. What had Colley seen? It suddenly dawned on me that I had not followed Sedgfield's maxim after all. I had not checked what Colley saw!

A cloud passed over the sun. I shivered. Or what he claims to have seen! I tried to dismiss the unwelcome idea, but it would not leave my mind. I had only Colley's word for what he saw from the gallery in the Drum House. Indeed I only had his word for the whole episode. Supposing -. No, he had to be genuine. Hadn't he? But suppose... No, not that... The bag, the bag! I sighed with relief. The part of the story about the travelling bag was true, as I had found it myself. Found it twice, actually, and returned it to his home. The sun came out again from behind the clouds. I could not mistrust Colley. I didn't, did I? No, of course not.

On the other hand, I thought as I entered my own office, that I ought to check the gallery, if only out of duty to the Foundation. No, that was overstating it. I had to admit that I was deeply curious about the whole business and would have to find out, if I could, for myself. I had to make sure that you could see so clearly down into the boardroom and its anterooms from fifty feet up in the Drum. We ought to know that in any case. We could not have board meetings, or any other private discussions, overheard by some listener high up in the gallery.

It was all rather exciting. A little plan of my own. There would no need to tell anyone about it. Yes, it would be a useful exercise, a good piece of research. "Always check what someone has told you." I decided there and then to take the earliest possible opportunity of doing just that.

A planning sub-committee kept me all afternoon. Strangely enough, we were in the board room, and as the professor and Sedgfield droned on with the accountants about the budget for the financial year after next, my gaze drifted several times up into the high Drum far above us. I could see the gallery easily the first few times I looked, but as the afternoon wore on, it became dusk up there, and I could hardly make out the line of the handrails.

By the time the meeting ended, it was becoming quite dark. The staff in the offices and the laboratories had finished for the day and gone home. Kaltz's lights were still on, of course, and Mrs Kingston was only just packing up her things preparatory to departing. She looked very smart, though I felt I should not comment on her appearance. She had changed into an expensive looking short evening gown, for the theatre or dinner, perhaps, in London. She gave me a few staccato messages, none of which required urgent attention, and left hurriedly before I could say more.

Now would be a good time to have a look round in the Drum. Sedgfield's car was already driving away, and the professor too was walking towards the car park. He seemed to be in a hurry to be off somewhere as well. Soon the only remaining lights were those across the lawns in Kaltz's laboratory. No doubt he would be on the premises for some hours yet, but he was sure to be more than pre-occupied with his research, safely in the distance.

I moved quickly across the reception hall and opened the door to the turret stairs without a sound. I don't remember why I thought it important to make no noise, but it did seem to be so at that time. It was as well that I took the precaution of bringing a flashlight with me, as it was completely dark on the stairs. I put out my hand, feeling for the guide rope that ran between buckeye fittings around the wall of the staircase. There was no handrail, and this had long ago been thought sufficient to guide anyone using the stairs. It would be easy to lose the steps and stumble down the steep stone treads. A body would pitch down and round, all the way to the bottom entrance door. I shut my mind to that idea, and gently took hold of the rope in my right hand.

I paused a moment to let my eyes become accustomed to the darkness. All was silent around me.

And then, a shudder of horror ran through me. Standing there motionless, holding the rope, I distinctly felt it move in my hand! Then a pause. Then another slight pull! Panic swept over me, but I stood rooted to the spot, still feeling the rope pulsating regularly. What did it mean? Whatever was happening? I began to think that maybe after all I was imagining it, when the rope started to move once again within my hands.

Then I realised what it was that was causing the movement. Somewhere, higher up on the staircase, someone was silently moving while holding the rope, climbing up the stairs or coming down! I froze, but realised that I could not stay where I was without being detected. I didn't want to be seen there, investigating quietly. It was important to remain unobserved, though I did not know why.

The slight movements began again. Listening hard, I heard a tiny sound, a feint creaking. I would have missed it altogether, if I had not been listening so carefully, half expecting to hear it and half dreading that I would not. I knew immediately what it was, and breathed an almost audible sigh of relief. Someone had opened the door on to the outer gallery. They had gone *up* the staircase!

Quickly I mounted the first few steps and withdrew into the door space leading to the mezzanine landing. Then the rope began to twitch again. The secretive explorer high above me was now descending the spiral stairs. Slowly the seconds ticked by. I pushed back further into the recess of the door space, hoping that they would not come that way. I edged still further back so that I would not be seen even if that happened.

Since I had heard the top gallery door creak, no further sound had penetrated the darkness. Whoever it was on the staircase was taking great care to descend without being detected. They could be up to no good, I thought. Otherwise why the secrecy? If they had occasion to be there, why not just walk boldly up and down, shining a light? But wasn't that exactly what I was doing, stealthily creeping about in the dark, quite needlessly? I watched and waited. And waited. And waited.

I was almost ready to give up and walk down normally into the entrance hall, when a sleeve rustled slightly as it brushed the wall near my left ear. A shape almost touched me as I stood motionless, hidden in the alcove. A feint gleam of light from the bottom door just penetrated to where I stood, holding my breath. The quiet sound passed by, a dark shape descending, step by step, with the utmost care and slowly. Then the bottom door opened. Peering round a bend in the staircase, I clearly saw a man going out into the reception hall. I knew him immediately. I could not restrain an audible gasp. The man was Dr Garton!

The front door of the Drum House closed quietly. Eventually I heard a car start up in the distance and lights flickered along the road between the trees as it drove away. All was silent. After five minutes or so of sitting alone in the darkened entrance hall, I took my flashlight and re-entered the doorway leading to the spiral stairs.

Quickly I climbed to the inner gallery, pausing briefly at the mezzanine doorway where I had hidden to check that no-one had entered while I had been downstairs. Everywhere was quiet and empty. I took no particular precaution to stay quiet, but avoided letting light from my torch shine outside the Drum. Fresh marks showed up in the dust of the inner gallery, both on the floor and the handrail. A particularly large patch of grime had been wiped from one place along the handrail, but there was little to see. There was nothing that had not been there for years, or so I thought at first.

Looking more closely at the floor by the wiped area of rail, I noticed a torn scrap of white paper, or perhaps card. There were a few letters printed on it. I recognised what it was, but could not even imagine what significance it had. It was the bent flap off the end of a cardboard box of ten pencils, a standard issue at the Foundation, but one I had introduced only a month ago. We were always having to find cheap pencils for the staff. Goodness knows what they did with them. Chew them to pieces, Sonia had speculated. What was Dr Garton doing with new pencils at this hour in the Drum House gallery? It didn't make any kind of sense to me.

Then I found one of the actual pencils, lying broken on the edge of the gallery, partly hanging over the drop. Carefully I retrieved it and put in my pocket. I looked over the handrail into the darkness below. But it was not darkness any longer. A desk-light had been switched on in one of the anterooms, the room where Colley said the body had lain. The professor was searching all over the floor, occasionally picking small objects up. I withdrew slightly so that he would not see me if he looked up. Not that he would be able to see anything in the gallery, as it was in total darkness. Then I realised what he was doing. He was collecting pencils from the floor.

What on earth was going on? Had he driven away and returned without making a sound? Perhaps the car I had heard driving off belonged to someone else, Kaltz perhaps? Dr Garton seemed to testing out some theory by dropping pencils. Possibly he had been aiming them from the gallery to see where they landed. The only explanation I could think of was that he was using them as substitutes for something else. A weapon? I began to shiver again, and felt uneasy. In case Garton came back up to the gallery for another try with the pencils, I moved silently back down to my hiding place in the mezzanine doorway. Garton however did not return to the stairs. After a few minutes, I heard a distant door close and soon he emerged into the reception hall. Without glancing backwards he stepped briskly to his car, parked now just outside the entrance steps, and drove away.

Later that evening, I pondered the events of the day in my bedroom. Colley was certainly to be trusted. I had now checked on what he told me. Not only had he seen the body from the gallery, but the professor knew about it too, and was testing out his theory as to how the killing had occurred. I was relieved to think that neither Colley nor the professor had been responsible. However, going carefully through what I had seen, there were some disturbing conclusions to be drawn. Garton knew about the body. Well that was all right. After all, hadn't Colley seen him at the mezzanine door on the day he made the discovery? No, that was Sedgefield. Colley had seen his name on his laboratory coat. How odd! Or had Garton been wearing Sedgefield's white coat? Sometimes they did get mixed up when they came back from the laundry. Perhaps, then, the professor had seen Colley there. Perhaps he had seen him enter the building. Perhaps he had seen him hide the bag under the box tree. Perhaps, even, he had retrieved the bag and brought it to the Drum House. Did Garton think Colley had killed the man?

Or had the professor followed me to the station that day, even though he had sent me, and seen me find the bag? That could surely not be the case, could it? If so, it meant one thing for certain. Dr Garton suspected that I was involved, but had said nothing about his suspicions. I was utterly downcast that my old friend thought I was involved in murder. Perhaps he had said nothing about it for friendship's sake. At least he had said nothing yet. What he intended to do, when he had finished investigating, I could not begin to guess.

And then, supposing after all it had been Sedgefield at the mezzanine door. I went to the kitchen to make coffee.

Chapter Six

The Widow at the Drum House

"Perhaps he's taken up bird-watching or something. I don't know what he gets up to in his spare time, do I?".

Sonia clearly did not like the way the conversation was going. Brian Fletcher-Smith was a handsome young man, and she had been more than a little excited when he first came over to the office. She thought he had brought the parcel as a present for her, and had opened it before realising her mistake. Now she was cross with Fletcher-Smith for letting her unwrap the brown paper. She felt foolish. "You might have said something, instead of just standing there, grinning like a fat ape. What Mr Steward is going to say when he sees it I don't know. Do you want to get me into trouble, or something?"

There had followed a pause and a giggle, and Sonia told her visitor that she had not meant *that* - he was really terrible. I had almost stopped listening. I had not intended eavesdropping at all. I was in the corridor quietly looking up payments records in the filing cabinets we kept there for lack of space in our own rooms. What Fletcher-Smith could be doing with parcels for me I could not imagine, but I knew that time would tell.

As the giggling continued from Sonia's room, I walked quietly back to my own desk, and busied myself with the payments records. After a few minutes, there came the expected footsteps, a knock on my door, and Sonia entered carrying a heap of string and brown paper. "Oh Mr Steward," she burst out. "I didn't know you were in today. I thought you had gone up to town with Professor Garton."

"No, Sonia, I changed my plans at the last minute. There are some things I had to do here first. I hope to go this afternoon if I've finished. Was there something you wanted to ask me?"

"It's this parcel that's come in from Malcolm Horning in the lab block. Brian Fletcher-Smith brought it across and I didn't realise it wasn't for me. That's why it's opened. I'm very sorry, but he didn't tell me till I'd undone it."

"That's all right Sonia. I don't suppose it's anything private. Did he say what it was? I wasn't expecting anything."

"Oh, it's not for you Mr Steward." Sonia became flustered again. "I suppose I'd better leave it with you. It's some binoculars for Arnold Springer."

"Binoculars for Springer? How very odd. Do you know anything about this, Sonia?"

She did not, and indeed she seemed to be as puzzled as I was. I rang Fletcher-Smith and asked what was going on. The binoculars were quite new and obviously expensive, and of course I was more than interested in anything concerning the still absent Springer.

"I see. Yes, thank you very much. I'll put them into safe keeping here for the time being. Yes. That's fine, thank you."

I told Sonia that everything was in order and that I would deal with the binoculars. No, she had not done anything wrong. It was a natural mistake to make. Everything was quite all right. No, I was not at all cross with her. Nor with Fletcher-Smith. No need to worry any more.

That was not quite true though, as I had to admit to myself. I wondered again about Springer and whether I ought not to start looking for a replacement. If he came back now, I would be justified in dismissing him. He had disappeared from time to time before now, although it was true he had then only been away for a few hours, a day at most. I looked again at his binoculars. Really he was such a strange young man. We knew so little about him, though we had seen him almost every working day. I suddenly realised I was thinking of him in the past tense, and wondered why I instinctively done so. Was he never coming back to the Drum House? Had he absconded for some serious reason in his private life? Was he perhaps even dead?

I didn't know that Springer was interested in bird-watching. He had never mentioned it. Nor did I know that Horning was an ornithologist either. I had taken little interest in my fellow members of staff, and resolved once more not to let things slip past me without noticing. It was generous of Springer to lend his expensive glasses to Horning, I supposed, but then he could well afford to do so from all appearances.

My reverie came to an abrupt end when Merryman opened his door and went noisily into his room, accompanied by two or three other people. Evidently somebody else thought I was away in London. I began to cast around for some excuse to see Merryman, when I heard my name mentioned. I paused with my hand on my own door for a moment, out of courtesy or perhaps out of curiosity.

"He's taken on a new lease of life, all this gadding about. He's up in London again today, isn't he? What do you think is at the back of it?" Malcolm Horning had obviously been questioning Merryman for some time, but without learning very much. "Old Steward is a bit on the sly side, don't you think? I mean, he never let's on, does he? I tell you, John, I bet he's got a lady friend up there in town somewhere."

"I don't know anything about it if he has," replied Merryman. "I don't really see that it's any of our business anyway. He can please himself what he does, as long as he's all right with us in the office. Which he is."

"Arnold said he was a crafty old so-and-so. He often used to tell us in the lab that he reckoned there was more to David Steward than met the eye."

"Oh, you know what Arnold Springer's like, Malcolm. Always stirring up trouble if he can. Anyway there's nobody more secretive than him, if that's what you're complaining about, is there?"

"Yes, you're right. Where is Arnold? Away on a project or something? We've not seen him over in the labs for weeks. I've had his binoculars for ages, and he's never been in to collect them. That's not like him, you know."

"I don't know where he is just at present. No doubt he's fixed it all up with the boss. He seems to have leave to go whenever he likes, and plenty of money to spend as well." Merryman must have known, or suspected, more than that, but was not going to betray our team's business to the laboratory staff. That was good work from Merryman. He really was a decent sort.

"Where does he get it from, do you think?" That was from Staniforth. I hadn't realised that he was in the room as well. It was quite a little party they were having while they thought I was away. I tiptoed back to my desk and waited for more. It would be interesting to see how Merryman bore up to questioning from his friends.

"His family are probably well off," said Horning."Janice says he's often at the bank paying in cheques and cash."

"Your little girl friend shouldn't be reporting on her bank's customers, Malcolm. I shall have to take my overdraft somewhere else if that's what happens."

Come on, Harry, that's not fair. She just happened to notice it that's all. She said nothing about the amounts. The cheques might be just for the odd quid or two for all I know. I'm not saying it was hush money or any ill-gotten gains, or anything like that, you know."

Staniforth had hooked his fish, as usual. He could always head Malcolm Horning in any direction he wanted. Sedgfield had noticed that, and said so to me and the professor more than once. There was nothing crafty about it, just careful management of the conversation. Horning was not going to let the subject alone. He liked to think he knew more about what went on at the Foundation than anybody, and still had a trump card to play. "Arnold Springer reckoned that he had a hold on somebody important. Someone who was willing to look after him to keep him happy, or perhaps to keep him quiet."

"How would Arnold know anything worth that," said Merryman. "You mean blackmail? You're making it up Malcolm."

"It's true, I tell you! He said old Mountford had told him. And you know how thick he was with Mountford, or at least used to be. It's a funny thing, you know, but they didn't seem as friendly recently."

"Arnold used to lodge somewhere up where Mountford lived, didn't he? When he first came to the Foundation I mean. I know he's got that posh flat now, but I mean when he first came here."

"Posh flat is right, and a live-in housekeeper to run it. Arnold's really got it made, wherever he gets his cash."

"She's his sister-in-law, you idiot. Don't go starting those rumours, for heaven's sake," retorted Merryman.

I began to wonder how I could intervene without embarrassment, when I caught sight of Sonia outside in the corridor, waving frantically but silently to Merryman and his visitors. It dawned on me that she was trying to signal that I had not gone to London but was sitting in my room, probably listening to every word. The conversation had become so animated, however, that she could not get their attention and went away. She need not have worried, however, as they had tired of discussing Foundation gossip and returned to their more usual topics of lunchtime conversation. Eventually Horning and Staniforth drifted off back towards the laboratory block, but I was unable to spare Merryman's blushes. I had thought of walking out quietly and coming back noisily, but a commotion in the corridor prevented those plans.

Footsteps, followed by an unnecessarily loud knock on my door, brought Sonia and another visitor. "Mrs Mountford to see you, Mr Steward. Says she came on the off-chance you'd be in, because she can't manage tomorrow as you said." There was a clatter from Merryman's room, and no doubt a tidying of his desk.

"That's fine, Sonia. Show her in, and perhaps you would bring us some coffee." I heard Merryman close his door quietly and I did the same behind Mrs Mountford. I ushered the widow to a chair and returned to my desk.

"I'm sorry to have to tell you, Mrs Mountford, that I have not been able to find any belongings of your husband's here in the offices. I imagine that any of his personal property that is still at the Foundation will be over in the laboratory block. I'll take you over there in a minute, if that's all right for you. But I just wondered if you could let me have any idea what it is that you think will still be here. I spoke to my own staff, and they were as I surprised as I was that you had not received Paul's belongings already. Mr Springer was asked to see to it, and I quite thought that he had brought everything to you."

Mrs Mountford had lost the humility I noticed when we last met, and seemed entirely at ease. It was rather myself now who was uneasy. I did not know how to explain that we appeared to have lost what was now her property.

"Don't fret about that, Mr Steward," she cooed. "I didn't suppose there would be any of Paul's things here in your own offices. No, I was hoping to get the chance of a word or two with Dr Kaltz." I was puzzled by her manner, and still could not decide whether she was naive or clever. Had she come here simply to collect her late husband's belongings, or was there a more sinister motive? Had she come to cause trouble? If so, for whom? Did she suspect that I was withholding something from her? Did she even suspect that I was in some way implicated in her husband's death? If so, why? Well, I knew one thing that she would have to forgo.

"I'm sorry again, Mrs Mountford, but I do not think that it will be possible to see Dr Kaltz. I'm not even sure if he's here, and even if he is whether he can speak to you…"

"He's here all right, Mr Steward. Make no mistake about that. And as for speaking to him, well we'll just have to see, won't we?" She asserted her confidence so strongly that I must have been visibly disconcerted. Her manner changed at once. She had perhaps realised that she had made a mistake, and again I could not decide what her motives were. "I'll just collect whatever there is, I mean, Mr Steward. You and all the staff have been so very kind."

I explained that the laboratories were not my direct responsibility, and that we would be seeing Dr Garton. I was glad that the professor had agreed to share my burden with me. I had half expected him to refuse, as he seemed to have been keeping his distance in recent weeks. Perhaps I had offended him in some way, although I could not think of any particular thing that I might have done to upset him. Usually he was direct and open with me, and I was mystified by his attitude. I began to think that he must indeed know all about the deaths at the Foundation and believe that I was connected with them in some dreadful way.

The professor received Mrs Mountford with great courtesy, and appeared to be genuinely concerned that her husband's property had not been sent to her. However he was equally at a loss to know precisely what that property might be. Mrs Mountford seemed to be struck almost dumb, and merely kept repeating that she just wanted Paul's things. She began to cry, and we both found it most distressing. Then she surprised us with an unexpected request.

"I'd like, if that's possible, to see where Paul died, please. I know it might be awkward for you, but I would - I would - so like - ."

"Of course, my dear," said the professor, and led her away to the end of the corridor where Mountford had worked. Inside much was unchanged, although Dr Garton had put in two temporary students who had been seconded from his old university to help him. Mrs Mountford made no comment, and signalled that she would like to leave. I was puzzled once more by her attitude, or rather her succession of different attitudes.

Was that really all she wanted? Perhaps she had been to shy or upset to ask just to see Mountford's room directly. There seemed to be nothing there she wanted to take with her. An old coat of Mountford's still hung behind the door. I felt embarrassed when I spotted it. The widow had seen it at the same moment, and yet made no comment. It was all very strange.

"Perhaps, if that is everything that you wished to see - ," began the professor. Clearly he was as mystified as I was about her behaviour. We ushered her out again into the corridor.

Suddenly the door at the far end opened, and out came Kaltz. His head was bowed as usual and he had not noticed us. That was hardly surprising in itself, but we rarely saw him emerge from his room at this time of day. Half way down the passage, almost at the entrance door, he stopped and raised his head. Both the professor and I stopped, expecting some dramatic reaction. That certainly happened, but not in the way we expected. Mrs Mountford continued walking towards Kaltz at a steady pace. Then Kaltz uttered a cry, and rushed forward towards her. We both started forward, thinking that Kaltz was capable of almost anything when surprised like that. To our utter amazement, he seized Mrs Mountford, clasped her to his chest and muttered to her his deep anguish at the loss of his comrade, her dear, dear husband. He hugged her closely and would not allow her to speak. Then with his left arm still firmly around her shoulders, he led her into his room.

Garton and I stood aghast in the corridor. For a minute or so, there was no sound at all from Kaltz's room. Then came a dreadful wailing, followed by raised voices. The shouting went on for several minutes. We tried to enter Kaltz's laboratory but he had locked the door on us. I suggested that I might go for help. The professor motioned me to stay where I was. Suddenly the door opened quietly, and out walked the widow. She seemed to be quite unruffled, and indeed I thought I detected the ghost of a smile on her face as she turned towards us.

"Thank you very much for letting me come to see you, and to see where poor Paul used to work," she said. There was no suggestion now that she wanted to reclaim any of her husband's physical possessions. It was evident that, whatever her purpose had been in coming to the Foundation, she had entirely achieved it. The professor muttered that it was no trouble, and led her back across the lawns to the Drum House.

I stayed behind in the laboratory block for a minute or two, trying to make sense of what had happened. Then the door of Kaltz's room slowly opened and he peered out into the corridor. I froze, and he did not immediately notice that I was there. Then he caught sight of me, rushed back through his door, and slammed it vigorously. The sound of bolts being drawn across the inside echoed down the deserted corridor. I shall never forget the sight of Kaltz at that doorway, nor of his face. It wore the expression of utter terror!

Chapter Seven

Questions Without Answers

Dukring the third week in January I happened to be in London for a week's conference in which the Foundation was participating. Professor Garton should have lectured to the meeting, but a Chinese scholar arrived unexpectedly with a distinguished contribution. Dr Garton stood down to fit him into the agenda. He wanted to stay on to hear other papers read, so I agreed that he should take over my secretarial duties.

Consequently I found myself free, and before returning to the Foundation, I decided to call at Palmyra Square. I knew that Colley had been confined to his home because of recurring difficulties with his leg, and suspected that he must be thoroughly bored. He was delighted to see me, and I soon found myself again in his comfortable study. He looked pale and drawn, and welcomed the chance to talk. Something was worrying him, and it soon proved, as I expected, to concern the mysterious events at the Drum House.

I asked about his health, but received no intelligible response. After falling silent for a while, he suddenly brightened and asked for further news at the Foundation. "I presume the Mountford lady returned for a second visit after I left the Dixons."

Trust you to know that it was the widow who had called!" I replied. "There was I worried by the prospect of interviewing Mountford's spectre!" I told him about our meeting and the subsequent strange visit to the Foundation.

"That's very interesting." Colley had listened thoughtfully. "I wonder what exactly it was she wanted. You say she didn't take any of Mountford's belongings with her. Not even his old coat. How very peculiar!

"H'm. That's ruined a promising theory I've been working on. I had the notion that she was after Mountford's laboratory notebooks, to search for something valuable in them..."

"You mean technical data that she could use in some way. Perhaps to patent it, or sell to an interested party. No, I've been thinking about that myself. But having spent some time with her, I don't think she would be capable of it. Although I must admit I can't decide whether or not she's up to something."

"She certainly is. She may be out of her depth, but we can be sure of that. The question is what? I'm not certain she really wanted to collect Mountford's belongings at all. Wasn't it just an excuse to get into the laboratory block? She strung you along with that story, I'd say. I gather that she's quite persuasive."

"And persistent. She was anxious to see me without delay, even if I was just a way of getting access to the laboratories."

Colley paused. "Yes, that's really odd if you think about it, isn't it? I mean, she took her time coming to see you. Why didn't she come earlier, or even speak to you at the funeral? No, something happened subsequently. She had to approach you as a matter of urgency. Now what could that be? I wonder..."

The fire crackled in the hearth. The warm light lit up the room. My eyes took in the antique bookshelves, obviously valuable, and the modern gadgetry, the computer, the telephones, the large monitor screen. This was the den of a busy man, sociable and clever. Colley must have many interests I knew nothing about. Important interests. I realised that I hardly knew him at all. Yet I trusted him. So did Sir Carlo Waybridge, but somehow I did not need that second opinion.

Colley struggled to raise himself in his chair. "My guess is that the Mountford lady was after something quite simple. She wanted to see Kaltz. She would have little chance of getting to him except by being there in the laboratory block."

"That's right," I agreed. "She knew he was there. She must have made it her business to find out. Do you think that was why she came on that particular day? We had actually agreed a later date."

"Probably so. What did she want with Kaltz though? You say there was a fearful row? And yet she went home satisfied, triumphant even. So she had the better of the encounter. Has Kaltz said anything, or reacted to the meeting in any way?"

"Good heavens no! Not that I would know anyway. I hardly ever see him. But I haven't heard anything. The laboratory staff might know. Do you want me to inquire?"

"Better not," replied Colley. "It might cause a few eyebrows to be raised. We don't want you to arouse any suspicions. Not at the moment, at least."

"Do you think someone in the laboratories does know? I mean, I could put out some discreet enquiries. It would be very interesting to know whether - ."

"No, please don't do any such thing!" Colley stood up in his chair and tried to walk. "It would be very foolish. Please do as I ask. Anything else could easily undo all our good work. Not to say put yourself in even more danger."

"Whatever do you mean, Colley?" I was alarmed both by his words and the vehement way he spoke them. There was no immediate reply, and I could tell by Colley's expression that he had already said too much. I felt isolated and afraid.

"Now don't worry, David," Colley's voice was soothing. "As I told you before, there is some chance that another attempt will be made to put you out of the way. So just be careful and act normally. That's all I'm asking from you. Surely that's not too much to expect? It may not happen, and indeed I think the chances are rather reduced. The villain probably now realises that they were after the wrong person - or persons. Yes, I think someone other than yourself, in fact two people are in some real peril. Steps will have to be taken."

67

"Very well. I'll do as you say, of course. Is there any help though that I can give about the others?"

"No. Leave that to us, myself and my associates, that is. As for you, soon there'll be someone to help. You are not going to be alone for much longer." A flicker of a smile came to Colley's face as he spoke the last sentence.

There was nothing more to be said on that subject. In any case there was another question I wanted to raise. "I've been thinking about the body you found in the Drum House."

"So have I. So have I," interrupted Colley. "I must admit that I'm baffled about that. There must be something we've overlooked. Or perhaps there's going to be some further clue about it. It's not a stable situation. The body will have to reappear sooner or later, and the villain will act accordingly."

"That's not what I meant," I said. "Someone must know what happened to it. What concerns me is that time's passing and nothing's turned up. Don't you think we should call in the police?"

"No! Certainly don't do that!" Colley was emphatic. "There may well come a time for that, but it's not yet. After all, what could we tell them? I saw the body, but there's no physical evidence, is there? And no corroboration. No, just be patient. The villain will make a false move if we play a waiting game, and give himself away. In the meantime, act normally, but be vigilant!"

"Do you think, just for the sake of argument, that Mountford was murdered? Suppose he had discovered something about the murder of the unknown man you saw, and then the murderer found out that he knew, and struck again."

"Do you think that's likely? I'm not so sure. All the signs were that Mountford died of natural causes. You said he had a bad heart condition, and his doctor thought he could die at any time."

"Yes, I suppose so. He was taking tablets for his heart condition. He had them with him at all times. He made quite a point about that and told everyone. I suppose that made sense. Yet I can't help feeling that the two deaths are linked." There was something nagging at the back of my mind. Something that I half-remembered noticing during Mrs Mountford's visit. I had to tell Colley, but it had gone again for the moment.

"There's no evidence for it, is there? That's what's important."

"Well then, here's another hypothesis. Suppose Mountford is not dead. Suppose he's still alive."

Colley looked up, startled, and told me to continue. He wheeled his chair to the window and stared out.

"Suppose Mountford killed the man in the Drum House and then faked his own death. Suppose he did that by killing Kaltz and assuming his identity. They were similar in age and appearance. We always said at the Foundation that they had been together so long - ".

"Yes, yes." Colley wheeled back to his desk. "But it doesn't seem likely, does it? Again there's no evidence, and where's the motive? And another point. Surely he couldn't continue the deception for long. Sooner or later he would have been found out."

"Not if it didn't have to be kept up for long," I persisted, thinking aloud. "He could easily enough maintain it for a few weeks, a month or two even. Kaltz was a solitary man, working alone and living alone, as far as we ever knew." A cold shiver came over me, and I stopped talking. "Colley," I said at length. "Why do I talk of Kaltz in the past tense, as though he really is dead? I don't like it, but somehow - ."

Colley smiled. "What I should be talking about is offering you a drink. What will you have?" And with that he passed on, with some force, to speak of other matters.

"Mountford was curiously wealthy, wasn't he?" he resumed. "Presumably it was inherited money, because he could hardly have left so much money in his will from what he earned at the Foundation."

"I don't know. Have you seen his will?" I didn't even know he had left one. Again I felt hopelessly inefficient and unobservant, especially when Colley handed me a copy. I read the details. It was staggering, all that money.

"Well, I'm blessed if I know where he got it. It certainly wasn't inherited. He came from a poor family in some Northern back street. His father was a miner, I think.

Mountford made his way to grammar school and university with scholarships. He was quite open about it, proud of it, and why not? He may not have been in the top flight as a researcher, but his achievement was remarkable in his own way."

"You don't think he might have had some source of money that was not, what shall we say, entirely above board? I wonder if he was blackmailing someone. We managed to get a look at his bank account, and it was rather interesting. There were payments every month, or every quarter, at regular intervals, from the same set of names. Quite substantial payments too, They would easily account for his having plenty of money. Maybe he wasn't what everyone would consider rich, but Mountford was a careful spender, it appears."

"I don't know what to think. It's not really likely that Mountford would blackmail anyone. I don't think he could have organised it. What names were those on his account? The people paying regular sums into Mountford's account, I mean. Can you tell me?"

"Confidentially, yes of course. But don't mention it outside these four walls." Colley opened his desk drawer and took some papers from a folder. "Fairbright. That's one. Then there's Coggleswick, and Besford R.I. General Southchester. And then two strange names. Must be code I suppose. Dorborough Free and SS&P. A few more. Let's see, nine, ten, eleven in all."

I burst out laughing. Colley dropped the papers into the drawer and looked astonished. "Why, don't you understand?" I said. "They're not people. They're institutes, research institutes, or hospitals. Coggleswick Institute and the Fairbright Centre - they specialise in

70

rheumatic disorders. That was Mountford's speciality. Besford Royal Infirmary, and Southchester General Hospital - they have research units attached. So does the Dorborough Free Hospital. And SS&P is Sperlitz Spellman and Palburg, the pharmaceutical giant."

Colley was impressed. "I see now. Yes of course. But then you are more likely than I am to know that, as I suppose you deal with them all at the Foundation."

"I wish we did. It would be wonderful! They would keep us going for years. They are all very prestigious organisations. I wish they were our clients, I can tell you! But we never managed to persuade them."

"But Mountford perhaps was more successful. I don't think there can be much doubt that he was. The entries in his bank account must be fees for professional services.

Mountford was acting as consultant for them, and had been doing so for years. There's an entry for Palburg, which must have been before they merged with Sperlitz Spellman. And that's a few years ago isn't it? I held some Palburg shares, and wished I'd kept them. I would have done well on them when they linked up."

"It was ten or eleven years ago. So Mountford was acting on the side as consultant. No wonder we never got them".

"That's not allowed, I take it?"

"Well, yes. It could be. After all Sedgfield is a private consultant and the professor is retained by our old hospital, but it should have been authorised by the directors. Then Mountford's salary would have been adjusted."

"You mean, the Foundation would have paid him less."

"A great deal less. With all these consultancies, I doubt if Sir Matthew and the other directors would have paid Mountford anything at all. His work at the Foundation might have been purely honorary had they known about this."

"There's something else about Mountford that I don't think any of you knew. He went through what they call a form of marriage - I think that's the expression - with the lady you know as Mrs Mountford. But he was married already. Had been for many years. The lady's name? A certain Miss A.I. Easton. That's all we know. Alice, I think."

"Is she still alive?" I asked.

"That I don't know. She was certainly alive last July when she divorced Mountford. Quite a complicated life your colleague led!"

I was staggered. All this was a revelation to me. I thought I knew Mountford. I saw him practically every day at the Foundation. We all did. He was quite sociable. Very talkative, when Kaltz let him. It was incredible.

"So you think that Mountford was killed because of these secret consultancies, or perhaps because of his marriages?" I asked Colley.

"I don't know. I don't even know that Mountford died of anything other than natural causes. There's no evidence."

"Perhaps Kaltz found out. Perhaps there was a row and Mountford was killed. Or perhaps Kaltz was killed and Mountford is now posing as Kaltz. Perhaps - ."

"Perhaps we should just lie low and say nothing. In fact I must insist on exactly that. Sooner or later the villain will show his hand, and then, if we are patient, we will have the necessary evidence."

Colley would say no more on the subject, and we talked of other matters again. He told me that he would need another operation on his leg and hoped to go abroad for several weeks in the summer to recuperate. He clearly hoped that the Drum House business would be satisfactorily resolved before then. I knew he was anxious not to let Sir Carlo down. We talked about Waybridge and his work in Australia. Colley had spent some months in Sydney, and told me stories of that time.

The clock chimed six. It was time for me to go. I found my coat and hat, and put on the scarf I had also brought. The weather was damp and cold even for a London January. Colley wheeled himself to the door to say goodbye, and could hardly disguise the discomfort that he was suffering.

I was just about to close the door, when I remembered the little incident that was nagging at the back of my mind. Preparing to go home had triggered off my recollection.

"Colley," I said. "There was something of Mountford's at the Foundation that did interest Mrs Mountford - I must go on calling her that - ."

"And why ever not?" he interrupted in a playful voice. "After all she is his widow. They married the week before he died, and properly that time."

I was so accustomed by then to Mountford's surprising behaviour that I barely took in this latest revelation. In any case, it was what Mrs Mountford had done that I wanted to report.

"The odd thing was that she saw it and recognised that it was Mountford's, and yet made no attempt to reclaim it."

"What are you talking about? What did she see at the Foundation? How do you know she recognised it, whatever it was?" It was Colley's turn to wait patiently for an answer, and I resolved to time it to produce the maximum effect on him.

"She saw something as soon as Kaltz came out of his room. I heard her murmur the words under her breath, almost inaudibly. She said Paul's scarf. I didn't see it at first. I looked along the pegs lining the corridor. Then I followed her gaze and saw the scarf. Kaltz was wearing it around his neck!"

Chapter Eight

A New Lodger at the Dixons

Breakfast in the Dixon household was bad tempered. Even on such cheerless Monday mornings, the table was usually good humoured. I had heard loud voices while dressing, and the heated discussion continued after I came downstairs and Mrs Dixon brought in the coffee.

"Funny time to be on holiday, nearly the end of January," grumbled Mrs Dixon.

"Now don't you start all that again. She's not on holiday. I've told you, she's a photographer."

"Well, I can tell you this much. If it wasn't for Mr Springer asking us, I would never have agreed to take her."

"It was Dr Sedgfield, not that pushy young Springer. Anyway, it's only supposed to be for a few weeks. Ten or twelve, Dr Sedgfield said, at the most. He was keen, and the extra money will come in handy. The Foundation's paying over the odds. It wouldn't do to upset Dr Sedgfield."

"Sedgfield's a nosy old woman." Mrs Dixon was determined to be disagreeable. "What the Foundation want with a photographer at this time of year I can't think, and that's all I'm saying on the subject."

"I think we'll find Dr Sedgfield had a good reason for making the appointment," I said. "After all, he is a chief scientist on the research staff at the Foundation, and very good at his job. I'm sure he didn't mean to impose on you, Mrs Dixon. If you don't want the new photographer here, you have only to say so. Would you like me to have a word with him?"

That was probably an unwise intervention, but I could not let her remark about Sedgfield pass without reproof. Mrs Dixon said nothing, but clattered the cups and plates.

"We meant no offence," said Mr Dixon. "We were just a bit surprised when Dr Sedgfield asked us to take in another person."

"That's all right," I replied. "I quite understand how you feel. It's good of you to accommodate a request like that. We all think highly of you and Mrs Dixon at the Foundation. I'm sure that's why Dr Sedgfield approached you."

"I never said I wasn't having her," announced Mrs Dixon. "Don't you say anything of that sort to Dr Sedgfield. It's been arranged now, Mr Steward, and that's that."

So we left the matter. I was puzzled however that my landlady had formed the impression that Arnold Springer had asked her. I wanted to explain that he had no authority to make any arrangement with the Dixons, or anybody else, without first consulting me. He was my assistant, after all, although nowadays he did seem to be quite independent, even hobnobbing with the directors. Mrs Kingston had told me she had seen him with a senior member of the board in an expensive London restaurant, although she declined to name him.

Even though Sedgfield had made the request, I still felt disgruntled. Over the last few years, I had grown accustomed to our regular little household of three, and I resented the idea of a newcomer almost as much as Mrs Dixon. At least Professor Garton had not given the instruction. After all, I was the Administrator, and he would fully understand that such matters fell within my jurisdiction. Really, things were becoming quite slack and disorganised. The old spirit at the Foundation seemed to be fading away.

Later in the day I met Sedgfield, and he immediately mentioned the subject of the new appointment. He appeared rather embarrassed and looked at me anxiously.

"I didn't mean to trespass on your territory," he told me. "I can't think why you weren't asked yourself to broach the matter to the Dixons. After all, you live there, and I hardly know them. It was most awkward. Really Waybridge is an extraordinary fellow…"

"Sir Carlo? He asked you?"

"Yes. I thought it rather odd myself. He simply came into my room and asked me, straight out. I appreciate that it's really your sphere of activity - ."

"Oh, that's all right. Please forget it. I'm sure Sir Carlo must have had some good reason. It doesn't matter."

Sedgfield went away, visibly relieved. But it did matter, I thought. I hoped that Waybridge wasn't going to make a habit of disrupting our routine unnecessarily. Recently his visits had become more frequent, and I imagined that was connected with the anxiety about the Foundation he had expressed to Colley. Well, probably he was right to be concerned. Anyway, he was backing Colley in the investigation, so everything would turn out well in the end. Or so I told myself.

Miss Dempster arrived at the Dixons two days later, in time for the evening meal. She had walked briskly all the way from the station, carrying a heavy load of photographic gear and a large suitcase, apparently without difficulty and certainly without fuss. Mrs Dixon took to her at once. "She might be only a little 'un," was her verdict, "but she's a well set up body. She'll not be a bit of trouble, that one." She glared at her husband, who totally ignored her and continued to read his newspaper. "We'll hardly notice she's here."

So it proved. Miss Dempster had quite a talent for blending quickly into the background wherever she happened to appear. And appear she seemed to do, in all sorts of places, as we were to find during the next few weeks. She was quite friendly, in an unobtrusive sort of way, and had the knack of getting information by gently starting a conversation and then sitting back. In this way, she acquired the reputation of being a good mixer and a better listener. These were the very qualities, carefully nurtured over the years, that led Colley to have her appointed, though none of us knew that at the time.

Within an hour arriving, she learned the layout of the area, the nature of the work done at the Foundation, and the life stories of many of the staff. The Dixons were only too delighted to tell her, and I too found myself unusually forthcoming on subjects I did not often discuss. Dixon went reluctantly into the kitchen to help his wife with the washing-up, and before I knew it, I had told Miss Dempster everything that she seemed to want me to tell her. It was odd to recall later that she had hardly spoken more than four or five sentences all evening.

Nominally Miss Dempster reported to me, but after she settled in, I saw less of her. An early riser, she had usually breakfasted and gone before I came down in the mornings. She was often out and about in the woods, photographing goodness knows what, as I took the short cut through the trees to the Foundation. When I decided to take the road instead, I sometimes had a glimpse of her nearby. Yet I did not have the slightest impression that she was keeping a watch on me. In that I was proved to be entirely wrong, and thankful for it. On my homeward walk, she occasionally caught up with me, whether or not I had been delayed in the office. When I went over to the service block or to the laboratories, she was often on the scene, setting up or dismantling her tripod and camera.

Once I recognised her technique, I tried to play a little game with Miss Dempster, rather as I had done, with some success, with Colley in Palmyra Square. After our first encounters, I steeled myself to say as little as possible, and try to persuade her to do the talking. It did not work out. Miss Dempster seemed impervious to my scheme. If I did not speak to her, she simply remained silent, until finally one of us walked away. There was nothing unfriendly about her. She gave the air of not wanting to waste my valuable time once I had told her whatever it was that I had to say. I soon gave up, and she became a habitual piece of the background at the Foundation.

No-one seemed to know what she was supposed to be doing, and no-one took much notice. That was exactly what she wanted.

My own staff were baffled by Miss Dempster, and became rather uncooperative. "She's a director's spy," Sonia told Merryman. "They've sent her in to check up on us."

"Oh I don't think she is," laughed Merryman, and then turned serious. "Though goodness knows what she's supposed to be doing here. It seems a waste of money when there's so much else they could spend it on." That was becoming a recurring theme of Merryman's. His growing family were no doubt expensive, and his salary wasn't as high as it might be. I made a mental note to try to get him a good pay rise in the following year's budget. He was doing well, coping with the extra workload put on him during Springer's continuing absence.

Mrs Kingston agreed with Merryman about the cost. She saw no point in having Miss Dempster around. She had no time for her at all. When Miss Dempster called in at my office to ask even the most basic things, Mrs Kingston snapped at her and could hardly bring herself to be civil. Eventually I had to call her in for a private chat.

"It was a decision of the directors," I told her, "and we must accept it with good grace. I don't suppose it can be an easy job for her - ."

"I don't see that it's a job at all. And as for being a decision of the directors, it seems to me to be the whim of one man. There was no discussion at the board meeting about her. She wasn't even mentioned. Sir Matthew knew nothing at all about it. He was very surprised." She paused and collected herself. "As I'm sure you know," she added.

I knew no such thing. Indeed I was surprised as much by Mrs Kingston's knowing about it as by Sir Matthew's reaction. I had not even been aware that the board had met. Hiding my discomfiture, I changed the subject.

"Is there something wrong, Mrs Kingston? You don't seem to have been quite yourself these last few days. I hope you don't mind?"

"I'm quite all right," she responded, but her eyes filled with unaccustomed tears. "Well, perhaps there is something. It has been troubling me all week, Mr Steward, ever since I found it."

"Found what? I do wish you'd tell me. You know that I would keep the matter strictly confidential if you wish. Surely you understand that?"

"Yes, of course." She straightened her jacket and sat upright in the chair. "It's to do with a letter I found last Wednesday. A very unpleasant letter. It came by hand for Sir Matthew. I wasn't in my room when it arrived, so I didn't see who brought it. The envelope was slipped into the tray on my desk where I collect items for sending on to him." She paused, in distress. "Oh Mr Steward, it was vile!"

"You read it? If it was sealed in an envelope shouldn't you simply have sent it on to him, no matter what it contained? It could have been highly personal."

"There was nothing on it to tell me that. It was just addressed to Sir Matthew. He instructed me a long time ago to open anything not personal or confidential, and to use my discretion whether or not I send any letter on. He doesn't want to be bothered by trivial post, circulars and that kind of thing. Of course, I would consult you if I wasn't sure."

I knew nothing about that arrangement either. Sir Matthew had never spoken to me on the subject. On the other hand, Mrs Kingston did act as his secretary when he came to England, and probably he gave her his instructions long ago. She had been on the Drum House staff for longer than I had.

I asked Mrs Kingston if she still had the letter. She looked startled for a moment, and then told me she had destroyed it. I asked her if she could tell me what it said.

"It was a dreadful little note. Hardly a letter. A vile demand for money, more money. It just said that if Sir Matthew didn't pay up quickly then the truth would be told."

I hesitated to inquire further. Mrs Kingston was obviously distressed, but I had the curious feeling that she was toying with me, leading me on to question her further, in a kind of game. Nevertheless I wanted to know more.

"Did you recognise the handwriting? Perhaps you could tell whether it was a man or a woman who'd written it."

"It wasn't written. It was typed."

"Well, perhaps we can check which typewriter was used, Mrs Kingston. I understand that each one has its peculiar characteristics. Could we not check on the machines here?"

"You don't understand, do you?" she snapped. "You take no notice of anything the secretaries do here. It was done on a printer. Someone had printed it out from a word processor. They used a daisy-wheel printer like mine. But it wasn't mine. At least they didn't use any of the daisy-wheels we have at the Foundation. I checked. Oh, very discreetly of course! I have said nothing to anyone else."

"Let's keep it that way, for the moment," I said. "I'm glad you've told me. Now please don't worry about it any more. If you find another letter of that kind, you are to bring it to me at once. Do you understand?"

Mrs Kingston dabbed her face with a lace handkerchief, and composed herself to go. She agreed to do as I asked, but somehow I felt certain that I would never see any similar letter, if one arrived. She had not taken me fully into her confidence, I thought, although she seemed genuinely relieved to have shared something with me.

I had intended to mention this incident to Colley, but he seemed to be away from home. At least he didn't answer the telephone. I could not immediately spare the time to visit him in London, as we were particularly busy in the office. Papers, baskets of them, covered my desk, and had to be stacked on a side table where I normally kept a few reference books.

As I lifted the books, to take them across to a cupboard, a sudden clattering noise came from behind the table. I reached beneath it, and picked up a leather case. It contained Springer's binoculars. Quickly I examined them, but no damage seemed to have been done. The glasses were clearly of a high quality, and well-padded in their luxurious case. I took them out and turned the focusing screw. They were really excellent, but the walls of my room were too close for me to be able to test them at long range. Being well past five o'clock, everyone else in the department had gone home. I took the binoculars into the deserted board room. I thought there would be no-one there, nor in the anterooms, to see me playing about with the glasses.

They focussed beautifully, revealing fine detail in the high Drum House ceiling. I had never seen its features so plainly. I scanned the entire ceiling. Then I swept the field of vision across the drum supporting the Drum. The walls bore little painted decoration at gallery level, but further down, the classical panels glowed brightly under high magnification. Every face and finger of the nymphs and dryads could be seen.

I turned slowly round on the board room floor, keeping the binoculars close to my eyes, scanning lower and lower levels. Suddenly the view was interrupted. A curious rectangle appeared among the baroque curves and twists, a jarring contrast to its surroundings. I continued circling the walls with the glasses held to my eyes, until I came back to the odd rectangle. This time, however, it was different. Now it framed a face, but one whose features contrasted sharply with the painted surroundings.

Suddenly I realised what I was looking at, and nearly dropped the binoculars in amazement. The rectangle was a small shutter covering an aperture in the Drum wall. Within that opening the face stared out - and its eyes blinked! It was a face I recognised. I saw it almost every day, when it allowed me. High up in the wall, someone was peering out. And that someone was Dr Kaltz!

A clatter of sound in the entrance doorway disturbed my gaze. The watcher disappeared abruptly, a panel replacing Kaltz's features. When the secret opening closed, its painted shutter exactly matched the surrounding picture.

I turned around. A small figure was bent over, picking up a tripod. Miss Dempster folded it up, collected her camera bag, and went out without saying a word.

Once back in my own room, I locked Springer's binoculars in a cupboard. I tidied my desk, put on my coat and set off home. There was no sign of Miss Dempster. I half-expected to find her waiting around the corner, but the road was as deserted as the driveway had been. At the Drum House entrance, the road is quite level, on a sort of plateau, but on rounding the next corner, it climbs steeply to the village. Ancient trees come close to the roadway, leaving no room for a footpath alongside. However, traffic is usually light and there had never been any accidents.

I was just beginning to climb the hill when a loud roaring began. A heavy van rounded the corner above me at great speed. The banks rose steeply at the roadside where I stood. Recent rain had made them too slippery to scale. I was helpless, with nowhere to go. Suddenly an arm grabbed my sleeve and dragged me up the bank. The van screamed by, just scraping my left leg, and was gone. I looked up to see Miss Dempster clinging on to my coat.

Unfortunately her valiant efforts were not entirely successful. She had undoubtedly saved my life, but I lost my grasp on her and fell down into the road, landing heavily on my back. I couldn't move. Intense pain shot through my body. Darkness closed in.

Chapter Nine

At the Hospital

I awoke to find myself in a hospital room. Colley and Miss Dempster were looking down at me, anxiously. The doctors and nurse had allowed them five minutes.

"So that makes three times," said Colley, when I finally managed to focus on my visitors, "and you were not so lucky at the latest attempt."

Colley and Miss Dempster stood together at the side of the bed. Obviously they knew each other well, though presenting a striking contrast. Colley had been disabled by losing a leg in an unexplained accident. Miss Dempster was strong and nimble. Their relationship was not personal but professional. What that profession was I could only guess. I knew little about them then, except that they were both highly intelligent. Colley told me later that they had worked together at the Drum House, many years before it was bought by the Cammering Foundation.

Through the haze I gradually focussed on an error in Colley's reckoning. "Four, not three," I muttered, "There have been four attempts at me. I didn't tell you about one at the airport, because it seemed doubtful. The professor rather talked me out of it - ."

"But now you think it was genuine?" Colley was suddenly alert, sitting on the edge of the hospital chair. "Perhaps you'd like to tell us more."

"We can leave number three now, if you're not up to snuff," said Miss Dempster. "Let's get you over number four."

"No, I'm fine," I said. "I'd rather tell you - ." I paused. A sharp pain shot through my right arm. I sank back on the pillows and closed my eyes.

"Leave him to recover," came Colley's voice. "Let him get over the last attempt before he talks to us."

"Let's hope it is the last," said Miss Dempster, "not just the latest."

"Oh go away," I groaned. Gradually the pain subsided, and I opened my eyes. "Sorry," I said.

"You should thank Dempster was keeping an eye on you, or you wouldn't be here at all. You owe her your life."

"No need for all that stuff," countered Miss Dempster briskly. I could see that Colley had embarrassed her.

"Yes, of course," I replied. "I am grateful. Naturally I am. I remember now. Glad you were there. Thanks again." I paused. More memories of the event returned. "What actually happened? The whole thing is a mystery to me."

"An unexpected development, ," Colley said. "I assumed we'd passed that phase. Luckily Dempster didn't. She went out on a limb about it, fortunately for you."

"Just what are you two up to?" I asked. "What's going on, and just why is someone trying to kill me?"

"We're simply being ourselves," replied Colley. "That answers your first question. As to what's going on, I'll give you a briefing when you're back on your paws."

"And question three?" I retorted. "Why me?"

"Ah, that's a question indeed." Colley frowned. "Basically because you know something, or at least the villain or villains thinks so. Something that's put them in danger, and they don't like it. Do you agree?" He turned to Miss Dempster.

"Not altogether," she said. "If that were the case, then several other people would be under threat as well. Assuming it's something he knows about the Foundation - ."

"Wait a moment," intervened Colley. "You've got a point there. All this may be totally unconnected with the Drum House. It may be in his private life. I wonder what he's..."

"Well, don't let's rush the jumps. Let's assume he's in danger because of what he knows about the Foundation. Is that really likely? No, it's not. There's not much he knows that half a dozen others don't. From what I can gather, he knows less about what goes on there than anybody else."

"All right. So what are you saying, Dempster?"

"I'm saying that it's not what he knows, but what he's doing at the Foundation that's putting him in danger."

"But he never does anything extraordinary, does he? He sticks to the same routine, year in year out. Prefers it that way. If you're correct, he'd have been finished off years ago."

"H'm. Suppose then that it's something new that he's trying to introduce."

"Rather unlikely. Nothing new has happened for ages. At least till I arrived on the scene that day."

"Nevertheless," persisted Miss Dempster, "there's a change somewhere. Not big perhaps. It may seem trivial. But there all the same. And somebody doesn't like it."

I struggled up into a sitting position. "I do wish," I said, "that you two would not discuss me and my work as though I were not here. Anybody would think I was dead already. It's not right. And there's another thing you're wrong about, at least in my humble opinion. Not that you want it."

"On the contrary," said Colley. "We'd like your opinion very much indeed. Sorry not to include you. We thought you'd parted company from us, just for the moment."

"Well," I continued. "It can't be something that only I know. Everything that I do at the Foundation is open to plenty of other people. All my own staff, particularly. I've discovered nothing that others don't know. I'm not doing anything underhand, or at least I wasn't. Not when they first started trying to kill me, I mean. That was before I ever saw Colley or his travelling bag."

"Yes, that checks," said Miss Dempster. "You're good at delegating. The work is shared out between a real team. I'll give you points for that."

I bristled. No points were needed for anything, I thought. I took a real pride in the way the Administration Department ran. The professor had not been the only one to comment favourably on that subject.

"My department has no secrets. Except the personal staff files, and Mrs Kingston sees them when she does my typing. Otherwise everything's open. We share and discuss the workload, even if I am team leader. So if it's something that I know or I'm doing, why pick on me? Why aren't the others under threat, Mrs Kingston, Sonia, Merryman, Springer - oh!"

"Quite so," said Colley. "You do see our point. Springer is still missing."

"So we are in danger! What's going on? You've got to tell me!" I tried to raise myself in the bed.

The nurse rushed in when she heard me shouting. "Now, now, Mr Steward. You really must rest. Lie down please." Turning to Colley, she announced firmly. "You will have to leave if he becomes excited again."

Colley reassured her, and said that they wouldn't stay much longer anyway. To me he added "Rest now, and get better. I'll tell you everything I know as soon as you are up and active again. We can't talk now. Give me a ring when you've recovered. In the meantime Dempster will keep us in touch." He winked. "She'll keep an eye on you."

That last remark did little to reassure me. When they had gone, I lay for a long time thinking. Things were seriously wrong at the Foundation. Yet everything seemed the same, routinely organised, a little dull perhaps, even for me? No, not dull. I enjoyed having one ordinary day after another. Yet something unusual occurred before that man died in the Drum House. Then Mountford. Two awful deaths. Year in, year out, with nothing untoward till then. Who was that man? Where was his body now?

The nurse brought a drink and gave me some tablets. I lay back again, trying to sort out all the events since the day I found Colley's travelling bag. Strange coincidence really, Colley revisiting the Drum House and finding that body. He'd strayed there by chance, getting on the wrong train and deciding on impulse to walk across the downs. Odd, but that's what Colley said. Perhaps he was wrong, or mistaken. After all, if there was a body there, it could have been a natural death, like Mountford's, or even an accident. Nothing to prove otherwise.

There was no evidence of a body, let alone of how the man died. Not like Mountford. Plenty of evidence there. Poor Mountford.

Poor Mountford? Well hardly so. Fairly rich Mountford. Quite wealthy Mountford. I never suspected he'd acquired all those consultancies on the side. He'd done better than the Foundation recently. Maybe that's why. Had Mountford diverted inquiries his own way? Again, no evidence.

Yet, hold on a minute! There might be evidence somewhere. Records would have to be kept, letters written, reports drafted, correspondence, phone calls, invoices, accounts. Mountford would never have bothered with such clerical work. He'd have put it aside, just as he did with Foundation records and reports. Yet the work would have to be done. He must have had clerical help. So who's his accomplice? Mrs Mountford? You could never tell with her. She wasn't as naive as she looked. Even so, she hardly seemed capable enough. No, it had to be someone on the spot, to answer phone calls, deal with his clients when he was away. In other words, someone at the Foundation.

Whoever assisted Mountford would need paying to make it worthwhile. Well paid? Unlikely. Not enough in it for both Mountford and the accomplice on the generous scale. But even small payments might be acceptable if you were short of cash. So who needed money? Merryman? He admitted to needing money. He moaned about it. No. He was genuine and honest. Springer then? Improbable. Crafty enough, but such work would be beneath him. He'd despise Mountford if he knew. He'd plenty of money already. An outside professional? No, too risky. A private accountant wouldn't know the Foundation's routines. One unlucky phone call, one stray letter, would give the game away. The first Mrs Mountford? What was her name? Alice Eastman, no Easton. Perhaps. Sooner or later she would show her face.

Another point to bear in mind. Mountford had died suddenly. Work would still be pending on some of his jobs. Accounts and reports would need completing. An innocent outsider would have raised the alarm weeks ago, and nothing had happened.

Mountford must have had inside help at the Foundation.

Suddenly a commotion broke out in the corridor. The nurse peeped round the door and withdrew her head. "Yes, it will be all right," I heard her say. "He is awake. But ten minutes only, mind. He's very tired just now."

I raised myself on my pillows to greet the new arrival. The nurse came in first, carrying a huge bunch of spring flowers. Behind her entered Mrs Mountford. Her gift safely arranged in a vase, she sat down nervously by my bed.

"Please forgive me for intruding, Mr Steward," she began. "I was in the neighbourhood and I thought I'd pop in to see how you're progressing. Nurse says you're doing well. We've all been so worried. Such a dreadful thing."

In the neighbourhood of an expensive florist's shop, I thought. Mrs Mountford had resumed the role of the lonely widow. I told her that it was kind to come, that the flowers were lovely, and that I was much better. That opening lasted several minutes, because of Mrs Mountford's continual exclamations that I was so kind, and that she had been dreadfully concerned. She was certainly worried, but not about me.

"I won't stay long, Mr Steward, but there's - well, I didn't really want to see how you are. Oh, that of course! How silly of me! I'm ever so pleased you're doing nicely. But I'm worried about what happened to Paul. I didn't tell you everything the day I came to see you. I didn't really believe it myself then - ."

"But now you do." I was determined not to help her along. This time she would have to manage without a stooge.

"Yes," she admitted. Then she paused, as though counting under her breath. Then she seemed to abandon pretence, and pour out her story.

"Paul didn't die of natural causes. He was killed, murdered! There ought to have been an inquest, but they covered it up. They didn't like him, you know. They held him back in his research. That spiteful old Kaltz, and - one or two others I could mention. They stopped him being a great scientist. He never had a chance at the Foundation. They used him up, and when he threatened to turn on them, they killed him!"

"I always thought Paul and Kaltz were good friends. They seemed to get on well. There weren't many people who could handle Kaltz like your husband did. I often wished I could. He's becoming quite a problem now."

"Paul hated Kaltz! It was mutual. Kaltz is a miserable old humbug! Everybody says he's a wonderful scientist, but it's all rubbish. His own work's nothing, nothing! Paul did all the good work, but no credit, I can tell you. Look at those papers they published - all by Kaltz et al, Kaltz et al, Cammering Kaltz et al. Who's al? I'll tell you. It's short for alia. And what's that mean? It means others! Paul never got mentioned. He never even got paid properly."

Her last remark surprised me. If true, it struck me as strange that she didn't question where all his money came from. Perhaps she knew the answer.

"But Paul's death was entirely natural, Mrs Mountford. The doctor said so. I know it's distressing for you. We were all terribly upset, but it was natural. He had a bad heart. He was taking strong, powerful tablets - ."

"Yes, but not the right ones! Somebody mixed his pills up. They'd taken out the real tablets and put in blanks - what do you call them?"

"Placebos. Yes we use them in clinical trials."

"They kept back the proper pills, so when Paul had his attack, he took the blanks, and they didn't - ." Mrs Mountford began to cry. I waited patiently. "Yes," she said finally. "He was murdered. I found some of the proper tablets in his case when Arnold Springer brought it me."

"I think there's some mistake - ," I began.

"There's been a mistake all right. They think I don't know but I do! They think I'm stupid, but I know they killed my poor husband. And I know why! He'd found out what they wanted keeping quiet. He'd got a hold on them at last, he told me. But it was too late. They killed him."

"But why? What had Paul discovered?"

"Now that I don't know, but it was real enough. Paul had been depressed for weeks, months. Then, just a few days before he died, he changed. He cheered up such a lot. Really chirpy he was. Like his old self. He'd got that toffee-nosed bunch down at the Foundation just where he wanted. That's what he told me. His very words."

Mrs Mountford started to cry again, and searched in her handbag for a handkerchief. In doing so, she dropped it noisily to the floor.

Jumping up, she knocked over her chair. The nurse rushed into the room, and there was a fuss. Mrs Mountford kept apologising. The nurse told her she must go. I needed to rest.

"Thanks again for the flowers," I said. "I'll think over what you say. When I get back to the office."

She bent low over me and whispered. "You look after yourself as well. They're out to do the same to you. Well, keep quiet about it all, and take care!"

The nurse led her out. I drifted into a half sleep, pondering what Mrs Mountford told me. Was she right? If Mountford was murdered, I could think of no reason why. Having secret consultancies didn't justify silencing him. Nor could I see anything dangerous in his marriages. I wondered if Mrs Mountford knew about Miss Alice Easton. Probably she did. I wondered if Kaltz knew as well.

My thoughts kept returning to Kaltz, and I couldn't get it out of my confused mind that he was dead. I must be delirious or still concussed. Maybe it was the sedative. Suppose Kaltz was dead though, not Mountford. Was Mountford masquerading as Kaltz? Perhaps he wanted to get away from his marital complications, or maybe there was trouble with his private clients. Had Mountford killed Kaltz? I could see why, if he had. Mountford had put up with Kaltz for years, even if he didn't hate him quite as much as his wife maintained. That story of hers about Kaltz not being up to his reputation and exploiting the superior ability of Mountford all seemed far-fetched. The truth of that would have emerged years ago, surely.

Suppose neither Kaltz nor Mountford were much good at their work. Sir Carlo had noticed that the Foundation's standards were slipping. Only recently though. Well, perhaps Mountford's talents had only recently declined. He was seriously ill, and no doubt very busy with all those consultancies.

Suppose, though, that Kaltz had discovered Mountford's secrets, his bigamy, his unofficial sidelines, perhaps even some fraud. Had he threatened to report him, so that Mountford had to kill him to prevent his ruin? If that's correct, Mountford would have been worried, frightened and desperate. But he had been cheerful and confident just before he died, or so Mrs Mountford said. It was all very perplexing.

The light faded in the hospital room. I too was in the dark about my inquiries. There was not much to tell Colley. I hoped he'd more to report to Waybridge. Strange how interested Colley had been in Kaltz. Much more than in Mountford. Well, perhaps there was something in the Mountford-Kaltz connection.

My reverie was interrupted. The nurse bustled in, switching on a dim light by the bed. I had lost count of the hours, but obviously it was now late in the day. I could not remember if I had eaten. I wasn't hungry anyway.

The nurse handed me a thermometer to put in my mouth while she timed my pulse against her watch. She released my hand and then tapped it lightly.

"Naughty boy! You must be getting better to play games like that," she laughed. Pulling the thermometer from my mouth, she reinserted it the other way round.

"You got the wrong end of the stick, as they say." She shook the thermometer and put it back in its holder. Then she wrote down figures on my chart, tidied the room again, and settled me down for the night. "You look flushed, Mr Steward. Do try to get a good night's sleep."

I couldn't sleep. The wrong end of the stick, indeed. Yes, that might be it! Suppose it was not Mountford who had killed Kaltz, but Kaltz who had killed Mountford!

After all, Mountford had discovered some secret of Kaltz's, Mrs Mountford said. But what if Mrs Mountford misheard her husband and was only half right? Suppose it was Kaltz who had built up all those secret consultancies and Mountford had found out! He was closest to Kaltz, in the best position to take accidental phone calls and see incriminating letters. Kaltz's enormous prestige would collapse overnight in scandal if Mountford spoke. The very Foundation itself would be in danger. Mountford would certainly have to be silenced.

Then another thought tried to arouse me as I dozed. If Kaltz killed Mountford, then one very sure thing followed. What thing? Come on, I told myself, get it a grip on it. It's gone again. Think man, think! If Kaltz killed Mountford, what's the coronary? No, that's wrong. The sedative began to take hold. So, quick man, think! Corollary, that's the word. What follows? If Kaltz killed Mountford - .

I sat bolt upright in bed, swaying with sleep. Colley must be told! We must keep watch now. Make sure. No more deaths. No more murders. If Kaltz killed Mountford, then one thing followed. Whether naive or devious, Mrs Mountford was in grave danger!

Chapter Ten

The Problem of Dr Kaltz

S lowly I recovered strength. I began to exercise my legs around the room. Then, as the days grew warmer, I took short trips into the hospital grounds. John Merryman came to see me every day, and Mrs Kingston was also a regular visitor. They kept me informed about events at the Drum House, and brought work for me, sometimes.

Colley did not come again. I wanted to discuss my deductions about Mountford and Kaltz. Also I had still not been able to tell him about the incident at the airport car park. I was more convinced than ever that it was a deliberate attempt to run me down, despite what the professor said.

Dr Garton had visited me twice, but seemed uneasy and uncertain what to say. We confined ourselves to bedside small talk. When I asked about the Foundation, he hedged and mumbled that I had better leave all that till I recovered. Our old friendship evaporated. He looked unhappy and worried, but gave no clue as to what was troubling him.

Miss Dempster came every other day, on the dot of visiting time, and left immediately the bell rang again. She was marvellously well organised. Always brisk and business-like. I didn't feel able to tell her about the airport incident. She had the habit of not commenting on what I said, which I found disconcerting. I couldn't tell what she thought, whether she agreed, even whether she had heard. However, I did mention the other matter that I wanted to pass quickly on to Colley.

As usual, Miss Dempster sat patiently in the bedside chair, mentally tape-recording every word. I had been telling her about my visitors, those I expected such as herself and my own staff, and unexpected ones such as the professor and Mrs Mountford. And of course Palmer, who drifted in one day with a greetings card and basket of fruit from the laboratory staff.

"Mrs Mountford is quite ill," announced Miss Dempster, when I paused. "Something she ate, I understand."

I was alarmed, and remembered the corollary I had worked out from the Mountford-Kaltz relationship. "Not dangerously ill, I hope?"

"She was quite ill, as I say. Fortunately help arrived in time, and she's making a good recovery now."

"Tell Colley about her. I've been thinking - ."

"Mr Dale already knows. There is no need to concern yourself. Everything has been put in hand."

"But you don't understand, either of you," I persisted. "Her life is in great danger. Colley must be told. Kaltz killed Mountford to shut him up. Mountford had discovered that Kaltz had a great many private consultancies unofficially and had been using Mountford's work as his own. Kaltz killed Mountford, but Mountford had told his wife. That's why they tried to poison her. She's in real danger! You must warn Colley and Sir Carlo!"

Miss Dempster sat for a moment, silent and without expression. Then she produced a notebook and made a few rapid entries. "I see. Thank you. I have made a note. Mr Dale will be informed," she said.

It was hardly satisfactory, but short of seeing Colley myself and telling him, there was nothing more I could do. I sat back, quite exhausted. Obviously my primary task was to get better and return to my desk at the Foundation. Kaltz would have to be watched.

A week later I was discharged from hospital, on condition that I did not overtax my strength and did only essential work for the time being. Mrs Dixon fussed around me all day, plumping up cushions, endlessly bringing me drinks, and constantly asking if I wanted anything. It was kind of her, but I found being at home very frustrating.

I began working longer and longer hours at the Drum House, and soon was back to normal. At least outwardly normal, but I still felt quite exhausted by the end of the day. Mrs Kingston and Merryman were kindness itself, driving me home in the evenings, and doing everything they could during the working day to lighten my workload.

The workload at the Drum House had become heavy. We were short-staffed of course, and were rapidly acquiring fresh consultancies and projects. We took over those that Colley had mentioned as being on Mountford's private list. It could hardly have been coincidence. I thought that Sir Carlo had been making discreet inquiries and arrangements. I also began to think I was wrong about Mountford and Kaltz. The consultancies must have been Mountford's. Kaltz would not have needed to relinquish them had they really been his.

Kaltz, in fact, showed no intention of giving up anything. He was becoming a real problem for us all at the Foundation. His antisocial behaviour, never easy to cope with, had become almost intolerable. Any less eminent member of staff would have been dismissed had they behaved in the same way.

I had to go over frequently to the laboratory block to try to deal with the problems he caused. He became a major nuisance. He would not allow anyone into his laboratory or adjoining rooms. The cleaners were firmly excluded, and they complained loudly. Kaltz was disagreeable with the scientific and medical staff too, and shunned their company totally. Whenever anyone approached, he rushed into his quarters and bolted the door. Small fires in his laboratory were reported by the security staff, and although they must have been minor, as Kaltz evidently dealt with them himself, the whole business was very worrying. The security guard, recently appointed on Sir Carlo's instructions, also reported that in the evenings Kaltz sometimes lit bonfires in the woods. He seemed to have a quantity of paper that he urgently needed to burn. However, nobody could find out what he was actually doing.

There was little I could do about him. My priority was to recover my health and strength fully, and I was determined not to worry about Kaltz. After all, Dr Garton and Ambrose Sedgfield worked in the same building, and both were senior to me. There were plenty of scientists and technicians around to act if Kaltz's behaviour went beyond all reason. Still, it was a bother for everyone, and really rather undignified. We all hoped that Sir Matthew, or one of the other senior directors, would come and decide finally what to do about him.

"We can't go on much longer like this," said Mrs Kingston. "Dr Kaltz is becoming a menace to the whole Foundation as well as to himself. I know it's not for me to suggest such a thing really, but wouldn't it be best for you and Dr Garton, as well as Dr Sedgfield, to see the directors and persuade them to retire Dr Kaltz?"

"That's not so easy," I replied. "From what the professor told me the other day, that's just what he and Sedgfield want. I agree with them that he should go. It would be the ideal solution. Kaltz had earned a decent retirement, and I gather that money would be no problem."

"I suppose he doesn't want to go quietly," Mrs Kingston hesitated. "What I mean is I shouldn't imagine he wants to retire, even on a good pension. But can't you all do something to make him to go?"

"It will be difficult persuading him," I said. "We'll have to see what can be done when the directors come." I was unwilling to go further, as I didn't like discussing Kaltz with Mrs Kingston, no matter how anxiously she urged me to act.

"Well, we'll have to leave it at that then," she said. I rather had the feeling that she had decided to put pressure herself on Cammering.

I was right. Two days later, she told me she had spoken to him on the phone, ostensibly about some urgent correspondence that had arrived for him. "Sir Matthew tells me that he intends coming over shortly," she announced, "but apparently he's unwell at the moment."

Nearly a month passed before there was any further development. Then I had to travel to Exeter at short notice. Problems had arisen over funding a group of overseas students for whom the Foundation was responsible. It was a nuisance, but I had to go. Normally I would have sent Springer, who would have enjoyed the trip, but he had still not reappeared. That was yet another matter to be sorted out with the directors.

On my return, I was annoyed to find that Cammering had paid his visit and returned home to France. He had stayed only briefly, Mrs Kingston explained. She had looked after him and chauffeured him around. I felt sure she would have taken the opportunity to press for Kaltz's retirement. If so, I guessed that she had been less than reassured. She looked worried, but didn't seem to want to tell me anything. I thought that perhaps another threatening anonymous letter had arrived.

In fact nobody wanted to talk about Sir Matthew's visit. The professor changed the subject abruptly. Sedgfield and the others would not discuss it. Even John Merryman looked distressed when I asked him how things had gone while I was away.

"Oh, all right, I suppose," he replied unconvincingly. "I kept out of the way as much as I could. After all, it's nothing to do with me."

Eventually it was Sonia who made the breakthrough for me. She too looked miserable, and I asked if she were ill. "It's not me. I'm fine!" she snapped, and turned away. "I think it's awful, carrying on like that!"

"Like what, Sonia? Who's carrying on?"

"Not for me to say. None of my business. I might have been told to keep my mouth shut, but you've still got your thoughts, haven't you? And what I say is - ."

"Thank you Sonia," interrupted Mrs Kingston. "Get on with your work please. I'll explain to Mr Steward."

"It was that dreadful old Dr Kaltz," retorted Sonia. "He gets worse and worse. He ought to be locked away."

"He is locked away," said Mrs Kingston. "That's the whole trouble!"

"You know what I mean. He's not a real doctor, you know. Not like Brian and the others. Not a medical doctor, anyway. Treating Sir Matthew like *that*, and him worth ten of old Kaltz. Now he is a real doctor, and a gentleman!" Cammering had evidently turned his famous charm on Sonia, probably by accident.

"That will be quite enough, Sonia," said Mrs Kingston. "Please go and attend to the reception desk. I will explain everything to Mr Steward, as I have said already." Sonia left the room. "At least I'll try," she added softly to me.

"Has Dr Kaltz been misbehaving again?" I asked her.

Mrs Kingston sighed. "Poor Sir Matthew. He went over to see Dr Kaltz as soon as we arrived at the Drum House. I drove to meet him at the airport, and had briefed him on the way here. He could hardly walk, but he was quite determined to go. Dr Kaltz was outside, for some unfathomable reason of his own. Fetching something or other from a store. He spotted Sir Matthew hobbling across the lawn towards him. He rushed inside like a madman, slammed and bolted the door, and refused to come out or even speak to Sir Matthew. It was a terrible scene."

"Where were the other staff? Not watching what was happening, I hope?"

"The senior staff were all out at the front of the building, I'm afraid. It was so embarrassing! Dr Sedgfield ordered a young workman to break a window at the back of the building. The boy climbed through and opened the front door, while Dr Garton stayed at Dr Kaltz's window. Then Sir Matthew went in at the front door, and disappeared for a while. He must have surprised Dr Kaltz. Somehow he appears to have reached Dr Kaltz's room. A dreadful row broke out. The two of them were shouting and screaming at each other. We couldn't hear clearly exactly what was said, but it was quite awful. We were all dumbfounded." Mrs Kingston paused, visibly distressed. I waited for a few moments for her to continue. She seemed lost in misery at the recollection.

"Sir Matthew Cammering and Dr Kaltz were quarrelling, I take it?" I asked.

"They certainly were. The shouting went on for nearly ten minutes. Then Sir Matthew staggered out. He had to be assisted back to the Drum House. He rested for a while in the board room, but would say nothing about what happened in the laboratory. He was quite exhausted, shattered by his ordeal. When he had rested, he told me he wanted to go to the airport and catch a flight home as quickly as possible."

"Thank you, Mrs Kingston, for telling me. And what you did for Sir Matthew," I said quietly when she finished. She went out, much distressed. Genuinely so, as far as I could tell.

We heard nothing from Cammering for several days. However, all thoughts of his visit were put aside by the terrible event that occurred on the very next day. Even now, I shudder to recall it.

Sonia brought us the first inkling that all was not well in the laboratory block. She met Fletcher-Smith on the lawn running to tell us that Kaltz's door was wide open and that he had disappeared. They couldn't get through to us on the phone. Sedgfield organised search parties to comb the grounds and the surrounding woods. Dr Garton took the opportunity to examine Kaltz's laboratory and his adjoining kitchen and bathroom. Everything was clean and tidy, and he found no clue as to where Kaltz had gone.

Mrs Kingston had been taking a lengthy phone call from one of our associates in a clinic. Sonia blurted out what had happened. Mrs Kingston's reaction was extraordinary. She turned pale when she heard the news, and clutched wildly for the wall. She swayed and nearly fainted, before managing to regain her usual composure.

"Stay here with Mrs Kingston, Sonia," I ordered. "We shall want you to take calls. John, come with me!" We got into Merryman's car and drove up the road to the village. I had the notion that Kaltz might have wandered off in that direction. There was nothing of him to be seen, however. We drove back, past the Drum House entrance and towards the station. Again we saw nothing of Kaltz, even though, on reaching the open downland, we could see for many miles.

"Drive back to the Foundation, John" I shouted.

"I'd better fill up the tank first," Merryman said. "I'm nearly out of fuel." We roared up the hill again, through the village, and drove out to the filling station on the far side. While he was paying the cashier, I noticed a distant plume of smoke rising from the woods below the road.

"That's the Foundation, isn't it?" I asked. Being a native of the district, John Merryman knew the country far better than I did.

"Just to this side," he replied. "Look, you can see the Drum House. The smoke's coming from something on the near side."

"Is it the laboratory block, or the service wing?"

"No. It's nearer to us, on the edge of the wood. If you look to your left... Oh no! Just look at that!"

I didn't need telling where to look. Suddenly a great sheet of flame erupted where the smoke had been, and the blast of an explosion shook the trees down in the valley below us. A vast cloud of black smoke climbed silently over the woodland and poured over the downs.

"Drive out to the road and wait for me," I shouted. "Point the car that way and keep the engine running!" I ran into the garage workshop, startling men working under a car. I seized the phone and dialled for the emergency services. I ran out, without explanation, between the astonished workmen. John was ready for me, and we roared off back towards the Drum House.

As we shot up the drive, flames roared high behind the service block. The whole woodland seemed to be ablaze. Even from the Drum House we could feel the tremendous heat.

"It's the laboratories, isn't it, John?"

"No, much further back. It's the solvent store."

He was right. Our own fire engine was on the scene pumping water hopelessly on to the inferno. Sedgfield had ordered the service wing and the laboratories to be evacuated, in case the wind changed direction. So far, however, they were far enough away to be safe. The heat here was searing. Trees exploded into fire. The undergrowth roared. Sparks and flames leapt in all directions. Dr Garton sent our fire team back to safety. There was nothing they could do. Soon a crescendo of sirens and bells sounded behind the Drum House. Fire engines and tenders appeared all over the grounds. Two ambulances arrived with them and stood by. The county police screamed up in several large cars and a van. The professionals took charge, and we were all summarily ordered to the car park by the Drum House.

"Thanks, John," I said. We were both covered in soot and shaking like leaves. "Let's go inside and see if the ladies are all right."

Mrs Kingston had recovered her poise. Sonia wanted to go up to the outer gallery in the Drum to watch the spectacle. I refused permission, explaining that we must be prepared to evacuate the building at a moment's notice. She came outside and stood with John and myself on the lawn. Fletcher-Smith appeared and put his arm round her waist. Mrs Kingston brought coffee out to us. We stood, drinking it in silence. All around the lawns, people were arriving in cars or on foot from the neighbourhood, anxious to help. They were kept back by a burly police sergeant, who was talking to Miss Dempster, of all people. She quickly disappeared when she spotted me, no doubt to fetch her cameras.

The fire raged for nearly three hours, and the brigade had considerable difficulty before they managed to bring it under control and extinguish the last embers. The devastation was extraordinary. When the smoke cleared and we were able to reach the site, no trace remained of the solvent store. The ferocity of the blaze had been increased by oil from fuel tanks. We feared at first that the Foundation would be entirely wrecked. At the seat of the fire, glass and indeed metal had melted in the intense heat, and everything combustible had disappeared. Thankfully no-one was injured except for minor cuts and burns. However, when the roll call was taken, one member of the Foundation staff was still missing. Dr Kaltz, or rather the little that remained of him, was not discovered for two days.

Questions were repeatedly asked as to why Kaltz had gone into the store at all. He should of course never have entered alone. Our rules made that entirely clear, as Garton pointed out at the preliminary inquiry. No member of staff could be blamed. Kaltz always refused to work with anyone after Mountford's death, and had made surreptitious visits to the stores for any supplies he needed for his experiments. Everyone realised how difficult it was to persuade Kaltz to conform with sensible rules. His personality, and the authority which sprang from his distinguished career made it almost impossible for any of us to interfere with his plans. He prided himself on being able to manage single-handedly, and had dismissed his technician after Mountford died. He was a law unto himself, as Sedgfield remarked, his independence bringing about his tragic fate.

The remains of his body were charred beyond recognition. At the inquest, identity was established from dental records. Characteristically that caused an immense amount of trouble. There were plenty of local dentists, and yet Kaltz had chosen one in Geneva, of all places. It transpired that he used to have treatment there on his rare visits to Switzerland, but the latest records were twenty years old.

Miss Dempster was in her element, photographing everything in sight, and listening avidly to discussions she had provoked. Comments were made about her lack of decorum. The ubiquitous tripod had even been set up in the ashes of the solvent store itself. In all the commotion with the police, the lawyers and the scientific press, we forgot to notify Cammering. I felt sure I had asked Mrs Kingston to telephone a message to him, while she said she thought I had done so. That was an oddly uncharacteristic confusion. She was becoming quite ill, I thought, pale and worried about Cammering and the Foundation. That was quite understandable. She had a long association with both, and had known Dr Kaltz for many years.

Still later, I remembered that I had also not told someone else, who should have been notified immediately. When the thought first came to me, I postponed telephoning Colley. For one thing, you never knew who was listening at the Foundation. I planned to go up to Palmyra Square as soon as possible and give him a first-hand account of the dramatic events.

Chapter Eleven

Miss Dempster disappears

Daffodils were in full bloom in their high window boxes, safe from tyres if not from the fumes of the Holborn traffic. I felt light at heart as I stepped briskly along the Gray's Inn Road. Spring was in the air, even here in central London. I was looking forward to another talk with Colley in his comfortable home. I rounded the corner into Palmyra Square, eager to see the March sunshine flooding his sitting room.

When I reached the doorway, my heart sank at once. Dust was blowing in the entrance. No-one had entered for several days. The bell echoed in his empty hall. Feeling alone and disheartened, I walked back slowly to the bus stop.

On the station platform at Victoria I met Mrs Kingston. She had taken the last few days of her leave, before the start of the new financial year when all holiday arrangements began again. We had never been close friends, though our daily work first brought us together years ago. We had little in common. She rather despised me, or at least that was my impression. I was, frankly, a little frightened of her. She always appeared to be so self-contained and efficient.

The train journey took three-quarters of an hour, and we travelled together with some embarrassment. She explained that she had been shopping alone in the West End. I muttered that I had been visiting a friend. She gave no sign of interest. Then, after exchanging comments on the weather, we lapsed into silence. I wished I had bought a newspaper to read. The magazine on her lap was left unopened. She stared sideways out of the window as the south-east London suburbs passed by.

Suddenly, without turning her head, she spoke. "I wonder what will happen to us, Mr Steward. The Foundation is finished now, isn't it? I expect we shall all have to look for jobs elsewhere."

"I don't see why," I answered, with some surprise. "The old partnership of Cammering and Kaltz has ended, but there's no reason why the Foundation shouldn't continue."

"I'm not so optimistic, I'm afraid. It's not just that Dr Kaltz has gone. I don't think Sir Matthew will want to continue. Do you?"

I had to confess I thought it doubtful. Cammering's health had markedly declined. Soon he would be unable to travel. But I refused to be downcast, I told her. "The professor or Dr Sedgfield could easily take over," I said. "We have plenty of work in hand. It's increasing, as a matter of fact. We're still turning out good research, you know."

"Busy, yes. But is it profitable? The quality of work isn't the same. You must be aware of that, more than I am. Standards have slipped from the old days, haven't they?" She continued staring out of the window. I made no reply. Then, turning towards me, she smiled and said "It's true. Carlo Waybridge thinks so, anyway."

"Sir Carlo? You've seen Sir Carlo?"

"I met him at lunch. I happened to catch his eye in the restaurant and he came over to my table. He seemed anxious to talk. He is bothered about something. He didn't elaborate, but I gather it's connected with the Foundation. He said he was becoming concerned about the reputation of the Foundation, and naturally about his own reputation as a senior director."

"Yes, I see that," I said. "Between ourselves, I think he may be right. The quality of the work does seem to be falling away. Not perhaps the actual quality, because the standard of advising and supporting hospitals and clinics seems to be as good as ever. Better and more efficient, in several ways. Our staff are well trained. If anything their standards and qualifications have improved. Certainly there has been no decline there."

"So what is the difference, then?" she ventured. "You seem to agree with Carlo Waybridge that there's been a falling off somewhere, that there's something not altogether satisfactory."

"Recently I've thought about that myself", I answered. "There's been less reported research of the highest international standard. What has appeared in the scientific or medical journals hasn't been quite up to standard for the Foundation. The data hasn't always been well explained. It's been spoilt sometimes by hurrying into print. And there seems to have been less inspiration".

"Less inspiration?" Mrs Kingston pondered the word. "Yes, I see. Do you think Sir Matthew and Dr Kaltz would win a Nobel prize today, if the old team were alive and well?"

"Yes, I honestly think they would. Though now it would be more of a team effort, the combined work of six or seven people, perhaps with scientists from outside the Foundation as co-workers and specialists."

"So you think there's been a shift away from twosomes like Cammering and Kaltz towards whole laboratory teams, with outside advice."

"I suppose so," I replied, "but that's not quite what I meant. The sophistication of our research is probably higher than ever. You'd expect that with all the latest gadgetry. But the pace seems more hectic, more laboured, more of a struggle than it should be. Sir Matthew contributed a great deal even by correspondence - theoretical stuff, calculations, interpretation and so on. He doesn't have the practical facilities at his cottage, but it fitted in beautifully with Dr Kaltz's laboratory work. Sir Matthew at his desk over in France. Dr Kaltz beavering away at his bench, working hard enough for two men. They harmonised well till the last."

"Yes, they integrated all right," Mrs Kingston replied quietly, almost to herself. Then she lifted her head and said more audibly, "The old team really finished long ago, you know." The train slowed suddenly and drew up at a small station. She got up quickly. "I have to get out here," she announced. "One or two things to do."

"Did you leave your car here?" I asked. I was rather anxious for her. She seemed so depressed and nervous.

"No, it's up at our station. I'll catch a later train from here."

As I continued my journey alone, I turned over in my mind what she had said. It was odd that Waybridge had confided in her, but then it was probably just polite conversation at a chance meeting. He didn't seem to have mentioned Colley's role to her, or putting in hand his investigations at the Foundation.

Probably her conclusion was right. It was hard to see what was going to happen now that Kaltz had gone. Sadness overwhelmed me. Nobody could really take his place.

The train stopped at my station. The weather was really lovely. The grass on the downs was green and springy to the step. The air was soft. Summer was just around the corner. My mood changed. We still had an excellent team at work. Sedgfield, Garton and the others could hold their own in any company. After all, the whole idea of the Foundation had been that the work should continue when Cammering and Kaltz were no more. We had good contracts, our finances were sound, and as for the administration, I could honestly say that everything had been running very smoothly.

Had been, yes. But was it still? Merryman was overloaded. I was barely convalescent. Springer had vanished. It would need a big effort to keep the machine running as well in the near future. I stepped out determinedly along the road.

Mrs Dixon had an elaborate afternoon tea ready for me when I reached home. She sat down opposite me at the table and poured herself a cup of tea. That was unusual.

"Is there something wrong?" I asked. "You look rather perturbed."

"I am perturbed, Mr Steward. I'm worried nearly out of my mind. Dixon says I must speak to you about it. It's Miss Dempster. She's gone."

"Gone? Whatever do you mean, Mrs Dixon?"

"Vanished. Cleared her room, and gone."

"That's very strange. I didn't know she'd finished her work. She said nothing about it to me." Then a thought struck me. "Does she owe you any money?"

"That she does not! Left it in her room in an envelope. Correct right up to date, including for a week's notice. But never a word, or a note to say why. Just the envelope with my name on it."

"Well, don't worry. I'm sure there's a good reason why she's gone. Miss Dempster is a very sensible person, you know. She understands what she's doing. Leave it with me, and I'll find out what's happened."

Mrs Dixon drank her tea and reluctantly went away. Yet another problem for me, I thought. Probably Colley will know what's behind the change of plan. But where was he?

My mail had been left on the hall table. Mrs Dixon must have forgotten about it, as she hadn't mentioned that it was there. Perhaps she was too upset by Miss Dempster's sudden departure. Normally she was punctilious about such matters. Today she had even left one letter in the basket behind the front door. I picked it up. It was certainly addressed to me, but had not come through the post. The envelope bore no stamp and must have been delivered by hand.

For a moment I thought of calling Mrs Dixon in and asking her how it came to be there. Then I decided to leave her in peace. There was no sense in agitating her feelings still more. I opened the sealed envelope. It contained a brief note from Colley.

"Please meet 12.30 tomorrow. Silver Swan. Urgent. Say nothing."

I put the note away carefully in my pocket. It would be good to see Colley again. There was so much to tell him, and I looked forward to hearing what he had been doing and where he had been. Urgent he had written. That sounded promising. Say nothing. That I didn't like too much. There was danger in this. The sun set in a misty sky. I took the note out again and burned it in the fireplace. Fortunately Mrs Dixon had lit the sitting room fire. A chilly evening was drawing in. Rather than go upstairs to my room, I stayed warming myself in front of the cheerful blaze. The smell of wood smoke from the burning logs drifted across to me. I dozed in the armchair. This was really a very comfortable place, I thought. I had been really happy here with the Dixons.

Had been? Why the past tense? I sat up in the chair. Suppose Mrs Kingston's worst fears were realised, and the Foundation closed down? No, that didn't bear thinking about. I didn't want these good days to stop. We would soon get this business sorted out, Colley and Sir Carlo would see to that. With my help, of course. I smiled. It was good to be needed, to be valued for what I alone could do.

Yet there was danger. Colley's note had an ominous edge. Say nothing. Surely we weren't still in physically peril? Colley had been reassuring, saying that he thought that phase was now over. Was it, though? He'd told me so before, and I went on to meet that van in the road.

I stayed before the fire, half asleep and mulling things over in my mind. There was something that I knew, or perhaps that I was doing. Surely that item was still there. I hadn't changed my routine significantly. Perhaps that van was somewhere out there too, still waiting for me. I shivered and drew my chair nearer to the fire.

Strange that it should be a van on both occasions. In the road, and at the airport car park. I must remember to tell Colley tomorrow, I mused.

I went through the event in my mind, seeing again the van trying to run me down in the car park. The professor and I had taken Cammering to the airport to catch his plane. We saw him safely into the departure lounge. As we walked back to the car, Garton had thrown the keys across to me and disappeared for a few minutes to buy an evening newspaper. I was half way up the ramp in the multi-storey car park when the white van appeared.

I am quite sure that it was no accident, as Dr Garton insisted. He had returned to find me pale and shaken. It was a sheer stroke of good fortune that I happened to be exactly level with our car, so I could quickly open the driver's door and dive in unharmed. I would never have reached it if I hadn't taken an unofficial short cut through the parking bays by stepping over a low concrete wall. Not so much step, as jump. I can't think what made me do it. It was entirely out of character. I am not usually so adventurous. Perhaps I was relieved that we had managed to get Sir Matthew to his plane. He was badly behind schedule on the last day of his visit, and we only just reached Gatwick in time. The silly thing about it was that we need not have raced there at all. Cammering had been given the wrong departure time, and there was an hour to spare.

The great man had not paid many visits to the Foundation in recent years. In fact it was his first since I had joined the staff. The professor, of course, had seen him several times. Indeed he had been appointed by him. Now I came to think of them, though, even those visits had been to Cammering's London hotel. It must have been many years since he came out to the Drum House itself. I remember having to arrange for the press in general, as well as the scientific journals, to come to the Foundation. It had been a lovely day in late August. I wanted a group photograph, with Cammering and Kaltz together again at the front, with all their colleagues and staff arrayed behind them. Such a pity it hadn't worked out! Kaltz had gone home early, misunderstanding my arrangements. Afterwards he blamed someone for telling him the wrong times. It was, of course, just one of his usual excuses for avoiding the limelight.

We managed to take a splendid picture of Sir Matthew, posed in the board room, but I myself was deeply disappointed. Cammering and Kaltz! That would have been so historic! The old Nobel prize-winners together again, perhaps for the last time. Both were elderly and in poor health. As I told everyone, we just had to get a picture. I wouldn't rest until they were safely recorded for posterity. I was determined to succeed when Cammering next visited us, even if I had to tie Kaltz down!

Then my thoughts returned to that famous team, Cammering and Kaltz. Always that way round, Cammering and Kaltz. Never Kaltz and Cammering. Colley once asked me why. I explained that it came from the way their scientific papers had been published. Names of authors were always given in strict alphabetical order. It was an established convention throughout the scientific world, I told him. Now it was just Cammering. Poor Kaltz! We could never have that final photograph. The old partnership had been broken for ever. Well, at least I could continue trying to find an old photograph of the two of them together. Nobody else seemed interested in my scheme, though. Garton was lukewarm, and Sedgfield thought it might be upsetting for Cammering. Someone had strongly opposed the idea. Who was it? I remember getting no support where I most expected it. I might have to drop the idea eventually, but it would be worth making a thorough search through the old record.

It was after eleven o'clock when Mrs Dixon came into the sitting room. "Come on now, Mr Steward. Time for bed. I didn't know you were still here." I had fallen asleep in the armchair. I shivered. The fire had gone out, and it was cold.

"Oh, it's you, Mrs Dixon," I exclaimed. "I must have dozed off." I yawned and stretched luxuriously.

"It will have done you the world of good. You must have needed the sleep. But shouldn't you be making your way to bed now? You'll rest much better there."

There was a noise outside. Bolts were being pushed into place and windows secured for the night. A sudden crash of breaking glass echoed in the kitchen. Mrs Dixon threw up her arms in despair. "You can't trust Dixon with anything! That's the milk bottles broken. He's supposed to be washing them. He's getting really awkward. He wouldn't let me do them. That's the trouble with men, you know. There's always one objecting to what's sensible, and it's always one you least expect."

I went upstairs to bed. I was drowsy, but unable to sleep. Something was trying to push to the front of my consciousness. Something half forgotten, yet very important.

What on earth was it?

Suddenly I remembered! There was no need to stay awake any longer. Mrs Dixon's words finally propelled it into consciousness. Someone had indeed objected. A man, yes. Someone I least expected. Firmly, but gently, one member of staff had persistently blocked all my attempts to get that photograph of Cammering and Kaltz taken. For a moment, the memory faded. Then I remembered again, though I did not understand. As I drifted into sleep, I recalled that it was a colleague in my own department who had been so uncooperative. And that colleague was Arnold Springer!

Chapter Twelve

At the Silver Swan

Hardly more than a village pub, the small hotel stood over a mile from the nearest hamlet and along several twisting lanes from the Foundation. I sometimes retreated there for a solitary lunch, to be quiet and think things over. No other members of staff came, and probably few knew it was there. I had almost forgotten it too. My life had changed since the strange business at the Drum House began, or rather since I became aware of it. On receiving Colley's note, I realised that I had missed being there, and enjoyed walking across the springy downland turf on that fine morning in early April. That Colley knew about the Silver Swan grieved me for a moment, but somehow I was not altogether surprised that he had suggested our meeting there. It was ideal for private conversation.

The hotel was almost deserted on that particular Tuesday. Easter visitors had not yet begun to arrive. Although busier in the evenings, there were few customers at midday. A scattering of locals gathered around the public bar. A few business men, eight or nine, lingered over their working lunches, but we had no trouble finding a corner where we could talk freely without any danger of being overheard.

"I have been speaking to Carlo Waybridge again", Colley began. "I told you he was anxious about the Foundation. I don't think I mentioned though that he'd been to see old Cammering while he was touring Europe last summer. He spent some time at Cammering's cottage. Apparently they got on well, once Carlo tracked the old fellow down. He lives in a remote place in the Maritime Alps, miles from anywhere. Not that he's always there. It seems he travels about a bit. His housekeeper and her husband often have the place to themselves for weeks at a time."

"That's rather strange. We thought he was pretty well a fixture there. His health isn't terribly good, you know."

"I don't suppose he goes very far. He takes off as the mood takes him, according to his housekeeper. She thinks that he has a lady friend somewhere."

"Oh, I don't think that's very likely," I said. He probably gets tired of being fussed over by the staff, and goes away for a bit of privacy. He has a lot of friends in France, indeed all over Europe, and he must receive a lot of invitations."

"You may be right," said Colley. "Anyway, Carlo Waybridge managed to find him, and they had a good old chinwag. Cammering was indignant at the suggestion that things were going adrift at your place, and wouldn't listen to any criticism. He spoke highly of you, by the way. Said the place had never run so well. Finding you was the best thing that pompous ass Garton ever done, he told Carlo."

"Pompous ass! I don't think that's fair, you know." I was flattered to hear the report about myself, however, but made no comment on it.

"His words, not mine, I assure you. It appears that Cammering regrets having appointed Garton. He thinks him disappointing, not producing enough good research. The two of them quarrelled last time Garton met him, according to Carlo."

Once again I realised that I had been living in a dream world, noticing nothing. "I'm surprised to hear that," was all I could say.

"I don't think I was," returned Colley. "I know he's a good friend of yours, but he strikes me as being not quite genuine. Rather too good to be true. Still, that's just my opinion. I don't know him as well as you do. Anyway, Carlo left Cammering's place to go to a pharmacological conference in Paris, and he asked me to meet him while he was there. Which I did."

Frankly I wasn't much interested in Waybridge's travels, nor his opinions. I began to think him rather unsound. If he could be so mistaken about the professor, perhaps he was misinformed about the

Foundation. Yet that couldn't be correct. There really was something wrong there, and Colley was sure that murder had actually been committed. Terrible pressures must lie beneath the surface.

"So you had an hour or two with Waybridge in Paris then?" I wished that Colley would get on with his story. I was bursting to tell him about the dramatic events at the Drum House, but already I knew him well enough not to hurry him.

"More than that. We spent most of a day chewing over the whole business. Was it really happening? When had it all started, and why? What was causing it, and will it go on? Oh yes, we thoroughly explored the whole mystery."

"So it is a mystery then, a real puzzle? Not just something we are dreaming about, making much from nothing?"

Colley did not answer immediately. Then he became solemn, and staring me straight in the eyes, told me that the problem was real enough, absolutely real. Serious too.

"Important decisions have to be made. In fact the whole future of the Foundation is threatened."

I said nothing. Mrs Kingston's fears were justified then. Again I had signally failed to see the obvious. The careers of all the staff at the Foundation, all our hopes and livelihoods, were confirmed as uncertain.

"You used the word mystery", Colley continued. "The threat to the Foundation, to some of its staff, did seem rather baffling at first. But it is a mystery no longer."

I stared at him. "You've solved it? You've found out what has been happening, who's behind these dreadful events, the murder, the attacks on myself - you know?"

"I'm still uncertain about the motive, but I do know who's responsible. So would you, if you'd only use your undoubted intelligence. Think what you know, what you have seen! Above all, think what you're planning to do!"

116

"I just can't remember. I really have tried. I don't know what I have seen," I groaned. "That at least is plain."

"You have the solution tucked away in your mind. All you have to do is to bring it out. I'm quite certain you know the answer. In fact, it was you who gave it to me."

I ate my meal in silence, hardly seeing what was on my plate. Clearly either I was being very stupid, or else Colley was playing one of his games again. I began to get cross.

"I'll tell you what I know", I shot back, "from the very beginning, that day I found your travelling bag." I poured out the events of the past few months, the four attempts on my life, the arrival of Miss Dempster, the allegations of Mrs Mountford, the disappearance of Springer, the heavy workload thrust on my department, the difficulties in trying to rearrange schedules and programmes. Then, although it soon became obvious that he already knew, I told him about the terrible fire in the solvent store and the loss of Dr Kaltz.

Colley leaned back in his chair. The log fire crackled in the grate. A shower of hailstones rattled on the window panes. "A concise account, if I may say so, but you omitted one important point, your very interesting remark - ." He paused for several seconds in thought. "No, let me go on now," he added. "I'll tell you what I've been doing first."

We refilled our glasses, and Colley continued. "After I returned from Paris last September, I spent three or four weeks in London, reading everything that I could find about Cammering and Kaltz, their prizewinning research, and the setting up of the Foundation. I ploughed through scores of journals from learned societies, mountains of press-cuttings, all the brochures and reports of your Foundation. Even the architectural plans of the Drum House and its extensions. I had just received a large box of photographs from a press collection, by courtesy of Carlo Waybridge, when I had a bit of bad luck. My artificial leg had been troubling me for some time. You know all about the surgical pads that I need. Well, I tried to carry on as normally as possible. However I happened to slip on the pavement - you know how tricky it can be in the Gray's Inn Road, with that early frost we had last November. I broke a bone in my ankle, my own ankle, and had to lie low in my flat for a while.

"Couldn't you have brought in some help? I would have been glad to do what I could. Any time. You have only to ask me."

"Very kind. I mean that. However, I could not ask you then, as we hadn't met, although of course I knew about you and your previous career with Dr Garton. That was really most interesting. Indeed for several days, dare I say it, you were the prime suspect," Colley chuckled.

I could feel the blood rising into my cheeks. "You have, I take it, now eliminated me from your inquiries?"

"Now don't get agitated. Of course I have. You want to know why? That's simple. It was because you returned my travelling bag. It was obvious then that you were totally innocent of the murder in the Drum House. A guilty person would have kept quiet about it, had they come across it. They would have worried, and waited to see if anything happened about it. But let us return to my side of the story. Where was I?"

"You were lying helpless and alone, stricken on your bed of pain."

"Hardly that. Certainly not helpless. I immediately telephoned my old colleague Enid Dempster and asked her to come in and do some of the leg work. She has helped me before, on several other little puzzles. I needed her to investigate the ground locally with great care, up at the Foundation."

"Hence all that nonsense about her conducting a photographic survey. She doesn't seem to know much about it."

"Was it so obvious? Oh dear, she assured me she knew how to handle a camera. It was the best we could come up with in the short time we had left."

"I don't think anyone else noticed, but I used to be quite handy with a camera myself. I was keen on amateur photography at college. I haven't kept it up, but at least I do know one end of a tripod from the other. With Miss Dempster it was like watching someone setting up a deckchair on a windswept beach." We both laughed. Then I recalled what Colley had just said. "What did you mean, the short time that there was left? What was so very urgent? What was going to happen?"

"It did happen. We didn't foresee that it would take the form of that disastrous inferno in the solvent store. We only knew that, very soon, there was a strong possibility that Dr Kaltz would be no longer with us."

"I might have known you'd heard about Kaltz. Miss Dempster will have made a full report, of course. You just can't dismiss the disaster like that! If you thought Kaltz might die, why didn't you try to stop it happening? He caused us all a great deal of trouble, more than he ever gave you. Yet we miss him. At least I do. It was a terrible end for the poor man."

"Yes, you're right, of course. I see that it's been traumatic for all of you who were there to see it happen."

"It's not just personal. A great partnership is over. Perhaps the Foundation is finished, as you say - . Yes, why weren't you there with us? You went swanning off somewhere. If Miss Dempster could manage to be around, why couldn't you? Now she's disappeared too."

"What! Dempster gone!" Colley sat up in his chair, and then relaxed again, smiling. "Oh, I see. No, I can explain that. She's fine - ."

"Well Mrs Dixon isn't. She's really upset. I had quite a job on my hands persuading her not to call the police."

"That would have been pointless. She has not disappeared, anyway. I know precisely where she is. I sent her to stay with Mrs Mountford."

"All I can say then is that you might have told me. I tried to contact you, and I find you're away on holiday or something. Really - ."

"Now stop barking at me, you old terrier. Chew your dog biscuits and calm down." The waiter had brought the cheese course, and we ate in silence again. Sullen on my part, I'm afraid. Colley seemed alternately cross and amused.

The waiter returned to collect the plates and then brought coffee. We argued about paying the bill. Colley insisted that he was the host. "I owe you that at least," he said. "I'm sorry not to have kept you in the picture, David. The fact is that I couldn't do so. I was prevented, deliberately. I was lured away from the Drum House on a fool's errand. A private message came to me, supposedly from Sir Matthew Cammering, to go at once to France to see him. His place takes some finding, I can tell you. Waybridge was right about that. When I finally reached him, Cammering knew nothing at all about it. He'd been away from home and had hardly got back himself when I arrived at his cottage."

"Oh, I see. That's rather worrying, isn't it? If somebody went to all that trouble to get you off the site, it means we're still in danger, aren't we?"

"I certainly am," said Colley firmly. "The villain must have rumbled me. But I don't think he's after you any more. The event that happened the other day has really put you out of danger, I would guess. It's no longer necessary to silence you."

I was mystified. "What do you mean? What event was that?"

"Don't you see it yet? The fire that finished off Kaltz. That means that you're no longer a threat."

I didn't understand at all. I sat back and drank the brandy that Colley fetched from the bar. "I want you to tell me the truth," I said. "I thought from our first meeting that we were to be partners in the matter, however it turns out. I'm not complaining, but I don't think you have been altogether frank with me."

"Sorry about that, but it was necessary, believe me." Colley leaned forward in his wheelchair, looking like a naughty schoolboy. Then he became very solemn. "However," he intoned, "I do not think that you have been entirely forthcoming with me. You have not told me everything."

"How can you say such a thing? I've told you everything that has happened as I know it. Everything that seemed to be of the slightest relevance! You must remember that I've been out of commission for a few weeks. Then you disappeared to France. I would have thought that your Miss Dempster would have been well able to supply anything that I might have withheld from you, however unwittingly!"

Colley grinned broadly. It always amuses him when I rise to his bait. "Now please don't get upset. There's really no need at all. You've been most helpful in this serious matter. At least I'm becoming convinced it is. Possibly very serious indeed. Dempster's also been playing another vital role, though quite different from yours. This business is going to take the talents of all three of us, if it turns out the way that seems likely. In any case, you must admit that she's proved useful to you. As in fact you have to her, - but more of that later."

"Yes, I see that, I think," I acquiesced. "I apologise for what I said. It was unfair. But what information haven't I given you? You mean that I discovered the hidden lookout in the Drum House? Surely Miss Dempster reported that. She saw me there."

"Yes, she did. I wasn't altogether surprised, though I didn't mention it to Sir Carlo. We had many other things to discuss, and he had to prepare for his conference. No, it wasn't that."

"Then I don't suppose it's significant. I really can't think of anything I haven't mentioned that I'm sure you don't already know. So tell me. What have I omitted to report?"

"A very singular occurrence. You have at no time mentioned to me the death of Arnold Springer."

"What?" I gasped. "Springer hasn't died. Disappeared, yes. We thought he was away in the Midlands, visiting a hospital where we have a joint research programme. Springer, or Merryman or myself often go there. It's one of our joint projects - ". I tailed off talking. I just could not believe the news. "Are you sure?", I asked eventually. "He's been away from the office for a long time I know, and I don't exactly know why or where he is. But not dead, surely? How? When?"

"Not just disappeared, I'm afraid," emphasised Colley. "Springer is not in Birmingham nor at any of your other research places. I've made extensive inquiries, I do assure you. Nor is he at home. His sister-in-law was very anxious about him, as he'd not been there for six months."

"Six months!" I was astonished. "But I saw him every working day. At least I did before he went to Birmingham, and that's not - ".

"He wasn't going home in the evenings even then. Are you quite sure you saw him regularly at work? Merryman says he was on sick leave for some time. He apparently called in to the Drum House late one afternoon to collect his papers for the Birmingham trip."

"I didn't see him myself, now I come to think about it. I'd forgotten. Yes, he rang in to say that he was unwell. I'm pretty sure he spoke to me himself. It wasn't his sister-in-law who telephoned. Didn't John Merryman see him when he came back, or Sonia?"

"Apparently not. Nobody at the Foundation has seen anything of Arnold Springer for six months. Except Mrs Kingston. She was working late one evening last November. She was busy with a phone call in reception when Springer hurried through the hall towards his room."

I was amazed. What was happening to us all, and our normally busy, perhaps slightly dull, routines at the Foundation? Since that secret visit of Colley's last autumn, the world seemed to be turning upside down. It was hard to think straight. We finished our drinks and left the dining room. Colley decided to walk back with me across the downs.

"You haven't changed your mind again, have you Colley? You did say that I was out of danger?"

He laughed. The fresh air had restored our good humour. "I don't think you are in any danger. Not unless you do something totally foolish. No, it's Mrs Mountford that we've got to keep tabs on. You were quite right in your conclusion about that. Dempster will perform that little task very well, though. At least for the time being. Later on, you and I must put our heads together. We're going to set a trap for the villain, and Eleanor Mountford will be the bait. I'm arranging it already, but I can't tell you any more just yet. Bear with me, please."

"I understand. I'm glad you think that my poor old addled brains are of service after all. I'm sorry if I went off the deep end a bit. I do appreciate now that you couldn't help being away when Kaltz died."

"You're too lenient with me. I can't forgive myself yet for falling for an old trick like that. I should have foreseen it. I didn't even check that message Cammering was supposed to have sent before I rushed off to France. I'd grown too confident that nobody knew what I was doing. We underestimated the villain, I'm sorry to admit. But at least one good thing came out of it."

"What was that? So that Kaltz could be murdered? I suppose his death wasn't accidental, was it?"

"He wasn't murdered. I'm sure of that. My involuntary absence made no difference there. No, the benefit I mean is that, although the villain knows what I'm doing, at least we've forced some action. Time must be running out. We've made it uncomfortable for him, and soon we'll see more fireworks. This time, however, I mean to be present and in complete control."

We had a pleasant and leisurely walk across the downland, strolling in the warm afternoon sunshine. We discussed much of what had happened at the Drum House over the last four or five months. I did most of the talking, I'm afraid, but Colley listened all the time. He commented occasionally, pointing out things that I hadn't properly put into place. I told him about the incident with the van in the car park.

I'd forgotten that I hadn't yet told him. He seemed particularly interested, and questioned me about it in detail.

Then I remembered something else that I hadn't told him, and which I particularly wanted to. "Will you be seeing Sir Carlo Waybridge soon, Colley?" I asked.

"Possibly, but I've made no definite arrangement. I'm bound to have another chat with him though, sooner or later. Why do you ask?"

"He's been rather talkative, I'm afraid. Perhaps too much so, although I hope not. He told Mrs Kingston about his anxieties concerning the Foundation. It seems to have troubled her a good deal since he spoke to her. She's quite depressed about the future." I went on to narrate my conversation with her in the train."

"H'm. Oh dear. That's unfortunate", said Colley. "However he doesn't seem to have mentioned anything to her about our investigations."

"No, I think that's right," I continued. "I suppose it's understandable she feels that way now Kaltz is dead. Cammering and Kaltz, the famous old partnership has gone for ever. Perhaps the Foundation will perpetuate their achievements. I hope so, and not just because of our jobs. It would be a great shame if Cammering and Kaltz were altogether forgotten."

"Cammering and Kaltz," muttered Colley. Always. Cammering and Kaltz for ever."

"Talking of my departmental staff - ."

"Were we? Do you mean, Cammering and Kaltz?"

"No, you idiot. I was telling you about Mrs Kingston. I do hope you paid attention. Talking of my departmental staff, what do you think I should do about finding a replacement for Arnold Springer. I was wondering about asking the directors for permission. Perhaps I should request temporary help rather than permanent at this stage - . What do you think? Colley, I said what do you - . Colley!"

I raised my head. Colley had not spoken for several minutes. He was staring across the downland with the strangest expression on his face. It was a mixture of elation and apprehension. "What is it? What's happened?" I had never seen him looking like that before.

"It's rather what's been happening!" he exclaimed, his face gleaming in the afternoon sunlight. "The motive, at last the motive! None of us, absolutely none of us, not one, had ever noticed! You have explained it all perfectly. It's all perfectly clear now." He stopped and stared hard at me. "No, most certainly do not ask for a replacement for Springer. Don't discuss it with anybody at all, not the directors, not your colleagues at the Foundation. No-one. Is that clear?"

"Yes, I suppose so. Though I don't see how I can have explained anything. Do you mean that you've seen the motive for all the trouble at the Foundation?"

"Trouble? Far more than that, David. Deception, fraud, and yes, murder! And it may still not have ended yet, I very much regret to say."

Now I was alarmed. "Not ended? But that's dreadful! Three deaths already, but not three murders, surely? Kaltz is dead, Mountford too, and that man you saw on the Drum House stairs. Too many deaths! Too many bodies!"

Colley looked straight at me. "There you are entirely wrong, my dear friend, my clever terrier. Too many bodies? No, don't you see? We've had one body too few!"

Chapter Thirteen

John Merryman is disgruntled

Easter was always a bore for me, and depressing too. In the shops people bought bread as if it would never be baked again. Chocolate eggs disappeared overnight from shop displays as if by magic. Caravans clogged the roads to the coast. Day visitors criss-crossed the Surrey downs. The Dixons spent even longer than usual in the garden, not relaxing and enjoying it, but exhausting themselves with endless digging and raking, weeding and planting.

I did not join in. They remembered my feeble efforts and I stayed out of their way. The kitchen porch filled with muddy boots. Meals became sketchy and ever more improvised. "Put the kettle on, there's a dear," Mrs Dixon boomed up at my window several times a day whenever I showed my head. "We're just ready for a nice cup of tea. Then we'll have a quick snack. No sense in wasting a nice day." I seldom went to public houses, but bank holidays like this were an exception. I escaped through the side door while the Dixons performed some complicated operation in a garden frame. Once clear of the house, I set off on foot across the downs, and rather to my surprise, eventually found myself again at the Silver Swan.

It was thronged and noisy, of course. No chance today of a quiet table in the nook where I had lunched with Colley. I managed to order a half-pint of bitter and took it outside through the jostling crowd. Perched at one end of a wooden bench, I drank the beer quickly. The wind was stronger now and rain threatened in the distance.

"Typical bank holiday weather, isn't it?" said a small feminine voice at my elbow. I looked up and saw Miss Dempster. I had lost much of my capacity for being surprised.

"Hullo, yes," I replied. Then a long pause. "I didn't expect to see you here."

"Don't see why," she said, quite tartly. "It's not a long walk."

Another pause. I never mastered the art of small talk, and Miss Dempster's habit of saying nothing unnecessary was disconcerting. "How are things going?" I managed eventually. "I expect you've been settling in at Mrs Mountford's. I haven't seen you at the Foundation. Is your work coming to an end?"

"When it is," she shot back, "the authorities will have a full report."

"Ah, yes," I replied, weakly. I wondered what authorities they might be. Colley for one, and Sir Carlo Waybridge, and no doubt several others.

"I shan't be around then to pick you up." She smiled.

A group of young girls at the next table turned round and giggled. I could feel my face reddening, but only partly with embarrassment. I had never really spoken to her about her rescuing me. It was difficult to thank someone adequately for saving your life. Especially someone so unforthcoming as Miss Dempster. I broached the subject, stammering my gratitude. She made me feel gauche and helpless, although I am sure it was not done deliberately. She was not superior or critical. She just wasn't interested in what I tried to say, although she stayed professionally polite.

"Enough said," she clipped the conversation short. "Anyway, let's hope there's no need now to watch for some joker trying to pop you off. That game should be over."

I thanked her again. She frowned. "You know Sir Matthew has resigned from the Foundation?" she said. "He's old and ill, you know."

"Thank you. No, I hadn't been told. Was that why you said -. "

"Must be off, now," she interrupted. "Going to rain soon. Best get back, smartish."

"Quite," I muttered. I drank the last of my beer, and handed in my glass at the bar counter through the thinning crowd. When I reached the door, Miss Dempster had gone. I set out over the heath.

A storm was brewing. I turned my collar up and strode purposefully. The wind blew stronger. Rain began to fall heavily. Then hailstones lashed the dry grasses at my feet. I pulled my hat down tightly on to my forehead.

I reflected on what Miss Dempster had told me, as my feet pounded the path. "Sir Matthew Cammering", I said aloud to myself. "Poor man. His life's work is over, but what a splendid achievement. Cammering and Kaltz. Well that's that. That famous team is finally no more. How grateful the world ought to be, even though they would be forgotten now. So many human lives saved. So many helped. So much - ." I felt my eyes brimming with tears, but that I could blame on the wind lashing the darkening landscape.

A mile nearer home I paused at the woodland's edge to catch my breath. I began to think of the future again. Was this the very end of the Foundation? Surely the work of Cammering and Kaltz must continue in other hands? Garton could take charge. No, even I realised that was unlikely. Another mile and I drew up again. What would become of my team, Merryman, Sonia, Mrs Kingston, myself? All would be dispersed, I supposed. I shivered under the swaying trees, and looked forward to reaching the safe haven of Mrs Dixon's kitchen, and teatime.

After the Easter break, I returned to the office to find my colleagues uniformly gloomy. Merryman looked despondent, and I guessed that he'd heard about Sir Matthew. Perhaps, though, he'd just spent a miserable weekend cooped up with his family. I said nothing about Springer. There was still no official explanation as to his whereabouts. Sonia had heard nothing on the office grapevine, although she knew Cammering had resigned. "Whatever is going to happen to us?" she wailed on and off all morning, taking every opportunity to consult Fletcher-Smith in the laboratory block. Mrs Kingston took up the same theme. "Everything is so uncertain. Poor Sir Matthew. You will let me know how I stand, won't you? I mean - ."

"Yes, Mrs Kingston," I cut her short, "but there's nothing I can tell you at the moment."

"Sir Carlo may be able to tell us something during his visit this afternoon."

"Waybridge!" I exclaimed. "You mean here's coming here!" Really it was amazing how Mrs Kingston and Sonia always got the important news first, as well as all the local gossip.

"Yes. He's with Dr Garton now, and a new assistant, a Mr Dale. Collingwood Dale he's called."

"Quite a mouthful, isn't it?" giggled Sonia. "I shall just call him Coll. He's really ever so handsome. It's such a pity though about his leg. He's quite lame, you know."

"Thank you Sonia," came back Mrs Kingston. "He's going to help Sir Carlo until a permanent decision is made. About the Foundation, and about us too, of course." With that she left the room, not a little pleased with herself.

"Thank you Mrs Kingston," I murmured to the closing door. I leaned back in my chair. Colley here, with Waybridge, and consulting with Garton! Things were moving quickly.

However, for once Mrs Kingston was misinformed. No announcement was made to the staff that afternoon, nor during the following week. We continued with our daily work as best as we good, although without directives from the board as to new contracts or negotiations. Merryman deputised for Springer again in Birmingham, as well as making his own rounds in East Anglia. I had to stand in for Garton, as well as coping with my own workload. The sun shone outside, but despondency filled the offices. We all felt tired and exhausted. I needed a holiday, but there was no chance of taking one at present. Not for any of us. The days slowly passed. It began to rain again. March ran into April.

By eight o'clock on one particular April morning, John Merryman had already managed to cut his face while shaving, trodden on the cat, and spilled milk on to his new jacket. He quarrelled with his wife and upset the baby. Finally his car refused to start and he arrived hot and tired at work, having walked through the rain. Normally mild-mannered, he reached his desk at the Foundation still fuming. The real problem, he reflected, was money, or rather the lack of it. He was amazed how much went on feeding, clothing and housing his family, even though he earned the reasonably good pay of a senior officer (administration) at the Cammering Foundation. Generally speaking, it was one of those mornings when getting out of bed was a mistake.

Merryman found himself entirely alone in the office. Springer had, of course, not re-appeared. Sonia was away ill. Mrs Kingston had to stand in for an absent secretary and was taking minutes at a meeting in the laboratory block. I had a dental appointment. Fortunately there were no phone calls. That was the usual pattern after Easter. Many of our clients and associates took a quiet early break before the school holidays started. John Merryman settled down in the quiet of the Drum House to write a report on his Birmingham visit.

About ten-thirty he made himself a cup of instant coffee. At five to eleven his ballpoint pen ran dry, and to his annoyance he found none left on his desk. He had no idea where the stationery was kept. Sonia or Mrs Kingston always attended to such trifles. He glanced at his watch, mildly surprised to find it hadn't stopped. Damn, he thought, he must finish the report by lunchtime. There would be no peace afterwards.

A final rummage through his desk confirmed his quandary. He was also running low on paper. My desk was locked, a habit I retained from my early training in hospital laboratories, but Springer's opened easily. Merryman's key fitted the lock. Indeed had he known it, half the desks at the Foundation opened with the same key. The directors had economised on office furniture.

The inside of Springer's desk surprised him. It was remarkably tidy, although containing very little. Quite unlike his own, which was a byword in the Drum House for being crammed and chaotic.

Obsessively neat, Springer had even lined the bottoms of his drawers with coloured paper. Really, wondered Merryman, how did the man find the time? Yet he often seemed to be out of his room, turning up again when least expected. He certainly had a wandering commission, the lucky devil. Merryman began to feel disgruntled again. He never got away from the place, except to see lousy clients like that lot in Birmingham. Springer had all the best jobs. Now he'd gone swanning off somewhere without even bothering to tell anyone, and nothing seemed to be happening about it. Well, Springer would have to take his fair share when he did come back to the office. Better say nothing now, though, he reflected. There would be another terrific row if Springer discovered he'd opened his desk. Merryman smiled, his ill temper evaporating. Crafty old Arnold would be furious if he knew the keys were the same. Serve him right. He was much too secretive, for ever thrusting papers into his top drawer when you walked unexpectedly into his room.

Pens were neatly bundled together in the middle drawer. The top drawer had been cleared. Curious, thought Merryman, because something had been lying there recently. Fresh marks scuffed the lining paper. In one corner the lining had been torn, and the jagged edge looked fresh. The white interior of the ripped paper was still clean, though the rest was dusty. Springer must have cleared the drawer in a hell of a hurry.

For days afterwards, Merryman fervently wished he'd resisted the impulse to lift the lining paper. Then he need never have known that a cheque lay underneath. He replaced it, and relocked the desk with his own key, but the row of zeros on the payment still vexed him. So much money, and paid on the personal account of Sir Matthew Cammering himself! Why did Springer get money like that, and not him? He worked far harder, and longer. Springer was always taking time off - two or three hours sometimes - when people thought he was still in his room. Nobody seemed to notice or to care.

The cheque continued to rankle in Merryman's mind. It was so unfair. He had been longer at the Foundation than Springer, and was three years older. Nobody ever found fault with his work, but the boss told Springer off several times about his lack of attention and scrappy work. It had got much worse in recent months. Not that it bothered Springer. He seemed to be well off, almost despising his Foundation salary. He didn't appear to need to work at all. There was that brand new car he bought last summer, and all those expensive foreign holidays. That wasn't all either. He'd bought his widowed sister-in-law, who did the housekeeping in Springer's bachelor flat, a real fur coat. Silly woman, wanting mink, when she could obviously do with some new furniture. Sonia had told him about the furniture, and about the mink, though she had the grace to admit her envy.

By the end of the week, Merryman was nearly bursting with his secret. He could not tell his wife. She would whine about his being passed over again and not getting a bonus cheque too. Worse still, she'd think he had been given it and spent it on himself. He could not bring himself to tell me when I returned, as that would mean admitting he had been rummaging through Springer's desk.

On the Friday morning, he was called into Dr Garton's study to be told about the new arrival, the temporary assistant. Merryman said he was sorry to hear that Sir Matthew Cammering had given up his connection with the Foundation, but Garton seemed to be taking his time to get to the real point. Surely he was going to tell him that he too would be receiving a bonus, a cheque like that in Springer's desk. However Garton wittered on and never mentioned it. Perhaps he would be handed it personally by Sir Matthew when he came round to thank all the staff, now that he had arrived at the Drum House. That would be one up on Arnold Springer, even though he'd got his earlier - then not bothered to take it with him.

Sir Carlo Waybridge had brought Cammering from France in his limousine, as he had obviously been unfit for the stress of flying. Merryman brightened when he noticed me alone in my office, not apparently busy. He hoped that I was feeling much better. I thanked him and told him I was. He hovered by the door. It was sad, wasn't it, about Sir Matthew? I agreed that it was, but had to be expected one day. Of course it did.

"Merryman," I said finally. "Is something bothering you? Did you want to tell me something? No? Are you sure? Oh well, if you'll excuse me, I must get on."

Alone once more, I turned again to the thought of working with our new temporary colleague, Mr Collingwood Dale. Colley had been set back by the wasted journey to France. He seemed puzzled also by Sir Matthew's return just before he reached the cottage. Really, Cammering was a strange man. Perhaps it was time that he retired, if his mind was going. Certainly he looked terribly unwell now he was here at the Foundation. Colley had said nothing in detail about his conversation with Cammering at the cottage. Then there was Colley's conviction that Springer was dead. That was still unexplained, but presumably he had evidence. I had the strong presentiment that something important was about to happen. Yes, it was good to have Sir Carlo's new temporary assistant close at hand.

Merryman took an early lunch in the service block canteen. That was unusual. Normally he went home for the midday break. It gave his wife, as he often explained, the chance for a little adult conversation. Service was always brisk in the canteen if you went soon after twelve o'clock. Consequently Merryman was back at the Drum House within twenty minutes. There was nothing else he could find to do. Furthermore it was raining again.

Colley told me afterwards how proud he was of recovering himself so commendably, but I knew he had been taken completely unawares when Merryman found him examining Springer's desk. It had been careless not to close the door. He remembered too late when he heard Merryman's footsteps and saw him glance in on his way past. Colley was cross with himself for miscalculating. He had to think quickly. Merryman had regained enough of his usual good humour, and was composed enough, to ask politely if he could be of any assistance. Colley hastily explained that Sir Matthew and Dr Garton had given permission for him to use the vacant desk.

Merryman and Colley got on very well together. By the end of the afternoon they were chatting away freely and confidentially. I could only hear the buzz of distant voices, but it was pleasant to hear such sounds in the office again. I had quite forgotten how things had been before all the trouble started, things taken for granted then. Colley could never be prevailed upon to say what Merryman thought of me. Sometimes he had a warped sense of humour, but I gathered from the twinkle in his eye that the opinion was not too unfavourable. Colley told Merryman about his artificial leg and how useful it was at fancy dress parties. Merryman confided in Colley about his domestic problems and how short of money he was. Finally, after much hesitation, he opened Springer's drawer and pulled out the cheque.

Colley was really excited by the discovery. He told me afterwards that it was a vital piece of the jigsaw. It also eliminated Merryman from suspicion in the case. Fortunately Merryman had been too preoccupied with his grievance to notice any change in Colley's manner. It had been quite a dilemma. The time had not yet come to disclose to Merryman everything he knew about Springer and the Foundation. Indeed it might never have been necessary to tell him. On the other hand, something would have to be said immediately, before his disaffection spread or led him to act unwisely. In any case, it was unfair to leave a valued employee totally in the dark without any explanation. Furthermore there was a risk that Merryman might inadvertently put himself, and the investigation, into serious jeopardy.

"Oh that," said Colley breezily. "Didn't you get yours? No? Well it's definitely on its way. A special farewell gift from Sir Matthew." Colley hoped Merryman hadn't noticed the November date on the cheque. In fact Merryman had been far too mesmerised by the size of the payment to notice anything of the kind.

"Will you let me have that? Springer shouldn't have left it lying around," said Colley. "I'll put it away for safe keeping. Now then, please don't mention this to anyone else. That's most important, you understand. I'm not authorised to talk about it yet, you see. I hope you don't mind my talking confidentially to you like this, but as a senior and responsible member of staff."

Merryman certainly didn't mind. On the contrary, he enjoyed sharing the secret, and would never have divulged it. The time would soon come, thought Colley, when great responsibility could be borne by those capable and sensible shoulders. It would be a pity to waste such talents.

Nevertheless, Colley was anxious. Springer must only just have received the cheque just before he disappeared, otherwise he would surely have banked it. He must not have had time. Something urgent had cropped up to delay him, and Colley could now guess accurately what that something was. He hoped fervently that none of the other cheques Cammering had signed were still lying around. The local bank might be induced to co-operate, if need be. He made a mental note to ask Waybridge to get a cheque made out for his new friend.

In the meantime all went well. Merryman beamed with relief. He received his very own cheque the next afternoon. At five o'clock he ran all the way to the village to buy his wife some flowers. Then he ran all the way home.

Chapter Fourteen

Sonia Sees a Ghost

S onia Ulrickson turned her shapely back to the reception desk, and sobbed. Above her, the blank silhouettes of Cammering and Kaltz, flanking the foundation plaque in the entrance hall, stonily ignored her bowed figure. Unperturbed by individual distress, the featureless heads united to commemorate the noble works of mankind.

She dabbed away her tears, turned the telephone exchange to autopilot, and rushed out to fetch her coat. Five minutes later she hurried away, outwardly composed again, but still unprepared for the usual lunchtime huddle in the canteen. She wasn't hungry, she told herself. Walking in the fresh air would do her good. Anyhow, it would just show some people that she couldn't be taken for granted! Flushed with determination, she plunged into the woods, taking a short cut to the road home.

Sonia rented a tiny room in a large villa divided into separate households. Her family lived on the northern side of London, too far away for her to live at home and travel to work each day. She hardly ever saw her parents now. At least she seldom talked about them, and Sonia was usually talkative. Her work at the Foundation was, frankly, menial. She was hardly more than part-time typist, part-time office girl, and not well paid. However, working in the Drum House carried a good deal of prestige. For that reason she kept up a slender superiority among her friends.

Although she would never have admitted it, she realised she was unlikely to make a good career where she worked. She was a sensible girl, for all her capricious ways and ready tongue. The administration at the Drum House would never provide a better vacancy, no matter how she struggled with shorthand and typing classes at the local evening college. Mrs Kingston would retire one day, she supposed, but she did not allow herself to think she would replace her. For one thing, she told herself, she didn't have influential friends. Mrs Kingston had known funny old Dr Kaltz (or was it Cammering?) long ago, before he became famous. For another, she didn't really go for all that posh hobnobbing. She would find the right boyfriend, she told herself, and settle down. Just like all her friends were doing. She sniffed the spring air among the fragrant pine trees, and felt happier again.

Discovering that bonuses had been paid to other members of the department had really shaken her. She hadn't intended listening to what that new man told John Merryman. She really had stayed only for two seconds after she walked in through the French window at the back of Arnold Springer's room. After all, that was her usual short cut when he was away. Everybody did it. Well, that was yesterday, and quite bad enough. Then today, she came in again the same way, quite thinking nice Mr Dale had already gone for lunch. She heard him and the boss together, inviting John to have lunch with them at the village pub or somewhere. She had only just managed to tiptoe out again unheard. The men walked out together through the reception hall, hardly giving her a second glance. Tears welled up and choked her as she remembered.

The main path through the woods was rather wetter than expected. Her shoes slipped and twisted in rough ground. She mustn't spoil them. They were nearly new. She couldn't afford to buy more just yet, being short of cash. Not like some people she could name! Sonia knew the woodlands well, having walked there with several young men at the Foundation or from the village. What about trying the old paved track higher up? A bit out of the way, but it would be drier. It took her near the back of the laboratory block, by the remains of the old solvent store. Few people went on that side of the building. The place seemed spooky, and she began to wish she hadn't come. Still, she must press on. She would show them!

Almost at once she regretted her decision. Her pulse had slowed once past the laboratories. The track was certainly much drier here, but more overgrown than lower down. Several obstacles blocked the original paved way, and the various diversions were confusing. Then a huge fallen tree, brought down in recent gales, blocked all the tracks completely. She had to fight through dense bushes, not quite knowing where she was heading. Sonia cried with frustration and dismay to find herself back at the laboratory block again. She plunged away into the undergrowth, striking out for the distant road. Her coat snagged on a dead branch, and she wasted several minutes unhooking herself. She shivered in the damp cold. The silence was eerie.

Just then she noticed movement nearby. She had been standing still for some time, so whoever was approaching had neither seen nor heard her. At first she could not tell his direction, but soon a man appeared on the other side of the fallen tree, hurrying along a parallel track. Clouds covered the sun, and the tops of the taller trees rustled in the gathering wind. Sonia crouched behind a thick bush and peered through its branches. She calculated that he would soon reappear behind the old tree, and continue towards the Drum House. Nothing happened at first, and Sonia thought he must have seen her and stopped. Fear gripped her. She shrank deeper into the bush. Then she saw more movement. He had not seen her, thank goodness. He was still hurrying along, making no sound. A sudden shaft of sunlight flashed through the trees. Sonia gasped in terror! For an instant she saw the figure clearly. Then he vanished again. But she had instantly recognised the man hurrying silently towards the Drum House. He was Dr Kaltz!

The strengthening wind flung branches across her path, catching Sonia's coat as she fled wildly away. The sun came out from behind the clouds, and gazed impassively upon woods and downland. Birds flew from the undergrowth, singing among becalmed branches and on tiled rooftops of the village houses.

At the local pub, Merryman and I finished an excellent lunch with Colley. It was good to be able to set John's mind at rest, even though he couldn't be told the real purpose behind the cheque discovered in Springer's desk. He was normally a placid person, not given to inquiring deeply nor particularly observant, but highly intelligent. A more likeable fellow than I had appreciated, his mind focussed on work and family. That made him a very useful member of staff. Indeed I told him so over lunch. Colley had appreciated Merryman's qualities at once. Feeling rather ashamed, I resolved to be less incompetent and complacent.

We reached our desks again shortly before two o'clock. Lunchtime had lasted longer than planned, certainly longer than was officially allowed. In the circumstances, I saw no cause for concern. It was good for us to be cheerful again. We ought to take the opportunity to be happy while we could. We would learn soon enough what the future contained. I rang for Sonia to bring in the afternoon's post and messages.

I had to ring again. Then for a third time. That was unusual. What had happened to the silly girl? This was really too bad. I had just got out of my chair to go and investigate, when the door flew open and Mrs Kingston entered in a state of considerable distress.

"What on earth - ", I began.

"Come quickly, Mr Steward. Please come at once," Mrs Kingston interrupted. "I need your help. I just don't know what to do. Perhaps I should ring for Dr Sedgfield or one of the other medics."

In the small room behind the reception desk, Sonia was sitting on a stool, shaking violently and sobbing, quietly but uncontrollably. I nodded and Mrs Kingston phoned for Dr Garton, who was fortunately in his room. He came down at once and gave Sonia a tablet. Eventually we were able to calm the hysterical girl. She poured out her story.

"She can't have seen a ghost." Mrs Kingston dismissed the account at once. "It's all nonsense. She's not been eating properly. Something's been worrying her these last few days. I don't know what it is, but she's not been herself for a week or two. Probably…"

"Probably boyfriend trouble," said Merryman innocently. I caught Mrs Kingston's eye. She realised it was not as simple as that, and I saw in her glance that she understood that I knew it too. The professor took Sonia home in his car. Mrs Kingston hovered in my doorway. From what John Merryman had told me earlier, I gathered that she had been trying hard to find me alone. All morning she had been in and out of my room, and had phoned through several times. Now she looked both concerned and relieved. Normally she was so strictly composed, bound in her own ladylike capability. I could never decide, on the rare occasions I had considered the matter, whether she really came from a socially superior family or whether it was an act perfected during thirty years of practice. However, she now looked so ill that I could not help feeling sympathy for her.

"Were you looking for me, Mrs Kingston? My meeting with Mr Dale went on longer than I expected." She frowned slightly at the mention of Colley's name, and I realised that I might have a problem there if I was not careful. "I was with Dr Garton for most of the morning. He called me over. He's becoming rather concerned about - ."

She did not want to hear about the professor's anxieties. "I need to go away for a few days," she interjected. "I was wondering whether it would be possible next week, if it's not too inconvenient. I know it's short notice - ," she trailed off.

"I'm not sure," I said. "Let me think about it." I had merely meant to consult my desk diary and check that Sonia or perhaps a girl from the laboratory block could cover for her at reception. I was almost sure someone would be available. Her reaction was, however, explosive.

"It's not often I ask! I really think you could put yourself out just for once! Can't you decide anything without having to ask Garton!" I was taken aback completely. I had not intended to be obstructive. She was on the point of bursting into tears. I cringed with embarrassment. This was so unlike her.

After a few moments she blurted out jerkily, holding back her tears "A person I know well … I have to attend... A friend of mine is going on a journey… I have been invited... If that's convenient of course, Mr Steward... I realise, as I say, that the notice is short... but it's unexpected...

and I be glad, very glad ... Just for a few days... Maybe the next few days next week? ... I have plenty of leave still in hand... I do think I'm entitled, after all that has ... But if it's inconvenient for you or the professor, of course I will quite understand. I do so much hope that you're not offended Mr Steward."

Her manner puzzled me. I wondered why she needed to hide the truth from me. She hadn't named the person concerned, and usually she spoke freely about her friends, many of whom were apparently wealthy and some quite well known. We both knew that all her annual leave was already booked in the office diary. Indeed I was certain she knew precisely how much leave everyone had at the Foundation. Her background was a mystery, but nobody bothered to ask questions. She had made herself almost indispensable, but we took her for granted, just as had recently been dramatically demonstrated in the case of Sonia Ulrickson. I really had to be less self-centred and take a greater interest in the hopes and fears of my colleagues.

"Certainly, Mrs Kingston," I tried to reassure her. "There's no difficulty at all. Of course not. Enter the dates in the diary, and that will be fine." Obviously she did not want to tell me where she was going. It was none of my business. Nevertheless I was curious. Colley would call me a terrier again. I had plenty to occupy me. Well, perhaps just one more try.

Going somewhere exciting?", I said as breezily as I could manage. I saw at once that it was a mistake. "Not that it is any of my business. Sorry to be so inquisitive."

"That's quite all right, Mr Steward," she beamed. Her act, or her personality, slipped back into place. She smiled at my transparent curiosity. It was almost too easy for her to deal with me, perhaps with us all. "I had been thinking how pleasant it would be to spend a little time on the Riviera."

No-one would disagree with that statement, I thought, but it had not answered my question. I tried again. "It's beautiful in Cannes or

Monte Carlo at this time of year, and of course St Tropez. Not that I know the French Riviera well. Or perhaps, Italy?"

"I have a – er - friend whose cousin lives in one of the main resorts," she said, smiling. She was enjoying this exchange. I was not going to be told, so I let the subject drop. I doubted the existence of the friend, but the destination was probably France. Unless it was Torquay. Oh, well, so be it. I failed to notice then that, without lying to me, she had again skilfully deflected my inquiry.

She returned to the reception desk, and I began to think, for some extraordinary reason, that she might be going to Cammering's house. I wondered why. If so, the visit had been arranged hurriedly. Sir Matthew had only just recently visited us and she could surely have found plenty of time then to talk to him. What had happened within the last few days? If there was something vital to tell him, why not telephone? She could have done that privately from her home. Perhaps she had something to take to him. Some object, something of value. Ah, now that was much more likely! Something to take quickly. Or to collect and bring back!

I began to see that I was a mere amateur in such speculations. Colley would have known the purpose of Mrs Kingston's trip already, or would have quickly deduced it from fewer facts than I'd been given, or possibly based on information from the reliable Miss Dempster. Perhaps he did know. At any rate, it soon appeared that I was on the wrong track, when the professor called in for one of his little chats with me during the course of the same afternoon.

"Sorry to bother you, David," he said, closing the door of my room behind him, "but I wanted a private word with you." He lowered his voice, and pulled his chair closer to my desk. Normally I was glad to see him when he dropped in like this, but his face was serious and I began to think that I was in some kind of trouble. I cast around in my mind for anything that I might have done to annoy him, or more likely something that I had forgotten to do that he regarded as important. At present, I had so much to think about.

142

I need not have worried however. He wanted some urgent assistance. He took up several minutes in small talk, asking me things about myself and the office of no interest to him. We had not seen much of each other over the past weeks. Of course, like myself, he had extra responsibilities thrust on him by recent events, especially in re-organising the unfinished scientific programme of Kaltz and Mountford. Our old friendship had faded, as our work took us in different directions. Really we never had much in common, I thought, and wondered why he taken me up in the first place. He looked small and rather silly now, fretting and uncertain what to say to me.

"Can I help you in some way, professor," I ventured, after an embarrassingly long pause. "Is there something bothering you?" I offered him a cup of tea.

The offer was brushed aside like an irritating fly. "Yes I rather imagine you can," he replied. "Keep this to yourself. Strictly to your own person, I mean. I can't explain now, but I don't expect to be away long."

He was making no sense, and I started to think that he might be ill. "You're going away, are you? On holiday, or is it business?" It was strange that he should be planning to leave the Foundation at this critical time. It must be vitally important.

"Business. Foundation business. Yes. Yes, important business. I must go over to France at once to see Matthew Cammering. I must see him privately, alone. I have to go this evening. It's very urgent, and for a special reason I can't tell you now. I'm not able to make the usual arrangements through your office. I wanted you to know, however, in case something - . Well, never mind that. But, as I say, please do keep what I have said a closely guarded secret. Between us, h'm?" He smiled feebly.

"Of course I will, professor. Can I help in some way with your plans or - er- arrangements?" He brightened at this, and I knew that I would regret my words.

"As a matter of fact," he said slowly, "you can. Would you - I don't like to bother you really at such short notice. You'll probably have other commitments, but would you be so good as to drive me to the airport? I have to leave in about an hour's time."

Rapidly I thought of credible excuses not to go with him. I did not like this at all. I didn't want to go to that car park again. Not yet, and not with Dr Garton. Dr Garton! No longer my friend the Professor! What was I thinking of? Panic took hold of me, as I recalled that attack made on me the last time I took him to Gatwick.

Fortunately he was examining his watch and did not see my face. I had controlled my consternation when he looked up for my answer. For the very first time in our long acquaintance I was going to let him down. For once I was not going to help him out. I felt a perverse thrill of pleasure.

"I'm awfully sorry, but I have to shoot off promptly this afternoon. I have a meeting. Going up to town. So sorry. Can I ring for a taxi for you?"

Garton flushed. I had deeply disconcerted him, either because I had thwarted his scheme or because I had reacted out of character. I could not decide which it was. Strangely, it didn't really matter. I felt peculiarly free. I didn't care. Maybe I had jeopardised my future career, but so what? It didn't look as though the Foundation would survive anyway, and I was not sure that I wanted similar work elsewhere.

Garton took a deep breath. "Oh, I see," he said. "Yes, of course. I thought you might be tied up with something. Well, never mind. If you can't, you can't. Thank you all the same." He paused, as though he had nearly forgotten. "And please, keep this to yourself."

He left the room, baffled. Immediately I regretted what I had done, and was about to call him back and tell him that I could manage to drive him after all. However, the phone rang, and the moment passed. I experienced a curious peace of mind as I picked up the receiver.

Sedgfield was inquiring after Mrs Kingston. I was about to tell him sharply, with my new confidence, that she was not with me, and that I had no idea where she might be, when the door burst open. Mrs Kingston herself rushed into the room. She signalled for me to tell Sedgfield that she would ring him back. Deeply puzzled, he rang off.

"Come and look at this, please," she urged. "Something very odd has happened in reception. Please come with me. Now." She ran out of my office.

I found her in the entrance hall, staring at a magnificent display of dried flowers. Our regular suppliers had brought them, at my request, as a change from ubiquitous daffodils. It had remained there for many weeks, as I had forgotten to ask for it to be changed. I seemed to be less interested now in such matters than formerly.

"Look at this, Mr Steward!" I began to explain that I would contact the suppliers to remove the display in due course, nearly adding that it was really no business of hers.

"No, you don't understand! Take another look. Don't you see it? Something odd, something that shouldn't be there?"

"Is this some kind of joke, Mrs Kingston?"

"Joke? Of course not, but some joker has put in an extra flower, if that's a joke."

Now that she pointed it out, there was something odd about the display. The balance was all wrong. Too much weight on one side. The composition was wrong. Mrs Kingston impatiently thrust her hand into the mass of everlasting petals and drew out a brown object. At first I quite thought that she had gone crazy and pulled the head off a flower. Then I stared. She was holding in her hand a plastic daisywheel.

"Don't you recognise it?" she shouted. "It's from our computer printer. It's what spins round to type the letters. There's a whole box of different kinds of typefaces."

"But what's it doing there? Who's taken it off your machine? How very strange."

"That's the whole point," she exclaimed excitedly. "It fits my printer, but it doesn't belong. I never use that typeface. Someone has been using my machine with this daisywheel on, and hidden it in the flower display!"

It was odd certainly, but what really baffled me was the expression on Mrs Kingston's face. She was not puzzled, nor worried. She was exultant!

Chapter Fifteen

The Terrier and the Hares

"You're falling into bad habits, David. You shouldn't be here like this at the weekend, you know." Dr Garton stood at the door of my room and gave a nervous laugh. "Did I startle you? I wondered who was moving around in the offices."

I looked up from my desk, more annoyed than alarmed. There was no peace and quiet for me at the Dixons. Colley had moved into Miss Dempster's old room. Mrs Dixon fussed over him, making sure that he was all right and that everything was suitable for him. Dixon was irritated, and marched off to the vegetable garden. I wanted to think things over, but there was no chance. Colley had admired the flower borders, and was given a grand tour by his new landlady. To make matters worse, he did seem genuinely interested. Now my refuge at the Drum House had been invaded. Garton had chosen a bad moment.

"I thought you were in France," I told him. "It must have been urgent for such a quick trip."

"Er, well..." began the professor. "...As a matter of fact, I didn't go after all. I gave the matter some further thought, and changed my mind. You didn't mention it to anyone?"

"You told me it was confidential. So naturally I didn't -."

"Good man. Don't want to feel foolish. Do you mind if I say something to you? I mean, in view of our long friendship?"

"I am rather busy. Won't it wait until Monday? On the other hand, if it's vital - ."

"No, it's perhaps not all that important." He hesitated. "Yes, we can have a word early next week, if you like. I can see you're rather occupied now, David."

I heard him close the outer door. His last word had stung me like a reproach. Perhaps I was too hard on the man. Something was clearly bothering him and he'd wanted to talk to me about it. I regretted rebuffing him, thinking that I was relishing my new independence unduly. Well, he'd gone now. And, after all, he had been behaving oddly and secretively in recent weeks. He'd not seen fit to take me into his confidence earlier, so why trouble with him now?

I shuffled papers around on my desk and leaned back in the chair. I must pull myself together, get organised. Mrs Kingston's remark about always needing to consult the professor had wounded me more deeply than I had thought. Even though I did feel quite semi-detached, I still wasn't in full control somehow. I must keep more aware of what happens, and use my brains before they became hopelessly lazy.

Brains. Colley had said that if I used them I would remember. What was it? Oh yes. Remember what I had seen or done that had been so crucial. So vital in sorting out what had been going on at the Foundation. I'd started hares running in the long grass all right. I smiled to myself at the pastoral scene, but only briefly. It wasn't really a pretty picture. I had put myself in serious danger. The last attempt to stop me doing - whatever it was - had nearly finished me completely.

Four attempts there had been altogether. I was convinced now that what happened at the airport was no accident. Garton really had dismissed it too lightly, perhaps even too anxiously. When did it happen, and what had I been doing then to trigger it? I sat upright, took out my pen and held it resolutely. Time to start thinking, set about using those famous brains, David, I told myself. Let's get it all down on paper and in the right chronological order. I found my diaries for the previous year and turned back the pages.

August 29th, yes. "To airport with Cammering and prof." What a relief it should have been to get Cammering there in time for his plane.

Then we discovered that we were too early, for some reason. What was it? Oh, yes. Mrs Kingston had confused the departure times. I remembered thinking that was a highly unusual thing for her to do, as she was normally so efficient. Something to do with the clock? No, that must be wrong. Perhaps she had simply forgotten the correct flight time in all the excitement of Sir Matthew's visit. Certainly it had been a hectic week for all of us. The press conferences had to be arranged at short notice, and Cammering made such a fuss about not wanting cameras flashing at him. I learned a lot about handling the media then, especially as I had never had to do the job before. Not even the scientific journalists. It would be easier next time. Assuming, that is, if there was a next time!

Come on, think, think! There'd been that fuss with Kaltz as well. He went home early and missed the photographers altogether. That was strange too, and out of character. Kaltz had never been known to leave the laboratory before the evening. Usually he worked there until eight or nine at night. Yet he calmly walked home in the middle of the afternoon and disappeared totally from the landscape. So then. That's a start. Quite a lot out of the ordinary happened just before I was nearly killed by a crazy driver in the airport car park. Taking that jump across the dividing wall as a short cut had saved my life. Must have been the relief after a strenuous week that made me so uncharacteristically frisky. I had just reached our car in time.

Garton had gone off somewhere. Where was it? Oh yes, to buy an evening newspaper. Now that was out of character too. He never read newspapers. In fact he prided himself on being oblivious to trivia, as he called it. So why - ?

The outer door slammed. A peal of laughter rang through the Drum House. I threw down my pen in exasperation and went out to investigate. In the entrance hall, Sonia and Fletcher-Smith rapidly disentangled themselves from an embrace.

"Oh Mr Steward!" Sonia cried. "You gave me such a shock, coming in like that! Ooh, my heart's thumping like mad." Fletcher-

Smith put his arm round her waist, and grinned broadly. "I just came back for my umbrella," he explained. "I left it in Sonia's room yesterday. It looks like rain. We're going into the woods. Walking."

"Quite," I replied I didn't know what to say, but felt that something was required. I was determined not to shrink into my former shell of indifference to my colleagues. Above all, I didn't want to remind him that yesterday was Saturday. "It is a lovely day," I eventually managed. "Such a shame I can't join you, but I have a lot of paperwork to catch up with. If you'll excuse me..." I retired quickly to my room.

My first attempt at social involvement had not been an overwhelming success. The giggling soon faded into the distance, however, and the outer door slammed. Sonia had obviously recovered from her shock to be venturing into the woods again, I thought. Then I blushed to recall that she now had an escort.

I returned to my deliberations over the four attempts on my life. So then, that was number one. Now, when was number two? I flicked through the diary pages, a lot of pages. Nothing till October 31st. That was the Halloween party, when I found poison in my glass. Now that was odd too, I thought, looking at my diary. "Meet Prof G in lab re ideas". What on earth did that entry mean? Ah yes, and still another strange thing. Garton never showed up. I put down the diary, appalled by the new thought that struck me. Suppose the drink had not been intended for me at all, but for Garton. I'd gone out somewhere, came back, and picked up the glass beaker of coffee, just assuming that it was mine! I must try to recall who was there - .

No. It was more important to remember what I'd been doing, before the party. That had led to the attempt, assuming that I was the intended victim. At first I couldn't remember anything. Yet that was out of character also, I thought. My going to a party! I hadn't even been invited - . Yes, though, I was asked to go. I remembered then. Someone came into my room and asked - . No, not there. In the car park. Staniforth. I was going home. It had rained all day. That's why I had the car. But what had I been doing?

The sun shone through the windows. The shadow of the Drum House would soon cut the afternoon light off from my room as the day drew on. I must get on. I recalled being anxious to complete a task on that October day too. I had a report to finish. I turned back a few pages in the diary and deciphered some notes I had entered. Ah yes, that was it! I'd had the idea for getting together a publicity booklet. I'd been planning a series of lectures at the Drum House. Seminars. To be given by distinguished scientists from our client firms and clinics. I'd put it to a board meeting. Some directors were keen, but one or two were unsure. Cammering thought Garton would be against it because of the extra workload. Even Sir Carlo was lukewarm. Nevertheless I persisted and was asked to pull a few ideas together and submit a report. I thought a publicity booklet would be ideal, to go with a draft brochure on the lectures. I'd looked out a few illustrations and written down some likely names. The majority of the board thought that was a good idea.

The sun disappeared behind the main building. A sudden breeze lifted the papers on my desk. The outer door had opened again, but quietly this time. I put down my pen, leaned back and waited. Slowly my door opened. I was just about to reprimand Sonia for disturbing me once more, when I received a considerable shock. Colley peeped round the door and grinned.

"Working away here on such a glorious day! You should be ashamed of yourself, leaving me, a poor old invalid, to do all that weeding and hoeing in the Dixonry."

"Colley, it's not funny! I'm trying to work, and there's just one interruption after another." He looked up quizzically. "I'm doing as you advised," I continued. "I'm working out what it was that I've seen or been doing that's so dangerous to somebody that they have to stop me."

Colley threw himself agilely into my visitor's chair. Working at the Foundation seemed to have improved his health considerably. Not to mention his spirits. "Show me!" he commanded. "You're writing something down."

I told him how I was arranging the four attacks in date order, and trying to discover what I had been doing before each date that was unusual. I explained what I had done so far. He pulled his chair round the desk to my side.

"That's excellent," he said. I looked up, thinking he was mocking me, but he had become serious. So what's next?" he asked, rubbing his hands together in anticipation.

"Number three attack took place ten days later, on November 8th. That was when the piece of railing fell from the gallery in the Drum House. You remember that I told you about it when I was ill at home."

"The important question, however, is what had you been doing before then? Remember, it must be something unusual, out of routine," Colley said.

"H'm. That's difficult." I turned backwards and forwards through my diary. "There's nothing at all new or different. Just working on the same things as I had done for several weeks. There were plans to relocate the solvent store further from the service block, and to build a new extension to the laboratories on the site. There were architect's plans I was collating for the board to see. Then there was that report for the directors on my proposals for the seminars." "I was writing it just before attempt number two.?"

I explained my intentions for the series of lectures to Colley. "Ideas for getting together scientists from various hospitals and research institutes we work with, to give a day, or perhaps several days, of lectures. Probably one day only, to begin with at least. We couldn't run a residential course because we have no hotel accommodation. Not yet, anyway, although I've had the architects draw up some plans for the board to study on that too."

"There'd have to be a theme, presumably, holding the day's lectures and talks together. It would take a lot of organising."

"Nothing we couldn't handle, I think. We'd want to run them basically as an exercise to boost the Foundation's image, although of course there'd be a serious scientific purpose. Lots of good ideas get sparked off by bringing people together in fairly informal surroundings, you know."

"So you'd expect to make a profit for the Foundation, would you?"

"Good heavens, no!" It would be strictly non-profit making. Once expenses were covered, of course."

"Sounds a bit dodgy to me. How did the board of directors react when you put it to them? Not with much enthusiasm, I'd guess. I can't see Carlo Waybridge, for one, letting his staff spill the beans on their latest projects to rival companies. Doesn't sound much like Cammering's style either, going in for publicity."

"Sir Matthew was quite interested, at first. Dr Garton rather put him off later. Waybridge didn't say much, but wasn't completely against. I suppose he wanted to wait for the costings and so on."

"Why did Garton discourage Cammering? Did he think it too ambitious?"

"No," I laughed. "On the contrary, he was as keen as me. He became enthusiastic, wanting to widen the scheme with a book or brochure on the history of Cammering, Kaltz, and the Foundation. Cammering tried to shut him up. Perhaps he was embarrassed, but I don't think it was altogether that. Anyway, he backtracked hard, and the end result was that they deferred making a decision."

"Which means they've ditched the whole caboodle, does it?"

"Well, it would have done, but I've been here long enough to know how the board operates. I managed to save something from the wreck, I'm glad to say. I persuaded them to let me continue working on draft plans, and sound out potential speakers for the lectures. Now, don't think me boastful, but I'm particularly proud about this one. I also managed to persuade them to let me to spend time collecting materials for the historical booklet! I wanted them to let me co-opt Merryman and Palmer, but they'd only agree to my doing it alone. Well, that's something, although it will take longer to track down old photographs, news reports and suchlike. Anyway, I'm determined to do my best. I made that quite clear to the directors."

"I'll give you a hand, if you like. On the quiet, of course. I've already done a fair bit along those lines myself. Remember?"

I gladly accepted Colley's offer. I knew his research would be meticulous, and I thought he would probably have access to sources that I might find difficult to reach.

"You'll be discreet, won't you?" I asked. "I don't want the scheme torpedoed now. I've too much credibility at stake."

"Point taken," said Colley. "Right then. That's number three attack. The fourth would be when Dempster yanked you off the road in front of the van. What date was that?"

"I shan't forget that in a hurry. January 30th. You know more about the actual event than I do, so I won't go over it again. As to what I'd been doing beforehand that caused the incident, the answer is that I don't know. I've racked my brains time and again, but can think of nothing. Simply the same old routine. I don't recall seeing anything unusual, or doing anything different from what I'd been working on for months. It's very baffling."

"Nothing new at the Foundation? No new projects? No new staff? No new clients?"

"No, nothing - except - well hardly new staff, I suppose. Your Miss Dempster appeared on the scene, of course. She caused quite a stir with her wretched tripods and - . Oh, good heavens!"

"And her cameras," added Colley. "That's what you were going to say. My dear friend, you've got it! It's the photography! That's what's scared the villain! You had to be stopped, at all costs, from collecting photographs for publication. But why?"

"Yes. I see now. That's the thread running through everything I was pushing hard with before each attack."

"They thought you'd given up the proposal after that near miss with the piece of railing in the Drum House. Well, in a way you had. Actively, I mean. Then I bring in Dempster, ostensibly as a photographer. The villain must have thought you'd taken her on, and meant business. All the time you really were not doing anything unusual. It was me that introduced the new threat. By accident I do assure you! And the result was nearly fatal. My dear David, what can I say?"

"Sorry would do for a start, right?" I said. "Then you can take me out and buy me a drink. A very large one!" I tidied my desk, and we went out.

Colley drove across the downs, and we parked at the Silver Swan. The place was fairly busy, but we found the corner table free. Colley returned from the bar with the drinks, and I felt pleased with myself. The terrier has brains, after all, I told myself repeatedly. Colley grew serious. "We're making progress, but not fast enough. Are you willing to help me in the next stage? Right, don't look so offended. I had assumed you were. But there's danger in it, David. I feel it only fair to warn you."

"Come on," I said. "The sooner this business is over the better for me."

"Good! Your seminar idea is excellent, but let's arrange one for a slightly different purpose. I think we should start as many hares running as we can, and see what happens. I want you to fix up a gathering of all the relevant people, and to do it without asking the board of directors. In fact you must only tell them at the very last minute, when it's too late for any of them to stop it. The later, the better. I want you to organise a distinguished gathering in celebration of the life and work of that great scientist."

" - that important member of the Foundation, the great and justly renowned Sir Matthew Cammering!"

"Cammering?" said Colley. "No. The scientist we are celebrating is Paul Mountford!"

Chapter Sixteen

Guests at Mrs Mountford's

Ambrose Sedgfield threw down his pen and sighed with relief. Correcting the proofs of your own publication was bad enough, but vetting a colleague's article for the scientific press was far worse. It was a labour of respect, however, for the memory of his old friend Paul Mountford. The experiments having all been completed, it was only necessary to check the draft text found in his laboratory notebooks. The problem was to guess whether these were Mountford's finalised observations or whether they might have been revised or expanded had he survived. Fortunately the work formed a neat piece of self-contained research, one of the best articles the Foundation had produced for many years.

"About time poor old Mountford got some credit," said Horning. "Kaltz would have wanted to get his name on it, even though it was all Mountford's work."

"They ought to do something to mark Mountford's life and work," said Fletcher-Smith. "There couldn't be a memorial service because Mountford stipulated in his will that he didn't want one. Eleanor Mountford told Sonia about it. But a bit of a get-together would be a good idea, don't you think?" The laboratory staff all agreed, but nothing more was discussed at that time. Once Sonia's name had been mentioned, the subject changed abruptly, and Fletcher-Smith once again came in for a good deal of banter. The two of them were increasingly seen together, whenever their work permitted it.

However, when the same idea occurred to Dr Sedgfield and he put it forward to the laboratory staff at their next weekly meeting, they were already receptive, and definite plans took shape. Dr Garton agreed to speak about Mountford's career and achievements, and found a pretext to persuade Sir Matthew Cammering, whom he met by chance at a symposium in London, to come out to the Foundation on the day chosen.

So it came about that the plan Colley had suggested was easily set in motion. All I had to do was to accept the task of organising it and making the practical arrangements. It was a simple matter, when the initial enthusiasm in the laboratories began to wane, to secure agreement that the whole affair be kept to our own staff at the Foundation. It was unanimously agreed also that there was no need to discuss it with the directors, as it was an informal matter among Mountford's former friends and colleagues. When the date was fixed and the final guest list proposed, neither Colley nor Miss Dempster was included. There was no deliberate intention of excluding them, but nobody but Merryman and I even thought of inviting them along. I mentioned this to Colley, and he decided I should not arouse suspicion by insisting on adding their names. I was disappointed, but, to keep down costs, we agreed to limit invitations to permanent staff only.

Mrs Mountford was delighted when I broke the news to her. There was no difficulty in persuading her to keep all the arrangements secret from the directors. "That will put their noses out of joint," she said. "If it was my choosing, I wouldn't invite them anyway." Eventually, however, she agreed reluctantly that Cammering should be included in the guest list.

The secret was indeed well kept, partly because Mrs Kingston was still away on leave, so she had no opportunity of hearing the plan being discussed nor of reporting its details to Sir Matthew. She had been due back at work for over a week, but had phoned in to say that she was ill. The Riviera trip, if it had ever actually existed, had evidently not improved her health.

The gathering was arranged to take place at the Drum House at seven in the evening. We were all to assemble in the board room for the formal proceedings, and drinks and a buffet supper were to be available in the anterooms. Garton had discovered that Cammering was still at his London hotel, and although surprised when told about the gathering, he agreed to attend. Mrs Kingston returned to the office on the same morning, looking frail and nervous, still too unwell to pursue for long her outspoken objections to the arrangements. She was disconcerted, I thought, because for once she had not been personally involved in organising an event at the Foundation.

At lunchtime on the day of the commemoration, everything was going smoothly. The atmosphere was quite light-hearted and indeed happy. Life at the Foundation had recently been rather depressing for everybody, and we were glad of an occasion to get together and celebrate. Then, at four o'clock, Miss Dempster rang me to impart bad news. Mrs Mountford, it appeared, had fallen in the house and was unable to walk. She was vague about what had actually happened, but I was given the impression that Mrs Mountford had broken an ankle.

"She's in fine fettle otherwise," reported Miss Dempster breezily. "Just can't move about on her feet. However, she's asked me to tell you to transfer the whole jollification to her house. There's plenty of room, and I can wheel Mrs Mountford on stage as required."

So that was it. I had no time to ponder the question as to what Miss Dempster had been up to, not to assess the role of Colley in the change of venue. Merryman, Sonia and I rang round all the staff to tell them about the revised plan. Nobody objected in the slightest. Most were sympathetic to Mrs Mountford, although nobody seemed to know her well. Indeed few had even seen her. Mountford himself had a posthumous popularity greater than anything he had enjoyed in life.

"I'm dying to see what the house is like," Sonia told her friends in the canteen. They had walked over there for their tea break, though normally the building was quiet in the afternoon except for laboratory staff, who were not supposed to eat or drink at their benches. The other girls agreed with her that Mrs Mountford must be awfully lonely in her large house, seeing nobody.

"That's what you think," confided Palmer. "My aunt saw her in the village yesterday. Mrs Mountford was very excited. Not just about the celebration do, she thought. There would be an important announcement. Something about a discovery."

"I wonder what she's found out that's so exciting," speculated Fletcher-Smith, who was sitting close to Sonia as usual. "It will really put the cat among the pigeons, unless it's just talk. Must be something that Mountford had discovered. Do you think it's some laboratory notebooks?"

"Shouldn't think so," said Palmer. "Mountford was never one for taking work home. Anyway Sedgy's got all we found to write up Mountford's last paper for the journal."

"Well, everything will be revealed no doubt this evening," said Horning. "I take it that we're all going to be there? Good. Then how about meeting up afterwards at the Rose and Crown?"

"Good idea," agreed Staniforth. "I expect the party at Ma Mountford's will be over by eight o'clock or eight thirty. Let's all meet together in the pub then. We'll need a proper drink by that time. The celebration will probably turn out to be a bit of a bore."

"Bet you it won't!" said Sonia. "What if Mrs Mountford's found a vital clue proving that Dr Mountford was murdered! It's going to be really exciting, and so mysterious. Ooooh!"

She clung closer to Fletcher-Smith and the general company laughed. "Anyway, that's what we think, me and Brian," Sonia pouted. "So you can think what you like. I bet Dr Sedgfield discovered something and told Mrs Mountford."

"Talking of Sedgfield," said Horning, "he's a bit shirty about the rumour that Mountford didn't die of natural causes. Do you know anything about it, any of you? I've no idea where the story came from."

"He heard Garton talking to his secretary the other day," explained Staniforth. "He was peeved about it as well. Said it was all idle speculation with no evidence to support it. You know what he's like. Never believes anything till it's thoroughly tested out. I bet he never drinks his coffee till he's stuck a thermometer in it."

160

"Yes, it was peculiar," agreed Palmer. "I heard Garton ranting on as well. He seemed annoyed beyond all reason. I mean, Mountford could have been done in by somebody, couldn't he? He was on heart drugs and his drawer was full of tablets. It would have been easy to stuff a few more into his drink."

"Trust you to be nosing around Mountford's room," said Horning. "You're worse than Arnie Springer for prying."

"Don't get me wrong," explained Palmer. "I wasn't snooping. Anyway, Mountford was always too careful for that. Arnold never got far with him. No, I once happened to see the pills in his drawer when I was with him. He'd called me in to check over some figures. You know how he hated that sort of thing. He opened the drawer to get a pen, and there they were. Dozens of them, rolling about among the pencils and things."

"I suppose Sedgy and Garton are bothered in case it reflects badly on the Foundation," said Fletcher-Smith. "If there's been any funny business, there'd have to be a public investigation to see what had happened. It's bad enough old man Cammering signing off so abruptly. If Mrs Mountford's got evidence of something serious that's been going on, the police will be called in. Then it will be curtains for the Foundation."

"And for us too," added Horning. "I'm starting to look around for a job somewhere else, I don't mind telling you. Aren't you others doing the same?"

"Oh don't!" exclaimed Sonia. "It would be awful if we have to go. I mean, we'd be spread about everywhere, and we're settled here. All our friends are here."

"Some more than others," said Horning, nudging Fletcher-Smith, who winked back at him. "Talk about being spread around everywhere!"

The subject of Mountford's death was also being discussed at the same time between their seniors in Dr Garton's room. The professor paced up and down, angrily. "We must put a stop to these rumours, Ambrose," he said. "They will get out of hand, and goodness knows what will happen then. Paul died of a heart attack. You know that. We all do. You must stop that silly woman in your office talking nonsense!"

"That won't be easy, Augustus," replied Sedgfield. "We would do better to ignore her, and all the others talking the same way. If there's nothing in it..."

"Which there certainly is not!"

"If there's nothing in it, then the stories will die down themselves. Trying to suppress them will only make things worse. It would look as if there was something to hide. And if there is something in them…"

"Then we are in trouble," said Dr Garton. "All of us. We'd all be in trouble."

"Anyway, let's see what Eleanor Mountford has to say for herself tonight. I expect it will prove to be something of nothing."

"I wish we weren't going there. Not to that house. Bleak, draughty place. Half the rooms will be shut up, and we'll be rattling around in the rest of them."

"I'd forgotten you'd been there before," said Sedgfield. "I've never seen the inside of the place. It certainly looks to be a big house from what you see from the road. I always wondered why Paul bought it."

"I always wondered how he could afford to buy it," snapped the professor. "After all, he was never used to living in a place like that. Very humble beginnings, some north country back street, he used to tell me."

"He told us all, Augustus. Quite often. Maybe that was why he bought the house."

"Perhaps so," I added. "Well, I'm going back to the office now. We'll all have to get away promptly at five, if we're to be in good time at Mrs Mountford's." Although I had been present, I had said nothing during the exchanges between Garton and Sedgfield. I felt uneasy about the professor's agitated manner and uncertain how much Colley and Miss Dempster were behind the Mountford rumours. Actual evidence may have been found to substantiate the stories. I hoped that Colley really did have the situation fully under control.

It had been an unpleasant day throughout. Apart from all this gossip and morbid excitement, anticipating the evening's meeting, I had the trouble of re-organising the venue. The morning had been no better either. At the senior committee meeting in the board room I had made no progress on my scheme to run seminars at the Drum House. The professor now roundly opposed the plan. He said that it would reflect badly on the Foundation, calling my proposal a barefaced touting for publicity. I was puzzled by the strength of feeling behind his stance. He appeared hostile to me personally. Curiously, he also seemed to be frightened.

Sedgfield was no help either. He wanted to postpone the plan now that Cammering had resigned. In fact he wanted to postpone deciding on everything, and even managed to defer authorising the architect's plans for my proposed new buildings on the old solvent store site. The other members took fright when Garton mentioned the financial uncertainties caused by Cammering's departure. We wasted time speculating idly about the future, and the whole meeting ran into the sand. When I set out my project for searching for photographs of Cammering and Kaltz, I got no support at all. Garton's chairmanship was feeble. I'm afraid I became quite angry and told them that I was absolutely determined to push ahead immediately with my plans. Garton turned purple with rage. He closed the meeting abruptly, and the committee members sidled thankfully away. When the others had gone, he harangued me about my persistence. The breach between us grew constantly wider. Even by mid-afternoon, his manner still rankled with me. I just could not bring myself to support him against Sedgfield over the rumours about Paul Mountford's death, though secretly I did agree that they ought to be stopped. I felt that such idle talk would not have been started by Colley, and I was uneasy that it might affect our own private inquiries.

Soon after seven o'clock, the staff assembled at Mrs Mountford's house. As the weather was fine and still warm, most of us were circulating between small groups on the large rear lawn, drinks in hand. At one end of the garden was a terrace, which I thought ideal for the speeches and presentation ceremony, but Dr Garton pronounced the acoustics unsuitable and decided that the formal proceedings must be held indoors.

Although the surrounding dark shrubs and trees might trap some of the sound, there would have been far more room for everyone outside. Fletcher-Smith had even brought his loudspeakers and microphone, but to no avail. The professor glowered at him, and insisted on moving indoors.

We all stood, consequently, in the entrance hall, tightly packed together. Double doors had been thrown open, connecting with the drawing room, so there was a good deal of space. Even so, several of the junior staff had to perch on the lower stairs. After an introductory announcement by Ambrose Sedgfield, Mrs Mountford was wheeled in to prolonged applause, pushed by Miss Dempster in a wheelchair I had last seen in Palmyra Square. The whole scene was ridiculous and theatrical. There was a general air of embarrassment among the assembled guests, mingled with uncertainty as to why exactly we were clapping our hands so vigorously.

The unease, however, did not extend to Eleanor Mountford. She sat smiling and waving regally, enjoying every minute. The secretive smile on her face looked ominous, and I had a deep sense of foreboding. The professor fought his way to the front of the crowd and began his speech. We tried to relax as best we could.

Garton went on at inordinate length about Mountford's achievements. Several of us were visibly surprised by his overblown praise, but it was apparent that many of the laboratory staff were accustomed to his style. Although Mountford had done a great deal of research, much of it excellent, he had always published it as part of a team with Cammering, Kaltz or both. As a junior member of the team, too. That, at least, was the general impression we had formed over the years. No-one had disliked Mountford. Indeed some of us had actually liked the man, finding him congenial company. Garton, however, was giving an address worthy of a far more distinguished scientist. It struck me that his oration was delivered not so much to honour Mountford as to propitiate his spirit. Such honouring as it contained was directed more at Cammering, or perhaps Kaltz. Listening to the speech was a weird experience. A general sigh rippled around when he finished, not entirely caused, I thought, by our standing for so long, hot and tired.

Mrs Mountford daintily thanked us for coming to her house, and for all the kind things that had been said about Paul. She was touched, she said. It was very nice. Very nice indeed, she was sure. Paul would have liked it. Paul, I thought, would have detested it. It was all wrong. What was she playing at now? Remarkably composed, she raised herself from the wheelchair, aided by Miss Dempster. Colley produced a reading desk. To our surprise, Mrs Mountford inched her way behind it, clutching a sheaf of notes. Unbelievably we were to be given another lecture. The Cammering Foundation, embodied by Garton, had been totally upstaged. The professor looked shattered.

"Please sit down, all of you," she cooed. "Where you can. There are some chairs - ." We all turned around in circles, looking for floor space. A few lucky ones found the chairs. More joined the people already perched on the staircase. Soon we were all seated somehow, and quietly awaited Mrs Mountford's revelations.

She began by saying how much she valued Dr Garton's words. Garton himself appeared deeply unhappy and worried. I caught a glimpse of Colley's face in the shadows under the stairs. He saw me, and held a finger to his lips. Everything was going to plan so far, and I began to relax.

Eleanor Mountford was in her natural element. She was a magnificent speaker. Her delivery and sense of timing were superb.

Gone was all trace of the silly widow act. There on centre stage was a consummate actress. If she was playing yet another role, she could certainly turn pretence into sincerity. She held us all captive. While she spoke we listened. Where she led we followed. When she paused we held our breath. No sound came from her audience. The slow ticking of the staircase clock echoed through the spellbound house.

She told us how she met Paul Mountford, how they shared their lives, how they discussed every detail of his hopes and dreams, how he talked of his plans and research. Then she broke off, tightly gripping the back of her chair. Miss Dempster stepped towards her, but was waved away imperiously. She took a deep breath, closed her eyes, and spoke again.

"All this work, all these plans, were frustrated by treachery. A traitor, a person trusted by Paul, had conspired to thwart him, to subjugate him, and in the end to silence him for ever. You thought Paul died of a heart attack. So he did. He was ill, that's true. But his medication kept him alive, working and healthy. His tablets were tampered with by that traitor. Paul died before his natural time because of that person, that fiend! And the name of that - ."

She paused again, swaying behind the reading desk. She took a few sips from a glass of water. No-one spoke. No-one moved. Eleanor Mountford recovered her composure. She opened her mouth, but no sound came. She clutched wildly at her throat, gasped violently, and collapsed heavily on to the floor. Dr Garton lunged forward to catch her as she fell, but Miss Dempster pushed him deftly away. She leaned over the slumped body, beckoning sideways for help. Colley and Merryman came quickly forward. Between them they picked up Mrs Mountford and carried her away. The audience erupted in an astonished babble. People got to their feet and started milling about in the crowd, chattering excitedly. I caught sight of Colley signalling me to come forward. I needed no second bidding. I strode to the reading desk and took control.

"Ladies and gentlemen. Your attention please! Quiet, everybody!" I announced. I even surprised myself by the note of command and dignity in my voice, which I scarcely recognised as my own. "Mrs Mountford has been taken ill. Out of respect, and also out of gratitude for what she has done for the Foundation and for us, please keep calm. Open the garden door! Thank you. Now kindly move outside, slowly and in good order. Wait on the lawn. I will call you back in a few minutes."

To my surprise, that is exactly what all the staff did. Although it was already quite dark outside, the room emptied quickly but quietly. Merryman, Colley and I stood alone at the foot of the stairs. I was shaking, but John was beaming with smiles. "Well done, Mr Steward," he said. "That was simply splendid." With that he clapped me vigorously on the back. "Well done indeed," echoed Colley, silently reappearing from a door under the stairs. And no more of the Mr Steward business, John. His name is David. Shake hands with him." He did so, slightly sheepishly. "Good work David," he muttered.

"Now then," announced Colley. "To work. Quickly. This is what we do. In a minute, get everybody back in here, David. Eleanor Mountford is going to make a dramatic re-entry. She's perfectly all right. What an actress!"

I felt my mouth open. "None of it, that speech, was true?"

"Parts of it," said Colley. She delivered my speech faultlessly. Improved on it in fact. Come on, pull yourself together. When she comes in, you make another announcement, David, and present her with this." He thrust a heavy metal object into my hands.

"It's - it's a photograph," I gasped. "In a superb silver frame. Where on earth did you get this, Colley? I've been looking for ages for something like this. It's a photograph of Cammering and Kaltz, and, good heavens, Mountford. It's simply wonderful!"

"Tell the audience that, and give it to her. Then stand back and brace yourself. Literally, I mean. Something ought to happen, but you get out of the way fast. Dempster will take care of Mrs Mountford. John and I will do what's necessary elsewhere."

"Where did you find it?" I still wanted to examine the picture. It was just what I wanted for the Foundation. Cammering and Kaltz were shaking hands and smiling. To one side stood Paul Mountford. That was all right for tonight's purposes. I'd get a copy made. We could enlarge it, block Mountford off. Yes, it would still balance well as a composition. It was just simply ideal! "But, Colley," I said, "there's..."

"Get a move on," shouted Colley. I thrust the photograph under my jacket and dashed into the garden to summon the staff back into the room. I took up my stand by the reading desk. "I have an announcement to make," I called out when the audience had settled down again. I am very glad to be able to tell you that Mrs Mountford has recovered. I want you all to welcome her back warmly. Here she comes!"

I clapped my hands together vigorously as Miss Dempster brought on Mrs Mountford, seated again in her wheelchair smiling and waving. Colley grabbed my sleeve and dragged me out of sight for a moment. "Tell them she can't say any more but that she wants them all to stay," he hissed. "There's a buffet laid on in the dining room, and drinks. No more speeches. Say that. Tell the audience what it is, and then present her with the photograph. Got that?"

"Tell them who's in the photograph too?"

"Yes. Yes. Yes. That's absolutely essential. Then hand it over and get out of the way. Quick." He pushed me away. I walked back to centre stage.

I made the announcement. I don't know where the nerve or the words came from, but I did it. I told the audience that I was making a presentation. I explained what it was, and who was in the picture. I even held it up to show the audience, though nobody would have seen it clearly. I remember making the presentation. So far, so good. Then I made the one mistake. I forgot to dash away quickly.

Mrs Mountford reached for the photograph, but Miss Dempster pulled the wheelchair suddenly backwards, and ran with the passenger to the kitchen. The picture fell to the floor. A velvet curtain behind the reading desk bulged forwards. A hand came out and grabbed the precious photograph. Instead of rushing away as instructed, I sprang forward to retrieve it. The curtain bulged out again, more violently. The supporting rail collapsed, and I fell forward. Someone hidden in the heavy velvet leapt on me. Blows rained down on my head and shoulders. Splinters of glass from the broken frame pierced the curtain, slashing my face and arms. I staggered to the floor, swathed in thick cloth. I could see nothing, but felt my assailant struggle free from the curtain. Unseen arms rolled me across the carpet. I was pulled upright. The curtain fell away.

Colley and John were holding me but I could hardly see them. Something warm and sticky dripped from my forehead. Their sleeves were covered with blood. I realised it was mine. Quickly they bundled me out through the kitchen door. Merryman's car appeared in the yard. Intense pains shot across my face and arms. It was growing dark. John leapt into the driving seat. We roared away from the house.

"Where, where?" I gasped.

"You're going to the hospital. Double quick. Sit back and shut up," Merryman ordered. Then he laughed loudly. "Sorry. Sit back and stay still," he said quietly in my ear. "Er, David," he added.

"Am I all right, John?"

"You're fine. You've got a few nasty cuts, but they'll soon sort you out. Oh, by the way, Colley said I was to tell you 'Well done'. And something else. 'Terrier'. Mean anything to you?"

At the bottom of the drive, by the turning into the road, two dim figures appeared from the shrubbery. I saw them briefly silhouetted in the car's headlights. John braked sharply to a halt. A woman stumbled round to his open window. "He'll be all right, won't he? He will be all right?" she said.

"Yes, Mrs Mountford," I heard John say. "David's badly cut, but he'll be okay."

"Thank God for that!" she cried, staggering back to the side of the drive, where the other figure stood motionless. "It's got to stop," sobbed Eleanor Mountford. "All this business, Alice. It's got to stop!" Her companion said nothing, but took her arm and led her away into the deepening twilight.

Chapter Seventeen

Colley Makes Friends

"No more, you two," said Kate Merryman. "Mr Dale has had quite enough for one day. It's off to bed for the pair of you!" With that, she ushered her children upstairs, and John Merryman closed the sitting room door.

I felt distinctly uneasy in the cosy domestic surroundings of the Merryman's home. I tried telling myself that it was because I had no experience of lively infants, indeed none of children at all. The real reason, however, was that I had never before set foot inside the house. Until Colley announced our invitation, it never occurred to me that the Merrymans might welcome my company.

"I don't know why you've involved me, Colley," I told him. "You go if you wish. After all, you seem to be getting along famously during office hours. I'm sure they've only included me out of politeness. It's you they really want."

"Now that's utter nonsense, David. Kate and John wouldn't have invited you if they didn't want you to join the party. John's been trying to ask you himself all week, but he's never had a suitable opportunity. He didn't feel able to march boldly into your room and request your company at the twins' birthday party."

"I don't see why. Well, I suppose I would have put him off with some excuse."

I didn't say anything to Colley, but I was secretly delighted by the Merrymans' invitation. It wasn't just that it fitted in with my plans to be more sociable with the staff. I positively enjoyed myself, and began to think how to repay the family. Mrs Dixon would not want the twins playing in her garden, and I quickly closed my mind to the idea of boisterous children among the chintz and china in her sitting room. For the very first time, I began thinking of setting up house for myself.

Colley was a model guest. Like an amiable uncle, he had romped around the house all afternoon. How he managed with his disability I couldn't imagine. He seemed tireless, although finally confessing to being worn out when teatime arrived. Later he had sat between the twins on the sofa, reading their favourite stories to them.

"You're a lucky fellow, John," said Colley. "Two fine kids and a beautiful wife. What more could a man wish for?"

"I hope they've not tired you out completely," he replied. "They do get rather excited, especially on their birthday." He glowed with young paternal pride.

Kate tiptoed back into the room and quietly closed the door. "I think they're asleep at last," she said. "They're exhausted. Thank you Colley, you've been marvellous. And you too, David. Now, who's for coffee?"

"Don't bother with that, Kate," I said. "I brought a couple of bottles of white wine. Colley took the liberty of putting them in your fridge. He's really making himself at home. You'll have to watch out, or you'll find yourself with a lodger!"

"Oh, much as I would like that, I'm afraid Mrs Dixon couldn't spare me," laughed Colley. I felt a slight twinge of envy. Mrs Dixon would hardly miss me, I thought. Perhaps I had been there too long. Again I pondered the idea of finding a house or a flat for myself. Then I remembered how uncertain the future was, and put the thought aside.

Colley wandered round the room, looking at the pictures and photographs. Kate had considerable talents with watercolour, but she seemed embarrassed at Colley's interest in them. "Don't look closely at my daubs, please," she cried. "I've no time for much painting these days." Obediently, Colley turned his attention to the framed photographs. He picked one up from the back of the shelf.

"That's taken on the beach," said John. "The twins were tiny then, crawling about on the sands. It must have been three years ago this last summer. No, two years ago. I remember now. Arnold and his sister-in-law came with us. I don't think he enjoyed it much. He never came with us on an outing again."

Colley examined the photograph carefully for a minute or more, his face becoming serious. He came into the centre of the room, and asked the Merrymans if he could borrow it for a while.

"Whatever for?" Kate asked. "We've better ones of the children, and I look a frightful mess."

"Kate, come and sit down. Here, with John. Thank you. David, do you mind too? There's something I have to tell you. Something unpleasant. And something I must ask you to keep absolutely to yourselves till I say otherwise. Understood?"

"Whatever is it, Colley?" I asked. He held the photograph close to his chest, hiding the picture. The Merrymans sat together on the sofa, holding hands and looking anxious.

"On the day that I came to the Drum House last October, I found a man's body on the stairs there. David knows about it already. Afterwards the body disappeared, and has never been seen since. I did not know whose body it was. David would have recognised his face immediately had he seen it. So would you, both of you. I'm afraid that the body was that of Arnold Springer, the man that you pointed out to me in this photograph."

"Arnold?" John gasped. "Arnold dead? He can't be! I know he's been missing for weeks, but…"

"Where is he now?" asked Kate quietly. Her face was as white as a sheet but she was firmly in control of herself.

"That I can't tell you. I think I know the answer, but I'm not saying anything until I'm quite sure and have positive evidence."

"So that's it," I said. "Poor Springer. Has his family been told? Have the police been brought in?"

"The police are fully informed. Action will be taken at the right time, but until then please, please, keep this strictly to yourselves."

"When did you find out?" asked John. "Had suspected for long that Arnold might be dead?"

"For several weeks, yes," replied Colley. "I was pretty sure about it, but I had no proof until you identified the man in this photograph. Remember that, unlike you three, I had never seen Springer alive. I am prepared now to swear on oath that it was Springer's body I saw on the stairs."

The room fell silent. I didn't know what to say. John looked amazed. Kate was near to tears. "He wasn't really a friend," she said at last. "I'm afraid we didn't like him much. He was so superior and scheming. But I'm sorry he's dead, and I'm sorry for his sister-in-law."

"Was he killed, Colley?" asked John. "I mean, did he fall down the Drum House stairs accidentally, or was he - ?"

"He was murdered," replied Colley. "He didn't fall on the staircase. I don't think he was killed there. The villain dumped him in a hurry, and later on, well, disposed of his body."

"How dreadful!" exclaimed Kate. "Who would want to do such a thing?" Her face suddenly took on a fierce expression. "John isn't in any danger, is he, Colley?"

"I'm fairly sure that he isn't, Kate. I would tell you at once, both of you, if I thought otherwise, I promise you."

"Presumably he'd discovered something that was a danger to his killer," I said. "Do you know how he died?"

"If my theory is correct, he was poisoned. There was no sign of violence on his body, and I understand that he had no history of serious illness."

"No, he was fit and well. He looked after his health," said John. "It's ironic, really, Colley. Do you think that cheque that I found in his drawer had anything to do with his death? I know you made out that it was a bonus of some kind, like the one I received later. I thought that at first, but afterwards I began to think that wasn't correct. For one thing, it was such a lot of money, and for another - ."

"You noticed the date on the cheque," said Colley.

"Yes. It didn't register at the time, but I remembered it later on. Do you think he was blackmailing somebody?"

"Almost certainly he was, but whether that was why he was killed, I don't really know. Somehow it doesn't quite hang together yet."

"He was sending those notes to Cammering, wasn't he?" I said. "The blackmailing letters, I mean. Using Mrs Kingston's word processor and printer, but with a daisywheel he supplied himself. That would be why it was hidden in the flower arrangement, the one Mrs Kingston found. You remember. I told you about it."

"But who put it there?" asked Colley. "From what you told me about the date on which the flower arrangement arrived, Springer was already dead. So who hid it?"

"Tell me about it," said John. I did so. There was a long silence. "There's something peculiar about that," he said eventually. "It's not - well, tidy. Whoever hid the daisywheel must have been in a hurry, a panic even. After all, it would have only been a matter of days before it was found."

"Mrs Kingston found it," I said. "Even if she hadn't, it would have been spotted when the flowers firm came to change the arrangement."

"Not necessarily," said Kate. "David didn't see it at first, even when Irene Kingston took him to it. John here wouldn't have found it in a month of Sundays. He'd never look twice at a flower arrangement. The florists might easily have taken the daisywheel away with the old display, and no-one would have been the wiser. It would have been a clever way of dumping the thing, wouldn't it?"

None of us could even guess the answer to that question. We drank the cold white wine. Then Kate made coffee. Colley and I washed the dishes. John Merryman paced up and down the room, frowning and worried.

"You've got to tell him everything," I said to Colley. Soon afterwards the four of us sat down together again, and Colley told the Merrymans everything that he knew about the events at the Foundation. At first I suspected that there was more that he hadn't said, but when I taxed him on the subject, he replied that he had only kept back a theory he was working on. When he had definite proof, he promised to tell us about it. In the meantime, we agreed to keep the conversation entirely to ourselves. Colley placed the photograph carefully in his overcoat pocket.

At half past eight, the doorbell rang. John went to the front door, and came back into the sitting room with Brian Fletcher-Smith and Sonia. They had called with birthday presents for the twins, they explained.

"Sorry we missed them, and the party," Fletcher-Smith said. "We didn't realise that it was so late."

"I took Brian shopping," added Sonia. "Poor dear. He hated it. So afterwards we went..."

"We don't want to know, thank you very much!" exclaimed Kate, laughing. "Really, Sonia, you are the limit! Show me what you've bought. And keep your voices down, if you don't mind. The twins have had enough excitement for one day!"

"Me too," said John Merryman, quietly to himself.

The mood lightened as Sonia told Kate where they had been, and the evening passed quickly and very pleasantly. It was late when Colley and I drove back to the Dixons.

"You enjoyed yourself, didn't you?" I asked Colley. "You're full of surprises. I didn't realise you'd be such a success with the children."

"You seemed reluctant to drag yourself away, too," he countered. "You're becoming positively sociable in your old age! Just as well you are. We're invited to Eleanor Mountford's on Tuesday. Just the three of us, this time, and Miss Dempster of course."

I overslept next morning. Colley was already at breakfast when I came downstairs. "Just as well it's Saturday," he said. "You'd be fit for nothing at the office, looking like that. Anyway, eat up as quickly as you can. I gather there's a bit of a domestic crisis. Mrs Dixon wants us out of the way."

It transpired that Mrs Scutter had been unable to attend to her duties at the Dixons on the previous day. She had called after lunchtime, when Mrs Dixon had returned from her usual shopping trip to the village to find the house exactly as she had left it. Mrs Scutter was now due at any moment, and Mrs Dixon wanted to remove herself, and anyone else who might hinder the work, from the interior of the house.

Colley, however, had never encountered Mrs Scutter before, and was curious to see what she was like. Mrs Dixon threw up her hands in mock resignation and fled into the furthest recesses of the garden. Colley lingered expectantly in the sitting room, and insisted that I stayed with him. We waited, half-heartedly reading the morning newspapers, for the arrival of the legendary lady.

In due course, in other words slightly later than promised, there was a clatter in the hall. A whirring noise began, as the vacuum cleaner sprang into action. The sitting room door burst open, and the din grew to a crescendo. Then it suddenly stopped altogether. Colley had stepped forward and pressed the power switch.

"Oh, it's you is it, Mr Steward? Thought you'd have more sense than frighten me like that. I choked, and pointed to the guilty party. "So you're Mr Dale, are you?" she continued. "Pleased to meet you, I'm sure. Hope you're better behaved than this one here. Right little terror he is".

She nodded at me and beamed relentlessly at Colley.

"How do you do," he said. "You're a busy lady. How do you come to be working on a lovely Saturday morning like this? You ought to be out and about with your young man, whoever the lucky fellow is, enjoying the Spring sunshine."

"Now then. Less of that," she said sternly, but visibly preened herself nevertheless. She sat down on the arm of a chair, more than ready for a chat. I hoped Mrs Dixon would stay in the garden. Mrs Scutter counted on her fingers. "Chance'd be a fine thing, Mr Dale. I've had such a job fitting everybody in this week, you'd never believe! Mrs Turnock asked me Wednesday 'stead of Tuesday, Miss Arbuthnot changed me to Monday and extra Thursday this week - I'm not doing it regular, I told her straight - and then Mrs Darlaston went away on holiday, so that's Tuesday. Then to crown it all, I had extra work to do at Mrs Easton's. So bang went Mrs Dixon's Friday. I told Miss Fordyce, I said, I wouldn't do it for anybody else but I'm not letting you down, fixed like you are, what with the funeral and all that caper. It was the least I could do, I said, and so it was. Mrs Mackerworth and old whosit Robertson just had to take pot luck. But you know what a gasbag she is. Well, perhaps you don't. I never could stand about gossiping myself, as I tell all my ladies. So anyway, dear, that's how I come to be here doing Mrs Dixon's Friday on a Saturday morning."

"My goodness, what a complicated life you lead!" said Colley. "You need a secretary to keep all those arrangements properly timetabled. How on earth do you remember it all?" Mrs Scutter chuckled, and patted her hair. I started to speak, but Colley signalled me frantically to stay silent. He had noticed the same name among the list of employers that I had. "So Miss Fordyce is dead, is she?", he asked, skirting around the key name.

"Indeed she is not, Mr Dale. She's as full of life as I am, and twice as natural, as they say. No, you've got me wrong. It was Mrs Easton's funeral. Miss Fordyce is her cousin, and she had to make all the arrangements. Poor thing, what a palaver for her!"

"She's the only relative, I suppose."

"That she's not! That's the whole pity of it, Mr Dale. She's got a daughter, Alice Easton as was, but she comes sailing in like a lady at the last minute, when everything had been done, down to the last refreshment. Too grand to get stuck in. Always was. I knew 'em when they lived over Kent way. Years ago, when poor old Dad was alive."

"I expect she's as busy as you are," persisted Colley. "She'll be married I dare say, with a family of her own to look after."

"Not her! She was married once, but never had a family. Bit of a mystery about that, dear. Some folk make out she was never properly married, if you take my meaning. Anyway, be that as maybe, she reckons herself married. Mrs Kingston she is nowadays."

"I know a Mrs Kingston. She works at the Cammering Foundation, but her name's Irene not Alice."

"Same difference," said Mrs Scutter. "That's the one. Stuck-up madam, they tell me. Miss Fordyce can't abide her. Alice Irene Easton she was baptised, but Alice'd be too old fashioned. So it's just Irene now."

"Didn't she marry a doctor or a scientist, something like that? I'd heard she was once the wife of one of the men at the Drum House."

"Can't tell you that, dear," said Mrs Scutter. "I only know the Eastons because my husband came from over where they lived, years ago. He used to tell me about them. Quite fond of the old lady he was. She'd been good to him as a boy, you see. That's why I went all that way to where she lived to clean for her. Hardly paid my bus fare, but she was a nice old thing. I shall miss her now she's gone, though I never saw her for years and years."

After a few more exchanges, Colley excused himself and we went outside. He was smiling broadly, and it was obvious that another missing piece of the jigsaw puzzle had fallen into place.

"The scientist was of course Mountford," I said. "Mrs Kingston was unlucky with Mrs Scutter's husband knowing them, So that's why she wanted time off work. To go to her own mother's funeral.

Somebody she knew had indeed been going on a journey. Why couldn't she tell me openly? There was no need for any secrecy."

"Ah, but there was," replied Colley. "A desperate need for secrecy. We knew Mountford's first wife was Alice Irene Easton, and she could not allow her connection with Mountford to be revealed. Can't you see why?"

I had to admit at first that I could not. Then an idea struck me. "She was Mountford's accomplice, wasn't she? Mrs Kingston helped him with his private consultancies."

"Yes, I think she did. But there must be more to it than that. We've got to rack our brains, both of us."

My mind was full of this new turn of events when I arrived back at the office. I had to prepare myself to be perfectly normal with Mrs Kingston, and I succeeded by reverting to my former indifference to my colleagues. Fortunately on Mondays I hardly saw her, as she took minutes of the laboratory meetings. I began to think instead of the gathering on the following evening at Mrs Mountford's house.

When that time arrived, Miss Dempster met us at the door and showed us into a small drawing room which I had not previously seen, where Mrs Mountford was playing the piano. She stood up at once and welcomed us warmly.

"How are you now, Mr Steward?" she asked. "I do hope you have fully recovered from your dreadful experience."

I thanked her and sank, at her command, into the cushions of a comfortable low chair. Colley stood at a long window looking out across the garden. I glanced around the charming room. It was comfortably furnished in an elegant yet cosy style, totally unlike the bleak dark-panelled Edwardian splendours of the staircase and the rooms we had used for the commemoration gathering. Clearly this was Eleanor Mountford's favourite room. I told her how unexpected it was. Rather like herself, I thought.

"Do you really like it? Paul didn't. He preferred the larger rooms. His study is enormous, and terribly cold in winter. Have you not seen it? I thought you had been here sometimes. Ah no, now I remember, it was Arnold Springer who used to keep him company. It must have been quite boring for a young man, but they spent hours in the study together. Discussing work, of course. At least that's all I ever heard on the rare occasions when I had to interrupt them." She paused, frowning for a moment. Then she relaxed again and smiled. "Would you care to see the rest of the house?"

I hesitated, not wishing to intrude, but Colley strode rapidly across the drawing room to join us. "Yes, we would indeed, Mrs Mountford," he said quickly. "If it's not troubling you too much."

"Not at all," she replied. "And please call me Eleanor. May I call you Colley and David? Oh, thank you. That's splendid. Will you follow me? Enid will make the tea for us. She's absolutely wonderful. I don't know how I will manage without her." Miss Dempster grinned sheepishly, and went into the kitchen.

The house was even larger than it appeared from the outside. The study was gigantic, yet could hardly hold all the books and filing cabinets it contained. Some of the rooms on the first floor were empty, but apart from those occupied by Mrs Mountford and Miss Dempster, several guest rooms were comfortably furnished too. We climbed a smaller staircase to the second floor, where all the rooms were empty and long disused, except for one at the head of the backstairs. This was sparsely but adequately furnished, rather like a student's bed-sitting room, and had been unoccupied for some considerable time.

Mrs Mountford saw my puzzled expression. "This was Arnold Springer's room, years ago. He stayed with us for a few months when he first came to the Foundation. We kept it for him even after he found his own place. Sometimes he came and spent a few nights here with us. I rather think he enjoyed getting away from his sister-in-law occasionally. He liked his privacy. Rather a lonely man, don't you think?"

Mrs Mountford led us down to the first floor again by a different staircase. When we reached the landing she turned and said "Perhaps you would like to see my little den. I chose somewhere well away from the rest of the house because of the noise I make. The clacking annoyed Paul. I think the continual clatter got on his nerves, but I personally find it strangely soothing and relaxing."

We entered a long low room at the back of the house, over a kitchen or service wing on the ground floor. Three wooden-framed weaving looms stood in the middle, and the walls were hung with partly finished work and weaving materials. Mrs Mountford was prevailed upon by Colley to give us a demonstration. Her expertise was surprising. I didn't myself find the noise made by the looms particularly soothing, and could sympathise with Paul Mountford, but she obviously enjoyed the work tremendously.

Colley asked whether the looms were electrically powered or whether she had to work them continuously herself. She explained that she could set them to operate automatically if she had to leave the room for anything. They could run for an hour or more unattended. I asked about the things she made, and she showed us some samples. Much of the work was in a distinctive pattern that she had designed herself. It seemed strangely familiar. "You've seen it before, haven't you David?" she said.

"I once made a scarf in that design, but only one. The pattern is really too small, and I didn't think it very successful. Arnold liked it, however, so I gave the scarf to him. He kept it after he left us. It was always rather special. I wonder what's become of him. Poor Arnold!"

Colley and I looked at each other anxiously. Eleanor Mountford caught the glance we exchanged and recognised what lay behind it. There was no sign in her today of the poor lonely widow, nor of the dramatic performer in the wheelchair. She was a self-possessed woman, clever and talented. Now she was undoubtedly her true self. All the rest had been play-acting.

Colley spoke. "Eleanor, I don't think it will be good news about Arnold Springer, you know. When we eventually get it, that is."

Her eyes filled with tears. She bowed her head. "No," she murmured. "I think you're right. I think he's dead." She looked up again and stared straight at my face. Her clear, sad voice echoed around the lonely house.

"I knew he must be dead that day you let me come to the Drum House, and I found Arnold's scarf in the laboratory."

Chapter Eighteen

Sir Matthew Holds a Seminar

T he most dramatic day in the life of the Foundation began quietly enough. Humdrum even. We held our weekly meeting in the laboratories to discuss the ongoing research. Augustus Garton chaired the discussion as usual, but appeared ill at ease, preoccupied with some other matter. At the coffee break, he excused himself and left the room abruptly on a transparent pretext. Ambrose Sedgfield took over the chair and steered us through the rest of the meeting, but it was clear that his mind also was not entirely on the agenda we were supposed to be discussing. He leaned back in his seat, and turned to the events at Mrs Mountford's on the night of the commemoration. The general torpor vanished in a buzz of interest.

"How are you, by the way, David?" he asked. "I hope you're pretty well recovered from, er, what happened that night. It was a bad business." I thanked him and said that I was fine, that the cuts from the glass had been superficial, and that no lasting harm had been done.

"Strange thing that," mused Fletcher-Smith. "Was there somebody behind the curtain having a go at you? I didn't see exactly what happened in all the rushing about."

"Of course there was," said Horning. "And they were very determined to get that photo you held up to show us. They certainly didn't want Mrs Mountford laying eyes on it, did they? I wonder why."

"Yes, that was odd," I admitted. "You know, now I come to think of it, there was something strange about the picture as well. I didn't get a good look at it, of course. I mean, there wasn't much time before it was snatched away and smashed up."

"You mean you hadn't seen it before that evening?" asked Horning. "But I thought it was an old photograph of Cammering and Kaltz with

Mountford that you'd found in the records somewhere. If you didn't discover it yourself, where did it come from?"

I could have kicked myself for being so careless. Now I would have to explain, and hope that what I said wouldn't upset Colley's arrangements, whatever they were. In the event, however, Fletcher-Smith came to my rescue. "I thought I saw Mr Dale hand it to you just before the presentation. Was that right? I suppose he'd come across it when he went through the records in the boardroom cupboards. I noticed him there one day, and he told me that's what he was doing. Seems quite a good sort, doesn't he? Do you think the directors will keep him on, now that Cammering's packed up?"

Sedgfield said he had no idea, and quickly tried to change the direction of the conversation. "I can't see the logic in that," he said tartly. "It's not possible yet to forecast what will happen."

"What happened to the photograph afterwards, I wonder?" persisted Horning. "Somebody retrieved it, presumably. After all, it looked like a good frame. Solid silver I'd say."

"Solid, certainly," I said. There was general good-humoured laughter. "But what happened to it I don't know. Vanished into thin air." I wondered who would be the first to try to stop this line of speculation.

"Oh I expect someone would retrieve it," Sedgfield said airily. "There'll be a rational explanation. We mustn't make too much of it. Probably someone just stumbled on the velvet curtain and fell on to you, David. Glad you're recovering satisfactorily. Well, if that's all for this morning, shall we adjourn?"

I didn't join them for lunch. For one thing, it would hardly be a convivial occasion, what with Garton dashing off so mysteriously and Sedgfield flexing his temporary authority. Also I wanted to get back to the Drum House to have a word with Mrs Kingston. She had taken to avoiding the canteen at lunchtime and having a sandwich sent to her desk. This, I reasoned, would be a perfect opportunity to ask her a few private questions. As I walked across the lawn, it struck me that

Sedgfield had been rather too dismissive, and I wondered how he knew the curtain was made of velvet.

Sonia met me at the door. "Oh Mr Steward! There's a message for you. Sir Matthew is coming here this afternoon. Mrs Kingston has gone to the airport to fetch him."

"Coming here? Did Mrs Kingston know about this?

"I don't know. Don't think so. She'd been trying to get him on the phone all morning. I thought he was supposed to be very ill. Anyway, she left this note for you, all private and sealed up."

"Thank you, Sonia. Please ask Mr Merryman to come in when he's back from lunch. And tell Mrs Kingston that I want to see her at once when she comes in."

"John's in his room now, Mr Steward. I'm going to bring him some sandwiches from the canteen. Shall I get you some as well? I'll make coffee for you both." I accepted her offer gladly. Really she was a nice, sensible girl. Merryman came in and I read the note.

"Cammering's arriving at any moment, John," I told him. "From what Mrs Kingston says here, he's holding a meeting this afternoon. He wants to address all the staff in the board room at three o'clock. Can you and Sonia tell everybody, please? I have to call a special directors' meeting tomorrow. Heaven knows how! I only hope I can get in touch with them all on the phone. I'll have to prise Mrs Kingston away from Cammering and enlist her services."

"Some kind of seminar, I suppose," said Merryman. "Looks as if events are moving fast."

Soon a car drew up and Mrs Kingston helped Sir Matthew into the Drum House. I went out to meet him. He seemed reasonably agile, but ill with worry. We settled him down and Mrs Kingston went over the arrangements with Sonia and John for the afternoon meeting. Three o'clock came, and Cammering walked slowly and painfully into the board room, where all the staff were assembled. Spontaneous applause erupted, and Sir Matthew was visibly moved with emotion.

"I thank all of you for that welcome," he began, in a clear sonorous voice. "I thank you for all you have done here at this Foundation, which commemorates the work of my dear friend Dr Kaltz as well as myself. The meeting the other evening to commemorate the achievements of our splendid colleague Paul Mountford filled me with deep pride in all of you and with thankfulness for his work. It was a grief to me that I could not attend myself, unfortunately, but I wish to honour his widow. I would be grateful therefore if you would invite her to the special meeting of the directors here tomorrow."

He paused, searching around for a moment. Then, having caught the attention of Mrs Kingston, standing at the back of the room by the door, he resumed his address. Mrs Kingston, I noticed, looked more nervous than ever. Sir Matthew's request had obviously taken her by surprise.

"I spoke of Dr Kaltz a moment ago. It was a pride and joy to me that we together established this Foundation long ago. Twenty years, to be precise. It is the anniversary next month, as some of you may know. You have seen the Foundation at work. Dr Kaltz never saw it. He never saw with his own eyes this place, our vision unfolding, and our work continuing. He died immediately before we finalised our plans. Yes, you may look astonished, but it is true. Dr Kaltz died twenty years ago last week."

The sensation echoed quietly around the high walls of the Drum. All of us were staggered by the announcement. I looked around for Colley, but could see no sign of him nor of Miss Dempster. A question quivered on the lips of everyone present. I tried to catch Garton's eye, willing him to look at me. He simply hung his head down and sat slumped in a chair. Someone else would have to speak for the staff.

"Sir Matthew," I heard myself calling out. Immediately everyone turned to where I stood and I had their undivided attention. Sedgfield and his staff waited expectantly.

Even Augustus Garton sat up, and looked first at me, then at Cammering. "Sir Matthew," I repeated. "There is a question which should be asked, if you will excuse my interruption. You say Dr Kaltz died before any of us came to work here at the Foundation. Tell me then, why was he working with us here for so long until his tragic death in the solvent store fire? If that man was not Dr Kaltz, who was he?"

All eyes swivelled back to Cammering. A ripple of relief and expectation surged around the room as I sat down. We all waited to hear my question answered.

"The man was myself. I took on the role of Kaltz." Cammering struck his chest hard. The sound echoed through the Drum, more an act of punishment than of pride. "I became Kaltz, my dear old friend." He paused and smiled. "It was not so difficult, you know. It was simple. We were quite alike, the same height and build. We came from the same country, the same stock, indeed from neighbouring villages. True he wore a beard and had whiter hair, but these are trivialities easily dealt with. I came over and worked in the laboratory myself. It was easy. Few people ever noticed my absence from my cottage in France. If they did, they never bothered to inquire where I went. No, that was easy, David. What was less easy, what was indeed most difficult, was to perform the work of Kaltz, to achieve the same standard of his research, to emulate his position in the scientific community."

He paused again, wiped his forehead, and drank a few sips of water. "Kaltz was the star, I was merely the impresario," he continued. "Oh yes, I know I had a few slight successes in the laboratory and in the clinics, but Kaltz was the genius. And modest, so modest. He hated the limelight. He wished for, he insisted upon, the obscurity of his laboratory. His name must not be bestowed on the Foundation. In our published papers he always must come second."

"That was why you changed your name from Kammering with a K to Cammering with a C," I said. The explanation had suddenly flashed upon me. The alphabetical order of authors on scientific and medical publications was always exact, as I had explained once to Colley. No wonder he had been so excited when I told him. Where was he now? Then another thought - . But I had to continue while I was on my feet. "So it became Cammering and Kaltz, the famous team, or just Cammering and alia, with other co-workers. Dr Kaltz acquiesced, did he?" Cammering nodded his head vigorously, but could not speak. "Mountford, however, did not? Even though his contribution was as great, greater than your own, even perhaps as great as Kaltz's, he always came third at best. Cammering, Kaltz and Mountford. C, K and M. Or worse, lost altogether in the *alia*?"

"Yes, David. You are correct. That is a most intelligent deduction. Quite within character, if I may say so. Your intelligence and capacity have always been, in my humble opinion, remarkable. I pay tribute to you, and trust that I can always count on you, as a friend both to myself and to our Foundation. You are correct indeed . I have to admit at last that, although I helped my old friend Kaltz, complied indeed with his earnest wishes, I hindered the career of our young associate Paul Mountford. He was outstandingly brilliant. His work was remarkable. I do not agree that it quite matched that of Kaltz, although mine it did surpass, yes. It has long been a grief to me that his rightful place was not acknowledged. We could not do so. I could not. The Foundation - ."

"The Foundation was based on a deception," I intervened. "How can you justify that?"

"To enable our work to go on. Whatever my faults, and they are great, our work had been - how to say? - not perhaps unhelpful to mankind?" He smiled disarmingly.

I was entirely won over. "Forgive me, if I spoke harshly. "I was thinking of Mountford."

"That I well understand. Ah, only too well, you know. You should all understand that it was imperative above all things that the Foundation be established and continue our work. We are mortal men, but our names could assist further work fruitful to all people. We dreamed of a kind of immortality. Was that foolish? The vanity of proud men? I hope not so entirely. But Paul Mountford, ah, that was a pity, yes. He was an unwitting accomplice, if it was deception as you call it. I took him into the team after Kaltz died. They met but once only. The meeting was photographed. I understand you saw the picture the other evening at Paul's house. You, David, would notice that the Kaltz in the photograph was not the same man who had been your colleague here at the Drum House. As to Paul Mountford, however, in the role of Kaltz, I promoted him, encouraged him, paid him, gave him everything he could have wished for. Except the first place of honour. He was M, after C and K. That was so, fortuitously, but if his surname had come alphabetically before C, then I could have done nothing for him. He would have remained, I say it not boastingly but as fact, he would have remained a nobody."

Cammering paused again. This time it was for longer, and he had to sit down. Garton went forward to him as though to take charge. Cammering waved him angrily away.

"David," he said in a frail but clear voice, "David is to take charge."

I moved to the rostrum at Cammering's side. As I walked calmly forward, I noticed that Garton and Sedgfield were engaged in angry discussion. I took my stance at an angle to the audience, so that I could see both them and Sir Matthew. Sedgfield sat down and looked expectantly at me, with a smile on his face. The rest of the staff also settled down quickly, except Augustus Garton, who rushed to the back of the room and disappeared. "Sir Matthew," I began. "There is another question that troubles me and, I think, everyone else here. Forgive me, but may I ask it? If you impersonated Dr Kaltz in the laboratory here at the Foundation, then who died in the fire? The dental records identified the victim as Dr Kaltz."

Cammering rose unsteadily to his feet and stood behind his chair, like a man in the witness box, or even the dock. It was not a picture that I particularly liked, but unpleasant questions would have to be put to the old man. In public, too. Before the assembled audience. That was only fair to the staff. We had all become involved. In any case, I realised that if they were sent away now, and we went into private session, their resentment would lead to damaging rumours that would spread rapidly through the Foundation and perhaps beyond. Rampant speculation was not in our best interests. Within the last few minutes I had done some furious thinking, the need for action clearing my thoughts wonderfully. I saw at last what had been happening to us all. Colley had been right. I did know the truth of it, if only I used my brains. The role of leader that had been thrust upon me so unexpectedly had clarified my thinking, and I saw how we must proceed. Only the final scene still remained clouded in uncertainty. "Sir Matthew", I said quietly. "May I repeat the question, please? Who died in the solvent store fire?"

Cammering paused, calmly searching for the correct words. It flashed upon me that we were not going to be told the whole truth if he could help it. He had decided to withhold something, and I was determined not to allow him to do so. "No-one died in the fire," he announced. A ripple of disbelief ran round the audience. "Yes, that is literally true. The body you found was that of, well, shall we just say of someone who had also taken upon themselves the role of Dr Kaltz. That person did not die in the blaze, however." He smiled and sat down.

This dissembling would have to stop. If the Foundation was to be saved, then the full facts must be told. Only Cammering could tell us the whole truth. Despite the pain it would cause him, I had to persist in my questioning.

"No," I said. "That man was dead already. He was killed in the Drum House. He was murdered in the anteroom next door to where we are sitting. His body was hidden on the turret stairs, and then stored in the cellar cold room underneath the service block. A room to which only Dr Kaltz - you yourself - had the key. Sir Matthew Cammering, did you kill that man? Did you kill Arnold Springer?" The room fell into an electrified silence. Somewhere, near the back of the audience, a woman began to sob quietly. Cammering stood up again and looked me straight in the eye. Here, I realised, was no prisoner in the dock, no hostile witness. Here was a great man, utterly in control of himself, even in this hour of his direst tragedy. He was also determined to protect somebody else, and I was equally determined that the Foundation must not allow this person to remain hidden.

"No, David. I solemnly tell it to you, and to you all. I did not kill Springer. The rest of what you say is true, although I am amazed that you know it. We found the body in the anteroom and hid it on the stairs as you say, but we did not kill him. He was already dead from poisoning. You look at me so accusingly. I will tell you more, but the name of the other person who is involved I will not disclose, not to you nor to anyone. The person who poisoned Springer was Paul Mountford. Yes, I know it is astounding, and I regret having to speak it. Your insistence alone draws the fact from me. It is for the good purpose of the Foundation that you ask these questions. I see that, and I will answer truthfully. But the identity of the other one involved I will never reveal. Paul Mountford killed Springer. He told me so himself, and I believe it to be true. I have a corroborating witness. He was not ashamed of it, not regretful. He detested Springer. Yet I believe also that the killing was entirely accidental. Poor Mountford was driven to do what he did by the treatment he received at my hands, I confess it. I did not understand the intensity of his resentment. I thought he was content with the second, or third, place. But, alas, his mind was unhinged. It was never Paul's intention to kill Springer. The poisoned drink was intended for another. It was the merest chance that Springer took it. I can say no more."

"Mountford never acquiesced in your arrangement to impersonate Kaltz, did he? He quickly realised the false position you had put him into. On the one hand, you had provided him with the means for his talents to earn him a high standard of living, far higher than he could have ever dreamed about in his humble beginnings. On the other hand, you deprived him of the recognition of those talents. His scientific ability and originality were always buried under the edifice you had constructed. Frustrated, he turned to other work, either for an outlet to gain credit for his abilities or to provide an alternative basis for financing his lifestyle should he sever his connection with the Foundation. He accepted consultancies, and with the help of another person - whose name I think you know - built up a series of lucrative connections - ."

"Paul did nothing wrong! Nothing illegal! There can be no proof that he diverted work away from the Foundation. He earned those consultancies of his own merit."

"That may well be so," I admitted, "but he was becoming a danger to the Foundation. He had made himself both financially and professionally independent. He was in a position to break his links with the Foundation he had come to loathe. And then, all at once, out of the blue, he learned a secret. Something that could free by destroying both the Foundation and your reputation. He discovered that you were impersonating Kaltz. What happened? Did he discover the old photograph showing the real Kaltz, the one that appeared in his own home, the picture that I was forcibly prevented from showing to all the staff?"

Cammering started to his feet. "I swear to you all that I was not present on that evening! I did not strike you down. I do not know how Paul discovered I was impersonating Kaltz. I have an idea that Springer might have told him, but I do not know why. As to how I found out about Paul's private consultancies, that was again an accident, the merest piece of bad luck for him. Paul had always scrupulously avoided taking on work from clients of the Foundation or from firms associated with them. It was that wretched takeover of Palburg that did it. They had been clients of his for years, and then suddenly they were bought up by Sperlitz Spellman. Paul's involvement was then brought to my attention."

"And you were furious," I said. "Sir Matthew, you and Mountford had an angry confrontation when you found out, didn't you? You saw at once the danger you were in. Mountford had to be silenced. Money would not do it. He had no need of further payment from you. Some other means had to be found, quickly. The directors were perhaps beginning to get wind of what was happening. Mountford's health was poor. He had not been taking his heart drugs as prescribed, and that made things worse. When he had his final attack, the tablets had been switched. Instead of the medication that would have saved him, he took useless placebos. He died in his laboratory. The person who switched the tablets murdered him. That person was…"

"No, no! Stop!" screamed a voice from the back of the room. Irene Kingston shrieked the words. Tears were gushing down her face. "Tell them the truth, Matthew, for the sake of all of us. Tell them! You didn't kill Paul. You didn't kill my husband. He died naturally, at his bench. Tell them, tell them who killed Arnold Springer! Tell them who's behind this, who drove you to do everything you did!"

"Irene, no!" shouted Cammering. "It is impossible. I will never tell - ."

"There was another false Kaltz," continued Mrs Kingston. "I will tell them, Matthew. I was the one you were with when we found Springer's body. I was with you when Paul confessed to poisoning the water that killed him. I am your corroborating witness. You found another imposter in Kaltz's room, after Mountford died. He was going to finish us all, and everything we had worked for over so many years. I have to tell them! It would have been the end of all your work and dreams. I am to blame. It was me who helped Paul in his secret consultancies. I was once married to him. I was the hidden threat to the Foundation. Now it's the end. It's all over!"

The door burst open. Irene Kingston rushed outside. The staircase door rebounded violently on its hinges against the outer wall, shattering the silence. We heard footsteps clattering up the stone steps. Mrs Kingston's head appeared momentarily at the top gallery. She turned away without a word. There was a rush to the open door of the board room. Heavier footsteps echoed on the staircase. Irene Kingston's voice screamed once more, from the outside gallery of the Drum. "No, no! Get back! It's too late!" she cried. Another scream echoed across the lawns outside the Drum House. Heavy footsteps slowly descended the stairs. After a long pause, Augustus Garton re-entered the boardroom.

Chapter Nineteen

Truth from a High Place

Sir Matthew Cammering struggled to his feet. Grey and shaking he pushed his chair away and stood before the assembled staff. "Augustus Garton," he called out in a strong voice. "Augustus Garton, will you favour us with your explanation for these extraordinary events? Close the door, please, and approach to the platform here!" Garton hesitated, starting nervously as the heavy boardroom doors slammed shut behind him. All eyes darted rapidly from his lonely figure at the back of the room to the authoritative figures at the front of the audience. Garton remained unmoving, abject and miserable beyond expression. I suddenly felt a wave of compassion for him.

I stood up again. "Professor," I said quietly. "Won't you please come forward to join us here, and tell us what you have to say?" Garton looked steadily at me, then glanced quickly around the room and back to the closed doors. At last, to my immense relief, he sighed and slowly walked forward through the silent assembly. Reaching the front, he turned and faced his colleagues. I willed him to speak the truth out loud. Clearly and boldly he began.

"Sir Matthew, David, colleagues," he announced. "I have to tell you that Mrs Kingston is safe, quite safe, and out of danger. She was prevented from falling. I took the precaution of climbing the turret stairs ahead of her. I was waiting for her at the top. When she arrived, I grabbed her as she was about to throw herself from the outside gallery. She is calm now. I have brought her safely to the ground, and given her a sedative. She is now in good hands, and will recover herself in a little while."

Cammering threw himself forward in his chair, but lacked the strength to stand up. "You are sure, Augustus? Quite sure that she is all right? She has nothing to blame herself for. It is entirely my fault! I have brought you all into this terrible danger! I have disgraced the Foundation!"

I stood up. "That is not so, Sir Matthew. If you will forgive me again for speaking out frankly, you are completely wrong. Your actions years ago did indeed begin this sorry business. The concealment of the truth by Mrs Kingston and the secret life of Paul Mountford were contributing factors, certainly. They can't be countenanced, even if they may be forgiven. But neither you, Sir Matthew, nor Mrs Kingston brought these terrible events upon us. Nor did Arnold Springer. Professor Garton, please tell us all you know. You have behaved strangely, and you owe us an explanation." I paused, waiting for him to speak. He looked anxiously around but stayed silent.

"Professor Garton," I repeated. "We are waiting for your explanation." Still he said nothing. I scribbled a few words down on a scrap of paper and passed it to him. He read it rapidly, and then read it again, as though not believing what he saw written there. I wrote a few more words on another sheet, and handed it to Merryman, who tapped Fletcher-Smith on the shoulder. Both men left the room, followed by Sonia Ulrickson. A hushed expectancy descended, and everyone turned to the three of us out in front. Cammering remained slumped in his seat. I waved towards Garton, indicating that he was to take over, and sat down. The professor stepped forward, specks of perspiration glinting on his face, and the veins of his neck bulging conspicuously. He started to speak.

"My colleagues. David Steward is right. I do owe you an explanation. He is also correct in saying that neither Sir Matthew nor Mrs Kingston is guilty of bringing this situation about, ill-advised though their actions may have been, both recently and in the distant past. They did not kill Arnold Springer or Paul Mountford. The guilty party is another person. Someone we all know. Someone we have all trusted implicitly. Someone who has broken that trust. I have known the truth for many weeks, but could not bring myself to contemplate it. I had no definite evidence. Now David has informed me, by this note passed to me, that he also knows the identity of the person really responsible." Garton wiped his forehead and took several deep breaths. He bowed his head. "Now everything is different. Everything is finished." We waited, not daring to disturb the intense silence, in case we missed his next words.

Suddenly he threw back his head and shouted out the words. "Everything is finished! The truth is known, and now it will be told!" Then he turned to face us all, and continued in a normal voice. "Sir Matthew Cammering, you told us that Arnold Springer was killed by my esteemed colleague Paul Mountford. That is true. Not only do I believe what you say, but I was told it by Mountford himself, just before he collapsed in his laboratory. We are told that Springer was killed accidentally, and that Mountford intended to kill Irene Kingston. That also is true. Springer died in the anteroom next door. That too is correct. I saw his body lying there on the floor. I did not know at first how he died. I knew the gallery railing was insecure, and I thought that part of it had fallen on him. A fragment of wood perhaps, or one of the long bolts or nails holding the rail in place."

"You experimented by dropping pencils from the gallery to the anteroom floor in order to test your theory," I said. "However they proved inconclusive, I think, and you remained puzzled by Springer's death."

Garton looked startled, and then relief broke over him. He smiled and sighed loudly. "Yes, and I remained so until today. I don't know how you found out, David, but, yes, what you say is true. And there is something else I should tell you about Springer. Something long ago from the past. I remembered having seen him before he came to the Foundation. As you know, once I worked in a London teaching hospital. I needn't burden you with the details. One day, a young man, a rising junior executive, arrived with a visiting delegation from a pharmaceutical firm. I remembered him particularly. I'm afraid he seemed to me rather brash and pushy, visibly ambitious even though he was only a very junior member of the team. That young man was of course Arnold Springer, and the company was Sperlitz Spellman.

Later I learned from a press report that Springer had been promoted rapidly within that firm. I was puzzled. I could not reconcile his rapid rise with his evident lack of real merit or ability. I became especially curious when Springer joined us here at the Foundation, but decided to say nothing. He could do little harm, I thought, as his post was non-technical. Oh dear! I do not mean to imply, David, that an administrative post is in any way inferior. It is just that I, er - ." He broke off, embarrassed and uncertain how to continue.

I got to my feet again and confirmed his story. Garton smiled with relief, sitting down gratefully. Cammering shuffled about nervously in his chair, and muttered a few words I could not catch. "Springer was inserted into the Foundation deliberately," I continued. "Not because of his qualities. Indeed, I regret to say because of his very lack of them. He was forced upon you, Sir Matthew, and upon me as his boss. You and I know, Dr Garton, who compelled Sir Matthew to take him on to the staff." Cammering went pale, and took a few sips from a glass of water. "That same person is responsible for the death of his wretched young accomplice Arnold Springer, for the murder of Paul Mountford, and for the attempted destruction of the Cammering Foundation. That same person is with us here today! Watching, listening, preparing, scheming. No, not among you in this room, but present nonetheless and hearing every word I say. That person is up there, in the store room, on the other side of that false window!"

I pointed to the opening, now slightly ajar. Everyone turned their heads and clearly saw the disjointed picture on the Drum wall. Momentarily I wondered whether I was wise to go on, unsure what would happen. I examined the expectant faces of my colleagues and friends before me. Drum House staff, the laboratory technicians, Sedgfield, Horning, Staniforth, the service workers, the canteen helpers, the engineers, the cleaners, the gardeners. Then, with me, alone in front of all these people, the worried faces of Cammering and Garton. I knew I had to go on if the Foundation was to be rescued. The truth must be told now, loudly and vigorously.

"Yes, up there, watching us, as he has watched and schemed for so long, using us as puppets in his ambitions. Come down here, Sir Carlo Waybridge! Won't you join us, and tell us your story for yourself? We are waiting, Waybridge!"

The secret window crashed open, but no face appeared. There came the sound of a scuffle in the mezzanine room. A distant door slammed shut and heavy footsteps pounded down the stone stairs. There came a loud cry. The heavy boardroom doors flew inwards. Waybridge stood in the doorway. He started backwards towards the outer door. "Stop him, stop him!" shouted Merryman, leaping from the reception desk to grab the fugitive. Waybridge lunged forward, catching him a heavy blow and knocking him to the floor. Waybridge dashed to the outer door. Fletcher-Smith ran after him, and grabbed his knees. Both men crashed to the ground, struggling violently. At first Fletcher-Smith managed to hold him, but suddenly Waybridge jumped to his feet and kicked at the other man's fingers. Then a figure climbed up on to the desk, lifted the flower display, and felled Waybridge with a mighty blow, shattering the huge vase.

Sonia Ulrickson threw down the fragment of the handle she still held, jumped nimbly off the desk, and rushed to comfort the bleeding Fletcher-Smith. In the confusion, Waybridge struggled slowly upright, only to sink again under the combined weight of Horning and Staniforth. Then, to the amazement of the crowd emerging from the boardroom, Detective Sergeant Enid Dempster, in full uniform, took two paces forward and calmly handcuffed Waybridge. More uniformed police surged into the reception hall, and escorted him outside.

"Thank you, all of you," she announced, "for your help. I have arrested Sir Carlo Waybridge on a holding charge for the moment. Further charges could follow. In the meantime, please remain here while my colleagues take statements. Now, if you will kindly resume your seats, Mr Steward will continue with his explanation, assisted where necessary by Professor Garton and my former superior officer, Detective Inspector Collingwood Dale.

"Retired," said Colley, stepping forward. "At least, I thought I had retired."

Within a few minutes, everyone had been seated in the boardroom again, and the turmoil of voices died down. I rose once more to address my audience. Stifling my surprise about Colley's true role, I set out, as lucidly as I could, the course of events that had led to the day's drama. After about fifteen minutes, I sat down again into a stunned silence. Colley again stepped forward. "Mr Steward is correct in every particular. He has told the story concisely and accurately with, if I may say so, courage and skill. The Foundation and all of you owe him a great debt of obligation." A tidal wave of cheering and clapping swept the room, in which Garton and Cammering vigorously joined. I felt totally overwhelmed. I simply thanked them and dismissed them, asking that they would stay on the premises for the time being and not communicate with anyone outside.

The audience trickled out, amid a clamour of excited voices. Colley and Augustus Garton took me to my own room, where Cammering and the senior staff were already waiting. We sat down on chairs that had been provided, on Colley's instructions as I later learned. Sonia, Brian Fletcher-Smith and John Merryman came in behind us. We all waited, uncertain what would happen next.

Colley stood up. "We are all glad to see that you have recovered, Mrs Kingston, and that you have been able to join us here." He described how he became involved with the Foundation. He had come across Sir Carlo Waybridge in Paris some years ago. Subsequently he met him several times socially, though they had never been more than passing acquaintances. He had disguised his surprise when Waybridge had approached him in confidence and asked him to investigate what he termed irregularities at the Foundation. "Despite the obvious care Waybridge had taken in his choice of investigator," Colley explained, "he had failed to learn that I was a former Detective Inspector prematurely retired because of a disability suffered on active service." He went on to tell of his difficulties in carrying out Waybridge's wishes, not only because of his troublesome leg but also because he had no direct knowledge of the Foundation. Yet he did not want to turn down the commission. That was when, he said, he had the great fortune of meeting me.

Embarrassed, I explained how I had traced Colley. He then took over the story again and told his audience how Detective Sergeant Dempster had been assigned at his request, first to protect me and later to look after Mrs Mountford. "It was," Colley told them, "an unwise choice of mine to present her as a photographer."

"We soon tumbled to that," said Horning. "She hardly knew one end of a camera from the other. And as for setting up a tripod, well - ." A ripple of laughter ran through the audience. "Did she ever have any film in her camera?" he asked.

Colley laughed too. "I doubt it," he replied, "but I wouldn't question her about it. She's quite sensitive to criticism sometimes, and she's much tougher than she looks when dealing with awkward customers."

"It was my persistence with photography that brought me into trouble," I explained. "Especially after we'd brought Miss Dempster in, ostensibly as a photographer. I see that now. I merely wanted to have a photo of Cammering and Kaltz together, to illustrate the history of the Foundation. Waybridge realised that, if my plan succeeded, I'd discover that Kaltz had never actually worked here. It would have ruined his own carefully laid plans to discredit and seize the Foundation. He had to silence me. So he organised the attempts to kill me. I suppose, though, he didn't do his own dirty work personally."

"Indeed he did," Colley said. "The villain was behind the wheel in the car park and on the hill. We found his fingerprints in the van, once we traced it. And he was most definitely there at Mrs Mountford's house. He was the man behind the curtain who hit you that evening. I know because I saw him. Ambrose Sedgfield noticed him too as he was fixing up the curtain. So did you!" He spun round to address Mrs Kingston.

She said nothing but nodded her head. Colley turned back to me. "It was smart of you to reassure the professor with that note, and smarter still to forewarn John and Brian. You didn't count on Sonia, though, doing splendid stuff with the pot! Not that I approve of course. You should leave that to the professionals. I wondered if she'd taken lessons from Dempster." Sonia giggled, and clung even closer to Fletcher-Smith.

"Well, I was completely wrong about it all," admitted Staniforth. "I realised that some funny business was going on, but I suspected that Dr Garton was behind it. How wrong can you get! Sorry about that."

"No need for apologies," smiled the professor. "I suppose I must have seemed suspicious. I thought at first it was Sir Matthew here. Well, in a way, he did begin everything, but I soon deduced it must be Waybridge. He wanted to discredit Sir Matthew and Paul Mountford, and then take over, didn't he?"

"Yes, that's about right," I said. "Poor Springer found out somehow that Mountford was running his private consultancies. Probably by snooping around in Paul's study when he lodged there. He'd know when Mountford was out, and Eleanor would hear nothing once she had set her weaving loom going."

"No, it must have been much earlier than that," said Merryman. "I'd guess that he found out by inquiring around his contacts in pharmaceutical companies. Oh yes, that's it! It was when Sperlitz Spellman took over Palburgs. He pushed his way up in Sperlitz Spellman till he got noticed by the chairman, who was none other than Sir Carlo Waybridge! Arnold must have told him about Mountford's private work for Palburgs, and then quietly uncovered the other consultancies once he was on to Mountford. Waybridge saw the possibilities for discrediting the Foundation. No wonder he promoted Arnold! I suppose then he insisted on transferring him here at the Drum House to find out more about Mountford's activities."

"I'm afraid you're right," said Cammering. "Waybridge was very insistent. He was a major source of revenue for us, through his widespread contacts, as well of course as being a senior member of the board. He covered himself, should he be suspected of unduly favouring Springer, by also insisting that Augustus Garton also be appointed. With all respect, my dear professor, I never understood until today why he did so. It was frankly never my wish to have you here." Garton flushed angrily, but Cammering waved him to be silent. "Not that I have ever regretted it," he continued. "You have more than proved your merit to be so appointed. Your work here has been of the utmost value to us, Augustus, and I thank you most sincerely for that. Naturally I add my apology for having so misjudged you."

Garton returned no response, but had been deeply wounded by Cammering's confession. I wondered how much longer he would wish to stay in his post. I knew he would be warmly received in any of several other institutes, and I realised suddenly how much I would miss my old friend should he decide to leave. Perhaps I too should consider finding a job somewhere else. I felt exhausted after the last few gruelling months, and did not relish the task of handling the imminent police investigation and then trying to build up morale again at the Drum House.

"There's one thing that still baffles me," said Ambrose Sedgfield, breaking the gloom that had descended. "If you, Sir Matthew, were impersonating Kaltz here in the labs, how did it happen that you met Kaltz that afternoon when you had that flaming row with him. After all, you could hardly have had one like that with yourself. Anyway we saw Kaltz in the building before you came across the lawns. Who was acting as Kaltz that day? It couldn't have been Mountford or Springer, as they were both dead, and it certainly wasn't you. So who was it?"

Cammering rose unsteadily to his feet. "Yes," he began, "that was so regrettable a meeting. I fear that I quite lost my temper. The man there was of course Waybridge himself. He had taken to impersonating Dr Kaltz. It was all part of his dreadful scheme to subdue me and destroy the Foundation. Naturally his laboratory work was total rubbish. That was why he operated there so secretly. Any of you would have unmasked his obvious deficiency as a scientist at once had he allowed you, Ambrose, or any of you other men to approach anywhere near him. He even dressed the part outside the premises and rehearsed it in the depths of the woodlands."

"Then that's who I saw in the woods, that day!" cried Sonia. "I knew I wasn't dreaming! Brian, I told you I wasn't crazy! I knew it was Dr Kaltz. Well, someone I thought was him." She sank down tearfully, and Fletcher-Smith put a comforting arm around her. "I'm glad I hit him with that vase," she sobbed. "It served him jolly well right!"

"And the blackmail, too," whispered a croaking voice at the back of the room. We turned round to see Mrs Kingston raising herself in her chair. "Tell them about the blackmail, Matthew. Paul thought I was responsible, as if I would ever have harmed him or you, Matthew. Poor dear, he'd become convinced I'd betrayed him. He never realised that Sir Carlo was behind it. Neither did I. That was why he tried to kill me with his tablets. Instead of which he killed Mr Springer. Well, he did us all a good service there! Then, when he needed his tablets they were useless. Sir Carlo had seen to that also. I'm glad he's been found out, and I hope he goes to jail for years and years and - ." She broke off. Sonia ran across to her and held her, quietly stroking her head.

"Yes, my dear, I will tell them," said Cammering. "I was being blackmailed by Springer and so was Paul Mountford. The letters were typed on Irene's machine with some typing wheel of his own. I confronted him, but it made no difference. He demanded more and more money. Cheque after cheque I wrote him out, so that he should not expose my deceit and ruin our Foundation. He became more greedy, and careless too. One cheque you found, Mr Merryman, as I understand from Mr Dale. I apologise for deceiving you too. However, the extra payment I then gave you was entirely deserved. I hope you accept my apology and that you will continue your excellent work here."

John Merryman blushed, and muttered something incoherent. I gathered, however, that the apology was accepted, and I was sincerely glad about that. I would need the talents of John Merryman, I realised, in the days that lay ahead. Not to mention his friendship.

Chapter Twenty

The End and the Beginning

The rest is quickly told. Next day the directors of the Cammering Foundation met in urgent secret session. Garton, Sedgfield and I were asked to wait in our offices until they had concluded their deliberations. Merryman and I sat in my room, hardly able to speak for apprehension and doubt about the future. Sonia brought us coffee and sandwiches, before hurrying off to the laboratories, where Fletcher-Smith and the others had been instructed to wait. We had been regaled with graphic descriptions of Brian's injuries and his rapid recovery. John, too, had been remarkably little injured, although he had several bad bruises. Mrs Kingston, now fully in command of herself again, was in with the directors, at Cammering's side, officially taking minutes.

Colley and Miss Dempster were nowhere on the premises. I could not telephone to Palmyra Square as we had been told strictly not to communicate with anyone outside. Kate Merryman had phoned in, but John had to say only that everything was all right, and that he would speak to her again as soon as he could. We heard on the portable radio Sonia produced from behind the reception desk that Sir Carlo Waybridge had been arrested in Surrey and charged with obstructing the police in certain inquiries they were making into his business affairs.

Eventually the door opened, and Mrs Kingston asked us to go to the boardroom. On the way there, we met the professor and the other scientific staff who had been similarly summoned. Several of the directors had gone. Sir Matthew was in the chair, and despite looking desperately ill, was firmly in control. We were all told to sit down, and then Cammering announced the directors' decision.

"I have insisted that I resign," he said. "I can continue no longer. It is enough for me now that the Foundation bear my name. My colleagues here have so persuaded me, though I would myself wish otherwise. However, that is immaterial, of no consequence. What is essential is that the work of the Foundation, however called, shall continue. That will be so. The staffing will necessarily change of course. None of us is beyond replacement. That must always be so in the nature of the world. No one person, I much regret to tell you, is to take my position. That is unfortunate, but it is the unanimous wish of the directors that my post be divided. My esteemed colleague Augustus Garton is offered the post of Medical Director. Alongside him, in equal authority, is to be an Executive Director, so that he can concentrate wholly on his scientific work. I hope that you will accept, Augustus, and that your work here will bring ever increasing distinction both to yourself and the Foundation."

Garton looked dumbfounded. "I had thought," he began, "that I should perhaps now seek elsewhere - . However, if it is your wish, and that of your colleagues on the board, and if my friends here - ."

"Oh shut up, Augustus," intervened Sedgfield. "Of course it's our wish. Just say yes! It's what we all want. You'll have all our support and good wishes, won't he?" He turned to the rest of us, and to his obvious pleasure and relief, applause broke out.

"In which case," beamed Garton, "I am naturally honoured to accept. We can discuss terms and conditions later. But, Sir Matthew, if I may, there is something I wish to insist on now. Indeed it is essential to my appointment. You spoke of an Executive Director to work alongside me. I must ask that the appointment be offered to the man who has done so much to deserve it. Indeed it is no exaggeration to say that he has saved the Foundation and all our work. The man of whom I speak is of course Mr David Steward!"

Now it was my turn to be staggered. "You have anticipated the decision we had already made," smiled Cammering. Utterly astonished, I sat still in my chair. Something hit me hard in the back. It was Colley's foot, his sound one. He had come quietly into the room, unnoticed . "Get up, you ass," he hissed, "and say you accept."

I did so, scarcely believing what I heard. I mumbled thank for their trust and confidence. There was more applause. Then came a sharp tug at my jacket, and I fell back in my seat. "Well done," whispered John and Colley together.

"There are two additional appointments we have to announce," continued Sir Matthew. We are asking Dr Fletcher-Smith to take the position of Deputy Medical Director and Mr Merryman that of Deputy Executive Director. All four of these new appointments will include seats on the board of the Foundation."

And that was almost the end of the story. Sir Matthew Cammering returned to France, accompanied by Irene Kingston. A few weeks later we heard that they had married in a quiet ceremony. Brian, secure in his new career, proposed soon afterwards to Sonia, and they were married before the year was out, amid rejoicings that were far from quiet. We all enjoyed ourselves at the wedding immensely. Colley then returned to the obscurity from which he had come, and I supposed him to be engaged on some other investigation. John and Kate Merryman became close friends of mine, and I have come to value their company and talents increasingly over the years.

As for me, I threw myself into my new responsibilities. The seminars and publications that I had planned for so long eventually became a reality. The Foundation flourished as never before, and soon the unpleasantness of the police case and the inevitable publicity which followed softened into seldom remembered history. Waybridge was disgraced and imprisoned, having been found guilty on charges of blackmail and fraud. His role in the deaths of Mountford and Springer was never fully proved in court, and the charges of murder were quietly dropped.

I decided to set up house independently at last. The Dixons, who had been tearful when Colley announced his departure, hardly commented when I left them. They seemed almost relieved that I was going. In a way, so was I. My old life lay behind. The future stretched before me.

Eleanor Mountford remained in her large house. I went to live there too. She had converted the place into apartments, I hasten to add, and I rented one of them.

Or rather, that had been my original intention.

Tom Askey

BV - #0023 - 201221 - C0 - 210/148/12 - PB - 9781913839505 - Gloss Lamination